THE CARDASSIAN COMMANDER STORMED INTO SISKO'S OFFICE.

"Gul Marak?" Sisko said, looking up at him.

"And you're Sisko," Marak stated with a sneer.

With effort, Sisko kept his anger out of his voice. "I believe you asked to meet with me?"

Marak tossed a data clip onto Sisko's desk. "The government of the Cardassian Empire has ordered me to communicate their demands to the United Federation of Planets. To you as their representative."

Sisko reached for the data clip, but Marak stopped him. "I can tell you what is says. My government demands the return of the station currently designated *Deep Space Nine*. I am authorized to assume command. Immediately."

Sisko stood, his calm eyes meeting the Cardassian commander's angry glare. "That demand," Sisko said quietly, "could lead to interstellar war."

Look for STAR TREK Fiction from Pocket Books

Star Trek: The Original Series

Star Trek: The Next Generation

Star Trek: Deep Space Nine

BETRAYAL

Lois Tilton

POCKET BOOKS
New York   London   Toronto   Sydney   Tokyo   Singapore

An *Original* Publication of POCKET BOOKS

 POCKET BOOKS, a division of Simon & Schuster Inc.
1230 Avenue of the Americas, New York, NY 10020

This book is published by Pocket Books, a division of
Simon & Schuster Inc., under exclusive license from
Paramount Pictures.

ISBN: 0-671-88117-5

First Pocket Books printing May 1994

10 9 8 7 6 5 4 3 2 1

POCKET and colophon are registered trademarks of
Simon & Schuster Inc.

Printed in the U.S.A.

BETRAYAL

Printed in the U.S.A.

PROLOGUE

HE MOVED THROUGH the space station without attracting notice, although he took notice of everything, everyone he passed. He had done this kind of thing many, many times before. He knew he was good. The fact gave him no particular pleasure or sense of pride. It was simply a fact.

He took the main turbolift out to the docking ring. The controls for the lift were marked in Cardassian characters. Everywhere he looked, there was some sign that the station had once been Cardassian, designed and built by Cardassians. It didn't matter that they had abandoned it, turned it over to Bajor. This place would always be Cardassian, even when all the signs and notices had been replaced by signs and notices in Bajoran and the Federation languages. Its spirit was Cardassian. Nothing they did could change that.

There was no ship docked at pylon two, and so no reason for anyone to be at the main cargo airlock. He did not intend for anyone to be killed or injured. It was not his purpose at this time. At other times, it had been.

Alone and unobserved, he took out the device. It fit easily into the palm of his hand. Small, inconspicuous, easy to overlook. He activated the arming switch and set it in place.

This was the first bomb.

CHAPTER
1

COMMANDER BENJAMIN SISKO finished fastening his dress uniform and pulled at the tight high collar in irritation. A quick glance into his mirror revealed his brows drawn together into a dark frown, an expression which had frequently given pause to both his enemies and his Starfleet subordinates.

Dammit, he thought, I didn't sign up for Starfleet to end up playing ambassador to half the sentient races in the galaxy!

Sisko did not, in truth, much resemble a diplomat at that moment. The face in the mirror belonged to a man who preferred to take the direct route straight to the heart of a problem, not tiptoe around it with half-lies and evasions and eloquent phrases that sounded good but committed the speaker to absolutely nothing.

And especially not wearing resplendent, uncomfortable dress uniforms.

But the fact remained: he was the commanding officer of the former Cardassian space station now

called Deep Space Nine, and thus the ranking representative of the United Federation of Planets in
Bajoran space, which positions entailed a number of
unwelcome duties and responsibilities, diplomacy
among them. And Benjamin Sisko was not a man to
shrink from any duty.

Still scowling, he searched in his drawer for a pair of
white gloves.

"Dad! That farking Cardassian replicator's fritzing
up again! It—"

"Jake! Watch your language!" Sisko snapped automatically as his teenaged son came into the bedroom.
The boy picked those words up from that Ferengi kid,
the father thought, a bad influence if there ever was
one. And Nog had doubtless picked them up from the
Cardassians, when the station was Cardassian, and
the personnel used to hang around in his uncle
Quark's casino. But it was also true that he was the
only other boy Jake's age on DS-Nine.

"I thought you said we could take the runabout out
today. You promised you'd let me take the conn!"

Sisko's irritation immediately changed to guilt as he
saw the stricken look on Jake's face, staring at the
dress uniform. It was true, he'd promised his son an
excursion away from the station. He hated to break his
word, but he had no real choice—not this time, at
least.

"I'm sorry. But an emergency's come up. I have to
greet the Kovassii delegation when they dock. There's
no way out of it."

Jake's scowl made him look even more like his
father at that moment. "You always say that! There's
always an emergency somewhere in this place!"

Sisko sighed wearily. "Jake, it's my job. You know
that. These trade negotiations are important. Don't
you think I'd rather be teaching you to pilot the

runabout than standing around in this ... *uniform* shaking hands with a bunch of self-important diplomats? But we don't always get to do what we'd like in this galaxy—or any other I know about."

"That's for sure!" Jake muttered. "Not around here, anyway."

Sisko's frown returned.

"Well, why do you have to be the one to meet this stupid delegation? Why can't somebody else do it? What about Major Kira?"

"Because I'm the station commander, that's why. Because that makes me the official representative of the Federation in this sector. The Kovassii are very touchy about protocol and security. And they're particularly nervous after that incident at the docking pylon."

"You mean the bomb?"

The commander's frown deepened. So much for security and secrecy in his command. It was impossible to keep anything quiet around this station. "I'd prefer it if you didn't mention the fact in public, but, yes, it was a bomb." Sisko sighed. It took a real fanatic to set off an explosive device on a space station full of civilians. It had gone off on docking pylon two, damaging the main airlock and forcing him to shut down the pylon just when the station was expecting an unprecedented number of ships to arrive for the trade negotiations. At least no one had gotten hurt, but it had taken every ounce of persuasive diplomacy Sisko possessed to talk the Kovassii delegation out of returning directly home to make an official report that Deep Space Nine was swarming with fanatical maniacs and terrorists. He had personally promised, as station commander, to guarantee their safety when they docked.

Thus the dress uniform, required by the delicate Kovassii sense of protocol and ritual. Thus his broken promise to his son.

"So why are all these delegations meeting here, anyway?" Jake asked, the sulky tone still in his voice. "If they want to negotiate with the Bajorans, why don't they just go down to the planet and have their meetings there?"

Sisko looked at him. "Is that a real question or just another complaint?"

A pause. "A real question, I guess."

"All right." Sisko touched his comm badge to activate it. "Sisko to Ops. Can you give me an ETA on the Kovassii ship?"

"They're cleared for pylon three, Commander. They should be docking in forty-five minutes. Their pilot seems to be taking, um, all due precautions in making his approach."

"You can inform the security detail that I'll be at the airlock when they come in, then. Sisko out."

He turned back to Jake. "All right, I have a few minutes. Look, the Cardassian occupation hurt the Bajorans in a lot of different ways. I don't mean just deaths and physical damage to their world, like the damage you can see here on the station. The Cardassians were ruthless. They didn't care if they left a single soul living on Bajor. At least here on DS-Nine they had to leave basic life-support systems intact.

"It was a brutal occupation. And if you learn one thing, Jake, learn this: Brutality only breeds more brutality. The Bajorans used to be a peaceful people. When the Cardassians first invaded, they had no idea how to fight back. But the occupation taught them to fight repression with terrorism. Three entire generations were bought up that way, living in exile and in forced-labor camps."

It was like one of those word-association tests, Sisko thought to himself:

Klingon / warrior
Bajoran / terrorist

"But I don't get it," Jake protested. "The Cardassians are gone now. The Bajorans won! They got their world back. So why are they still fighting and blowing things up?"

"That's what I'm trying to explain. Strange things can happen to people when they've spent their whole lives fighting for a cause. Think about it: Now that you've won, who gets to pick up the pieces? Who gets to put them back together again? Who gets which share of what little there is left?

"They have peace now, but they can't quite remember what peace used to be like. Some of them have forgotten any other way of resolving a dispute. Violence can turn into a way of life. And, besides, only a minority of the Bajorans are involved in all this factional infighting. But the entire world suffers from their reputation. Too many people think all Bajorans are terrorists."

"So I guess the Kovassii wouldn't want Major Kira to meet them at the airlock, huh?"

Sisko tried to suppress his grin, but he knew that Jake's remark was only the truth. Major Kira Nerys, his first officer, was a Bajoran, not a Federation officer. Deep Space Nine was officially a Bajoran station, although it was under Federation administration, and the joint command reflected that complicated fact.

It was also true that Kira, before she had put on the

uniform of an officer in the service of the provisional Bajoran government, had been an active member of the Shakaar resistance group, which was for all intents and purposes a terrorist organization dedicated to driving out the Cardassian occupiers by any means possible. No, the touchy Kovassii ambassadors certainly would not be pleased to discover that Major Kira was personally escorting them onto the station.

"The point is, Jake, this station is the one place that belongs to all the Bajorans, not just some group or order or faction. When the delegates come here, they're meeting at the nearest thing to a neutral zone in all Bajoran space. And what keeps it that way is the presence of the Federation. Our presence. If Starfleet were to abandon Deep Space Nine, the Bajorans might blow it apart fighting over which faction would assume control."

"Or the Cardassians would move in and take it over to get hold of the wormhole to the Gamma Quadrant," Jake added knowledgeably.

"Or the Cardassians would take it over, right. And what keeps them from doing that now? You know the station doesn't have the weapons to defend itself against Cardassian warship. But because we're here, the entire Federation is here, behind us.

"And that," he concluded, "is why I have to wear this damnable uniform and go to that airlock to bow and shake hands with the Kovassii delegation. Because I'm the official Federation representative and that's my job."

"Uh, Dad?"

"What?"

"Why the gloves?"

Sisko stared at the gloves. "Oh, right." As he started to pull them onto his hands he said, "It's a protocol thing with the Kovassii. They think displaying bare hands is offensive, for some reason." Flexing his fingers, he went out into the other room, about to leave, when he noticed the sputtering lights of the Cardassian-built food replicator.

"What's the matter with that thing *now?*" he muttered, coming closer and hitting the Reset control.

"No, wait! That's what I was going to tell you, the replicator's—"

But it was too late. A foaming pinkish blob materialized on the tray, spattering Sisko's gleaming white gloves.

"—fritzed again," Jake concluded unnecessarily.

Sisko took a deep breath but controlled his language in the presence of his son.

Just then his communicator beeped. "Commander? The Kovassii ship is expected to dock in ten minutes."

Sisko exhaled forcefully. "Be right there," he informed Ops. Then, to Jake, "Clean up that mess, would you? And I don't want you hanging around the Promenade with Nog, either. You have your n-space topography problems to finish, if I'm not mistaken."

"Yes, sir," said Jake unhappily as his father left their quarters.

Left alone, he brooded on his injustices. The replicator was broken again, so there wasn't anything to eat. This stupid station was full of Cardassian junk, and none of it ever worked right. And those topography problems were *hard.* He'd been going to ask Dad to help him with them, but Dad was never around long enough. He was always in a hurry. There was always some stupid emergency.

And now no trip in the runabout. It wasn't fair.

I should have known I wouldn't get to go, he

thought. Nothing good ever happens around this place.

But at least on the Promenade, there was usually some excitement. And kiosks where he could get something to eat. And if he was lucky, if he hurried, he might even run into Nog.

CHAPTER
2

SISKO WISHED that Jake hadn't reminded him about the bomb at the docking pylon. This was *not* the time he needed things like that to be happening.

The turbolift was slow, as it often was. Sisko hit the control again, impatiently, and looked up and down the corridor, with its bare-metal look and exposed lighting. Cardassian architecture was utilitarian, almost grim.

Thinking of the bomb, he tapped his comm badge again. "Sisko to Kira."

"Commander?"

He thought he could detect an impatient undertone in the shortness of her response: Now what was he interrupting her for? "The Kovassii delegation is just about to dock. I assume that your security team has already checked and cleared pylon three."

"It's been done, Commander."

"Any leads yet on who might have planted that bomb?"

"Nothing yet." Now the impatience was even more noticeable.

"Thank you, Major. Sisko out." And under his breath, he muttered, "Damn."

Major Kira was a highly competent officer, and they worked together well—except for those few occasions when she decided not to take orders. So why had he felt the necessity to call her up just now, second-guessing her? He knew better. A good commander doesn't do that kind of thing.

But Sisko knew why. In her years with the Bajoran resistance movement, Kira had undoubtedly planted her own quota of bombs. There had never been a firm line drawn between resistance and terrorism by the Bajorans fighting the Cardassian occupation. This, on the one hand, made her particularly well qualified to carry on the investigation. Her contacts within the various resistance groups were extensive. But these same connections meant that the terrorist they were looking for might be a former comrade.

When he'd first met her, Sisko might even have suspected Kira of complicity with the bombers, whoever they were—and it was generally agreed that they were most likely Bajorans. After all, what better position could a saboteur hold than the station's first officer, in ultimate charge of security matters?

He remembered quite clearly the very first time he'd encountered Major Kira Nerys, with the station in chaos after the Cardassian departure: torn cables hanging from the walls, consoles smashed in, broken components crushed underfoot. She had stated quite flatly at the time that she didn't believe the Federation had any business on Deep Space Nine. As far as she was concerned, the station was Bajoran territory, Starfleet officers were present only at the provisional government's invitation, and the government had made a mistake in issuing it.

Sisko had asked for her opinion. And had gotten it.

But recent events had made them more sure of one another. Kira had proved herself more than once, had backed him up when he needed it—even against Bajorans.

When the Cardassians had abandoned Bajoran space, they hadn't realized they were giving up access to the limitless wealth promised by the Gamma Quadrant wormhole. This was a mistake they were determined to rectify, and it was only the presence of the Federation Starfleet that prevented them from trying to seize the station outright. Kira knew this, and she had come to regard the Federation presence as a necessity, despite the objections of some more intransigent Bajoran isolationists.

No, Kira wasn't working with the terrorists. But— what if the evidence pointed at former comrades? Members of her own resistance group? Could she turn them in? More important, would her objectivity be able to override her sense of loyalty?

Loyalties. They weren't a simple matter, as Sisko knew. Still troubled, he hit the control for the turbolift to take him up to the docking pylon.

Sisko out.

Major Kira switched off her communicator with an angry slap. What did Sisko think, that she hadn't checked the other pylons? All the airlocks? What kind of incompetent did he think she was?

"Just keep out of my hair and let me do my job, *Commander.*"

The station's security chief looked up. "Did you say something, Major?"

"What? No. Sorry, Odo, just mumbling to myself."

Odo snorted with amusement, then continued with his task of collecting the scattered fragments from the explosion. Kira grimaced wryly. She knew what Odo had heard.

Now she pressed the palms of her hands against her eyes. She was tired. After the explosion, they'd sealed off the area to search through the wreckage, but it was a long, tedious job.

The pylon's whole locking level was a wreck. There were shards and slivers of the airlock driven into the corridor ceiling and walls, scattered across dozens of meters. The station was frankly lucky that there hadn't been a hull breach. And, so far, if there were bomb fragments among the pieces, they hadn't been able to identify them. Possibly the computer could, when it completed its analysis. For now, though, they were searching for any possible clue to the origin of the device, the identity of the person who'd planted it. Whoever it was, she *wanted* them. She and Odo both.

Their motives weren't identical. Odo would have been more than happy to arrest whoever the bomber turned out to be: Cardassian, Bajoran, or even Ferengi. But Odo wasn't Bajoran. He wore a Bajoran uniform, he looked Bajoran—superficially. But Odo could look like anything he pleased. His shape-shifting ability was quite useful in his position of security chief, but he had held that position under the Cardassians, as well. Odo cared passionately about justice, about upholding the law, but his feelings simply couldn't be Bajoran.

Not like Kira's. For her, the reasons were personal. Deep Space Nine was Bajoran territory now. She had put in too much effort, too much blood to let anyone destroy it. Not the Cardassians, and not any Bajoran fanatics, either. Maybe the bomber hadn't been a

Bajoran. There was no evidence, no proof. But in her heart, Kira was afraid he was.

In so many ways, it had been easier fighting the Cardassians. Then, you knew who your enemies were. Now the Bajorans were turning on each other, fighting for control of the pitiful remnants of their civilization. Hardly a week went by without some kind of protest, demonstration, or near-riot somewhere on Bajor. Even here on the station. What better way to express your feelings than to set off a bomb or shoot your opponents? There were times when Kira wasn't altogether proud of her own people, times when she was almost ready to admit that they needed the Federation to step in and protect them from themselves.

Almost.

Sitting back on her heels, she glanced out through the viewport. Studded with lights, blazing against the dark background of space, was the high arch of docking pylon three, with the Kovassii ship snugged up to the airlock. Aliens. Trade delegations. Sisko would be up there now, playing his role as station commander, all suited up in his fancy Starfleet dress uniform, sleek and clean and bowing to the Kovassii delegates come to negotiate for access to the wormhole. She resented their presence bitterly, the more so because she knew how necessary it was. Bajor needed the trade to recover from the ruinous Cardassian occupation.

For sixty years, they had raped her world, driven her people into slavery or exile, crushed her civilization under their boots with the sadistic pleasure of their kind. And in all that time, who had protested, who had raised a hand to stop the slaughter, who had cared about one poor, isolated world and its people? But now that the Bajorans had finally driven off their oppressors, now that they were finally free, what happened? The Federation discovered a wormhole to the Gamma Quadrant in Bajoran space. Suddenly Bajor was standing at the gate to unimaginable wealth, and now every planet in known space was sending representatives to try to get in on it.

Quick angry tears stood in her eyes as Kira silently cursed the aliens, all of them. *Where were you when we were being slaughtered? Where were you then?*

"Major?"

Kira exhaled wearily, raking her fingers back through her dark, short-cropped hair.

"Sorry, Odo. Sometimes . . ." She turned and looked around at the shattered airlock. "Tell me, do you think there's any real chance of finding any more evidence in all this mess?"

"We can only look. If it's here, we'll find it."

Kira sighed and knelt down next to him, aiming her probe to sweep another section of the floor. So little to go on. So many fragments. Everything obliterated. No identifiable cells for DNA typing, nothing to connect the bomb to its maker. Too many uncertainties. It could have been a timed or a remote-control device, planted any time in the last few months. It could even have been left here by the Cardassians, as a particularly nasty surprise for the station's new owners.

But Kira knew she couldn't afford to make that assumption. If there were terrorists on the station now, they had to be apprehended. Because they would certainly strike again. Kira knew her own people. They weren't the kind to give up after striking a single blow.

Time to stop looking and start thinking. She sat back on her heels again. "This was a political statement, Odo."

"Major?"

"This bomb. Whoever set it, they weren't trying to

blow up the station. No one got hurt. They didn't even manage to breach the airlock."

"Are you sure they didn't just slip up? It could have been meant to be an attack on the Kovassii ship. Maybe their timing was off."

"That's possible. But I just don't think so. It's just a feeling I have."

"I prefer to look at the evidence, myself."

"Well, then maybe between the two of us, we'll find something. But look where this bomb was placed. And it wasn't even powerful enough to put a hole in the airlock, let alone the hull of a ship. I mean, I could have done a better job when I was twelve years old!" And had, which she didn't bother to mention. *"If* that's what I was trying to do."

"So," said Odo, "either we have a particularly incompetent terrorist on the station—"

"Or we have someone who knows exactly what they're doing."

"Making a statement."

"That's what I think, yes."

"Which is?"

"I'm not sure." Kira sighed and rubbed her forehead again. "Maybe it's someone who wants to disrupt the trade negotiations. To keep Bajor out of the Federation."

"That's one theory. But this bomb was placed in the airlock where the Kovassii ship was going to dock. It could have been one of their enemies. Maybe some trade rival trying to frighten them away from exploiting the wormhole. Or a personal enemy of the ambassador. You see a political statement here, Major, because you view the situation in political terms. I tend to view it in criminal terms. That's my perspective."

"It's possible," she admitted. "But if this was an

enemy of the Kovassii, how could they have known in advance which docking pylon the ship would be assigned to?" A sudden thought made her frown. "Unless—they planted bombs on all six pylons. To make sure. But we checked, we found nothing." For an instant, she suffered a sharp pang of doubt, remembering Sisko's officious call to check up on her. But was she *sure* there hadn't been another bomb? What if they'd somehow overlooked it in their search?

"No, you're right," Odo said. "There was nothing." He paused. "Unless . . ."

"Unless what?"

"Unless they went back and removed all the other devices, before we searched. Or unless they have an accomplice working in Ops who let them know where the Kovassii ship was scheduled to dock."

Kira shook her head. "Too many theories. Not enough evidence."

"Does it make it simpler if we assume a political motive?"

Kira laughed curtly. "Hardly. You can pin a political motive on half the Bajorans on this station. And they probably all know how to plant a bomb."

"So you do believe it was a Bajoran."

"I *hate* to believe it. Unfortunately, I know us too well." She paused. "I can barely think of where to begin. With all the different factions here on the station: the isolationists, the religious parties—"

Her reply was interrupted by the beep of her communicator. She heard: "O'Brien to Kira."

"Yes, Chief?"

"Major, I don't want to disrupt your investigation . . ." Which, of course, is exactly what you're doing, Kira thought sourly. ". . . but I wonder if you could give me an estimated time you'll be finished up there on pylon two. That airlock is going to have to be rebuilt before we can start to dock ships there again, and we have more delegations scheduled to show up within the next few days. I'd like to start work as soon as possible."

Kira sighed in resignation. O'Brien, as chief of station operations, had his job to do, just as she had hers. "Actually, I think we're just about finished, Chief. You can have your repair crews up here as soon as you like."

CHAPTER
3

SISKO REACHED the docking area without incident. The rest of the reception group was already assembled at the pylon three airlock: a wide corridor junction bare of carpeting or other amenities, not at all the kind of plush reception area the Kovassii would prefer. A pair of security officers in reassuring Starfleet uniforms stood at alert, and safely behind them was the notable representative of the current provisional Bajoran government, Ambassador Hnada Dels. Hnada was wearing an emblem of state on a chain around her neck, and she kept straightening it, visibly nervous.

Everything seemed to be in order, although Sisko felt a distinct ethical discomfort looking at the security contingent, both Starfleet personnel. Kovassii insecurities had demanded it, but this was a Bajoran station, and they were going to have to get used to that fact if they planned to conduct trade through the Gamma Quadrant wormhole. He was sorry now that he'd given in to their demands.

Hnada seemed to be trying to catch his eye. Sisko stepped over to her. "Madame Ambassador?"

"Commander Sisko, I hope the Kovassii delegates will accept our apologies over the explosion. They have to realize that the authorized representatives of the Bajoran people were not in any way responsible—"

"Ambassador, I can assure you that the best thing you could do would be simply not to refer to the incident at all."

"You're sure? I don't want to offend them. The Tellarites demanded an official apology when those demonstrators splashed blood on their robes, you know. And the Andorian insisted on fighting a duel."

"Yes, I'm aware. But in this case, the fact that the Kovassii are willing to continue the negotiations means that they're unofficially pretending nothing ever happened. If you were to bring the matter up now, they'd have to notice it officially, which would mean the entire delegation would be dishonored and forced to return home."

"I see. Thank you, Commander." Hnada gave him a slight, wan smile. "Your help in these protocol matters has made so much difference. We *have* to do well in these negotiations, but so many different races, so many different customs—"

"Commander, the airlock's engaged now."

Everyone resumed their proper positions, while Sisko inwardly gave thanks that he'd managed to stay awake during the interminable Academy lectures on diplomatic protocol.

The Cardassian-built airlock door resembled a large toothed gear. Now it rolled open with the usual slight hiss as air pressure equalized. A moment later, a cautious humanoid head emerged, crowned with a luxuriant topknot of silver hair. Wide silvery eyes peered closely at the reception party, narrowing at the sight of the Bajorans, dilating again as they rested on Sisko's dress uniform. The commander's gloveless hands were folded carefully behind his back.

The Kovassii disappeared again into the airlock, but reemerged only a moment later. He folded at the waist in a deep bow. A second Kovassii came out, bowed likewise, but not so deeply. A third. The final Kovassii to step from the lock had his hair arranged in the most elaborate topknot Sisko had ever seen, from which it flowed down like a fountain. His robe was a gleaming, spotless white. His eyes met Sisko's and he bowed at a slight angle.

Sisko returned the bow and stepped forward to greet the ambassador. "Your Excellency, welcome to the Bajoran system and to Deep Space Nine. Allow me to present to you the representatives of the Bajoran provisional government. This is Her Excellency, Ambassador Hnada Dels."

There were tentative bows on both sides. Sisko was about to continue with the introductions when his communicator beeped. His jaw tightened in irritation. He'd given strict orders not to be interrupted. Unless it was a grave emergency. If this wasn't serious . . .

"Commander, this is Dax, in Ops. We have a situation developing here."

A situation. He bowed again to the Kovassii ambassador, more deeply this time, in recognition of the breach of protocol. "Your Excellency, I'm very sorry, but if you'll excuse me, a situation has developed that requires my urgent attention. I'm sure you'll understand."

He stepped aside to answer the call, leaving the two ambassadors face-to-face with no Federation intermediary, vowing to himself that heads would roll if this wasn't really an emergency. But there was no officer on the station that Sisko trusted more implicitly than Lieutenant Dax. If she was interrupting him, he was sure there was a good reason.

"Sisko here. What's going on?"

"Commander, there's a Cardassian Galor-class warship approaching the station at point two-two impulse. They've informed us that they plan to dock."

Sisko felt an adrenaline surge of alarm. Why were they coming in so fast? Were they planning to attack the station? Ram it? Sisko was well aware that standard Cardassian doctrine was to strike first and let the survivors ask questions later. But he hadn't believed the local commander, Gul Dukat, was likely to use such tactics, unprovoked. Dukat had been prefect of DS-Nine under the Cardassian occupation. He was a dangerous but known quantity.

"Call Yellow Alert. Do you have ID on that ship? Is it Gul Dukat?"

"Hailing them now." A pause. "I'm not getting an answer, but scan says it's a different ship."

Sisko's sense of urgency grew acute. The Cardassian government had been unstable since their loss of the wormhole and the failure of their previous attempts to take it over. The ruling party had been overthrown and a new junta come to power, more belligerent than the last. There had been accusations of treason, and even executions.

Suddenly Gul Dukat's absence took on new, ominous implications. Sisko was about to consider issuing a Red Alert when Ops reported back. "Sir, the Cardassian is decelerating. We've established contact now. The ship's name is the *Swift Striker*, Gul Marak in command."

"I'll be right there."

"Yes, sir."

He turned back to the diplomats. "Your Excellencies, it does appear that there's an emergency which requires my presence in Operations."

The Kovassii all looked at each other in obvious alarm. "Not another bomb!" the ambassador asked, glancing back toward the airlock and the safety of his ship.

"Nothing like that!" Sisko assured them quickly. "An incoming ship is in violation of the traffic regulations. This is nothing that should interfere with your negotiations."

He turned to the senior security officer. "Chief Phongsit, would you please escort Their Excellencies to the meeting rooms?"

Then he tapped his comm badge again. "Ops, this is Sisko. Beam me down there now."

He stepped off the transporter pad to see the entire staff in Ops glance up at his arrival. With the station on Alert status, all available officers were present, seated and standing at their stations around the gleaming blue-lit display of the operations table. Over the whole scene loomed the huge main viewscreen, displaying the ominous image of a Cardassian Galor-class warship: with its spreading wings forward, it made Sisko think of a dinosaur from the floor of Earth's primordial oceans, armored in rough metal plates. But he had fought against such ships and knew that despite their crude appearance, they were efficient in battle.

He went immediately to his position at the master console, relieved to be abandoning diplomacy to take up his role as station commander. As Lieutenant Dax came up to meet him, he ordered, "All right, let me see what's been going on here."

"This is what we have," Dax told him, calling up a recording onto the screen. The image displayed was of the Cardassian ship, at a greater distance. Sisko heard Dax's voice, requesting identification.

The Cardassian officer who appeared on the screen had a predatory look, with a sharp-bridged nose and thin, cruel lips. Sisko wondered briefly if many Cardassian infants were born sneering.

"This is Gul Marak, commanding the Cardassian dreadnought *Swift Striker*. We intend to dock at this station within ninety minutes."

Dax's voice on the recording said, "Gul Marak, we advise you that your incoming velocity is well in excess of the safety limit specified in our navigation regulations. There is civilian traffic in the vicinity. Please reduce delta-V immediately."

But the Cardassian's image disappeared from the screen with no reply, and the replay ended, replaced again by the real-time view of the incoming ship.

"What's their current approach velocity?" Sisko demanded.

"Point fifteen impulse, Commander."

"Hmm." Still dangerously fast, but the Cardassians were probably just indulging in a typical display of flashy aggression, Sisko decided. Deliberate provocation was part of their style. They liked to see whom they could intimidate at a first meeting.

But at the moment there was another complication. If Gul Marak meant to dock his ship, where was the station going to find the room to accommodate it? Deep Space Nine was getting crowded with all these delegations arriving, and there were only six docking pylons suitable for a ship the size of a Galor-class. The Cardassian warship would strain the available facilities. This was just another complication Sisko didn't need.

He turned to O'Brien. "Chief, I don't suppose pylon two is in any kind of shape to be used right now?"

O'Brien shook his head. "No, sir," he said emphatically. "I can't say when it will be, either. Those airlock doors were blown to hell and we don't have replacements."

"Then what about six?"

"Well, we've still been seeing those fluctuations in the power-junction nodes to the turbolifts in that sector."

"It'll have to do," Sisko decided. Docking pylon six was on the "down" side of the station, directly opposite the Kovassii ship. Repairs and maintenance had been neglected in those sectors as the operations staff coped with one crisis after another. But uninvited guests couldn't be too picky about their accommodations.

"I hope the lifts do go down again," O'Brien said under his breath. "Let the Cardies walk all the way to the core. It'd do them good."

Sisko shot him an intimidating look, but said nothing. He knew the reasons for his engineer's attitude toward the Cardassians.

A moment later the communications technician said, "Commander Sisko, Gul Marak insists on speaking to you. Personally."

"Open channel."

Marak's thin nostrils were flaring in indignation. The corded tendons on his neck seemed to throb with it. "Commander, my ship was just ordered by some *Bajoran* to dock at pylon six. I command a Galor-class dreadnought, not some filthy mining tub! I warn you, this insult is insupportable!"

Sisko took a breath. "Gul Marak, you can observe the situation for yourself. Pylon two is out of commission due to a recent accident. The other facilities are either occupied by ships already docked, or committed to incoming traffic. And I'll point out that you've

26

arrived here without prior notice and without an invitation from this station. Under these circumstances, if I were you, I'd take the berth that's available."

Sisko cut the transmission and exhaled with distinct satisfaction. He'd learned some time ago that there was no use being too polite with the Cardassians. They only took it as weakness and used it against you. And this Gul Marak looked exactly like the kind of Cardassian who was going to cause trouble.

"I'll be in my office," he announced, heading for the stairs.

It was ironic, he thought a few moments later, looking around the room with its plenipotentiary's view of the Operations Center below. Not too long ago, this had been Gul Dukat's seat of command. Sisko had never before harbored any warm thoughts for Dukat, but at the moment, right after his encounter with Gul Marak, he almost missed the former Cardassian prefect. By now, he knew how to deal with Dukat.

What had happened to him, anyway? Had he been stripped of his command, or even arrested by a new government? Why was this Gul Marak suddenly showing up in Bajoran space?

Just then he spotted Major Kira as she stepped out of the turbolift into Ops, looking slightly out of breath.

Sisko tapped his comm badge. "Major? Could you come up to my office?" He knew that Kira was still, in her heart, at war with the Cardassians, and most likely, of anyone on the station, to have up-to-date intelligence on the enemy.

She looked up at him from the floor below. "I'll be right up."

He could hear her coming up the metal stairs,

taking them in a hurry. "There's an alert?" she demanded as she came into the office. "A Cardassian ship?"

"Nothing urgent. Not anymore. Please, Major, sit down. I'd like you to take a look at this." He replayed the encounter with the *Swift Striker* on his desk console. "Do you know this Cardassian officer?"

"Gul Marak." Kira frowned, a gesture that always emphasized her Bajoran features. "No. I don't recognize him. But the name—it sounds familiar." She passed a hand over her eyes, blinking wearily.

Sisko noticed it and realized that she had probably been investigating the bombing for the last twenty-eight hours without rest. "Thank you, Major. That'll be all now. Get some sleep if you can."

The Bajoran officer straightened at once, aware that she'd been caught in a moment of weakness. Kira didn't admit to weakness. "There's an alert on the station," she said stiffly.

Sisko gave her a hard look. "I intend to cancel the alert as soon as the *Swift Striker* is safely docked."

"With Cardassians on the station, there'll be a need for increased security."

"Then it'd be a good idea for you to get some rest now, before they get here," he insisted, in a tone that didn't invite argument.

Kira left the office reluctantly. Sisko tapped his fingers on his desk, thought for a moment. "Computer, get me a report on the current Cardassian political situation. I want to know how this Gul Marak is connected to the new ruling party."

The computer voice answered: "There are two individuals named Marak in office with the current Cardassian government. Both are members of the Revanche party. One is a deputy to the new war minister, the other is on the Loyalty Investigation

Board. The Gul Marak commanding the *Swift Striker* is the cousin of the deputy war minister."

"And what about Gul Dukat?"

"Records show no Gul Dukat currently holding a Cardassian command."

"What? Has he been cashiered? Arrested?"

"No further information on Dukat is available."

Sisko paused. "I want to be kept advised on this matter."

"Acknowledged."

Sisko tapped on the edge of the desk again. Finally he gave his communicator a thoughtful touch. "Dax? This is Sisko. Are you free to discuss something with me?"

"I can be right there."

Sisko brightened noticeably when she came into the room. An uninformed observer might have attributed this reaction to the fact that Jadzia Dax was an exceptionally beautiful humanoid woman, but the truth was that he had a hard time relating to her as a female at all. Years ago, another Dax had been his mentor, and now part of that Dax resided as a symbiont within this one. It was a confusing situation, and he hadn't completely come to terms with it yet.

But Dax was currently the only one on the station he could sit down and discuss things with, person to person. With Dax, he didn't have to constantly maintain the role of commander.

"You have a problem, Benjamin?"

He sighed. "It looks like I've been neglecting developments in the Cardassian political situation. It seems that our new friend Gul Marak is part of this new Revanche party that's taken power, and I don't think he's just come to pay a routine courtesy call."

"You expect trouble?"

He nodded. "It looks like Gul Dukat may have been

relieved of his command. Maybe even arrested, I don't know."

"That would be hard to believe. Could they be blaming him for failing to take over the wormhole?"

Dax and Sisko exchanged a glance full of shared memory. It had been the two of them together who first discovered the wormhole to the Gamma Quadrant, while they were investigating an area of unexplained neutrino disturbances.

"I suppose it might be something like that," he said. "Computer, have there been many Cardassians arrested since the Revanche party took over?"

"Records show that one hundred and fourteen individuals associated with the former administration have been charged with treason. There have been eighty-three executions. The guilty persons all confessed to accepting payoffs from the Bajorans and the Federation in exchange for turning over Deep Space Nine and control of the wormhole."

"That's absurd!" Sisko exclaimed. "Payoffs? To turn over the wormhole? No one knew the wormhole even existed until after the Cardassians gave up the system!"

"Not quite entirely absurd, Benjamin," Dax told him. "Consider: We know that the wormhole is an anomaly, artificially maintained by beings with the capacity for communication with humanoid species. The Bajorans have worshiped them for millennia. Isn't it conceivable, from the Cardassian point of view, that the 'gods' passed on the secret to their believers? That they waited to manifest the wormhole, in collusion with the Bajorans and possibly the Federation, until Cardassians had ceded control? Isn't this a more plausible explanation than mere coincidence?"

Sisko, who didn't believe in coincidence when it

came to the Bajoran prophets, grudgingly admitted that her analysis made sense. But the thought of all those confessions to a nonexistent crime, and the methods by which they had likely been obtained, made him feel slightly ill.

"And this is Gul Marak's faction," he said grimly. "I don't like it, Old Man. I just wish I knew what his plan was."

"We can't afford to provoke him. Or react to any provocation on his part."

"No," Sisko agreed. "And I don't think it's a coincidence that he's showed up just when these trade negotiations are going on, either." He pulled at his tight collar. "I'm going to go get out of this thing."

Kira Nerys's quarters were spare, uncluttered by worldly possessions. The only personal object visible was a picture of her family—what had been left of her family by that time—taken in the refugee camp where they stayed when she was very young: three or four years old, from the looks of the picture. She couldn't remember. Half of the faces belonged to strangers whose names she didn't know, but they could have been brothers, uncles, grandparents. So many that she'd lost. That the Cardassians had taken from her.

Marak. She couldn't get the name out of her mind. Lying sleepless on the thin, hard pad that was her bed, Kira could close her eyes, but the images persisted:

I was very small. Someone was carrying me. There was a crowd—I think we were waiting in line, maybe for water. There was never enough food or water in the camps. Life was mostly waiting in lines.

Suddenly there was screaming. People started to run. It was a panic. Then I was on the ground. They were kicking me, stepping on me, trying to run away.

People started to fall. Some of them fell on top of

me. I couldn't get any air. I pushed—pushed the body off me so I could breathe.

Then I saw them. The Cardassians. They were shooting the people running away. Making them fall down. I cried when I saw them fall.

And now this face on Sisko's viewscreen: Gul Marak. The same dark, armored uniform. It had been years, but Kira's gut always clenched at the sight of that uniform, at the sight of a Cardassian face.

Rationally, Kira knew it couldn't have been this same Gul Marak at the camp. It had been too long ago. From what she'd seen in Sisko's office, the *Swift Striker's* captain was close to her own age.

The Federation tried to claim that the Cardassians weren't the enemy anymore. Kira would never believe it. As long as she lived, they would be the enemy. As long as she could still remember.

And she would always remember. That was the curse of her past, that she couldn't close her eyes and make the images go away.

Only the names were lost.

CHAPTER
4

IT WASN'T SAFE TO SLEEP.

Berat closed his eyes and lay very still, trying to slow his breathing so they couldn't be sure whether he was awake or not. He ached with weariness. He simply ached.

He was assigned to the bunk nearest to the head, so he was constantly hearing the rush and gurgle of the sewer conduit, the voices of the men going in and out to relieve themselves, the sound of their boots clanging on the bare deck plates. When he was an engineering officer, he'd been used to having a cubicle to himself, no matter if it was just four walls, but there was no privacy for anyone here in the lower-deck barracks, with the metal bunks lined up in double rows and the lighting element sputtering faintly overhead. And of course all of them had to pass by him on their way in and out of the head, so that every time he heard their footsteps he would never know when someone would decide to deliberately "trip" over his bunk or commit some other petty act of harassment just for the amusement of it.

Amusement could easily get bloody on the lower deck of a Cardassian warship. One of the favorite tricks was tossing a blanket over the victim and holding him down while the rest of them beat the struggling form. If he survived the blows and the suffocation, he still wouldn't be able to identify his assailants. They'd already done that to him more than once since he'd been brought onto the *Swift Striker*. They might do it again, at any time. Whenever the men started drinking, when someone got into a fight or lost money gambling, or after the Gul had given another one of his rousing inspirational speeches about recovering lost Cardassian territory.

He had dared, once, to report a beating, but all it had gotten him was extra punishment duty for fighting. And then retaliation, later, in the dark. They laughed as their heavy boots thudded into his ribs, mocking him in the crude Cardassian language used on the lower decks. "You gonna report this, too, are you, traitor? You gonna report *this?*" It was all the more amusing because they knew he'd been an officer before he was broken, a rare opportunity for vengeance that the much-abused denizens of the lower deck greatly appreciated.

It wasn't safe in the dark, wasn't safe in the head or the shower or anywhere they could catch him alone. It wasn't safe here, in his bunk, to sleep.

And it was all going to get worse. Berat knew it, because it was common knowledge that the ship was heading into Bajoran space, to the station the enemy was now calling Deep Space Nine. The closer to Bajor, the worse it was for him.

Lower-deck rumors were spreading that Gul Marak was heading there to deliver an ultimatum to the

Federation: Turn over the stolen wormhole or face the might of the Cardassian fleet. It had happened again today. He was coming into the head to fix a broken ventilator, and a couple of crewmen were talking: "Gul's gonna blast'm if they don't hand it over."

The other nodded agreement: "Vaporize those filthy Bajoran scum."

Then, seeing him, they both went silent, fixing him with hostile stares. "What are you looking at, *traitor*? What are you doing, anyway? Spying on us? For your Bajoran friends?"

Berat was tainted with guilt, even if there was nothing they could prove. He knew it was no coincidence that he was assigned to this ship, to this commander, to this mission. They were setting him up. *Something* was supposed to happen once they got to DS-Nine, and then, somehow, he was going to be the one to take the blame. To be dragged home in chains for execution.

The way his father had been executed. And two of his uncles and his brother.

When their government fell, at first it seemed that Berat was lucky, assigned as systems control officer to Farside Station—on the other side of Cardassian space from the Bajoran sector. There was no evidence to link him personally to the wormhole sellout scandal. But of course it was all politics. As soon as the Revanchists had consolidated their power, he was stripped of his commission. Even after he had signed the denunciation. Which still made him burn with shame, remembering. They had made him watch, of course. The whole thing. One of them had handed him a stone. *"You aren't soft on traitors, are you?"*

And he'd thrown it. Aimed to miss, but—to his eternal disgrace, he'd thrown it.

Now, lying in his bunk, reliving it all, Berat found it

hard to swallow, even to breathe. The *Swift Striker* was already in Bajoran space.

Footsteps came down the corridor, armored boots ringing on the deck. Berat tensed. The footsteps paused at his bunk, and the bare metal frame suddenly rang with the force of a kick.

"Berat! On your feet, scrag!"

He recognized Subofficer Halek's voice. He would recognize that voice on his last night in hell. But there was no time to think, only to react. In an instant, Berat had leaped to his feet, was standing at rigid attention by the side of the bunk, eyes straight forward, not meeting Halek's. Inside, where they couldn't see it, his heart was racing, his gut was churning with apprehension and fear. But it was death to let them see weakness.

"What the flakk are you doing in your farking bunk when you're supposed to be on duty?"

"Sub, I was on duty the last two shifts."

"Well, you're on now. Let's go! Don't just stand there taking up space on the deck! I've got a job for you." Halek slapped his data clip smugly.

Berat knew better than to protest. He supposed there was a sewer backup in one of the heads, or some other filthy job that no one else wanted to take on. As quickly as possible under Halek's hostile glare, he got into his soiled fatigue uniform. He already knew he wouldn't be given time to make up his bunk, and that he'd be blackmarked on account of it, on account of the dirty uniform that he hadn't had time to get cleaned. By this time, it didn't much matter. He'd already accumulated enough black marks on his record to keep him on nonstop punishment details for the rest of his natural life span, which he didn't expect to reach.

But he was shocked when Halek ordered him, "Get over to the main docking airlock and strip it down. I want a complete point-by-point maintenance checkout—every motor element, every seal." This was normally a job for a skilled two-man engineering crew, not a single low-grade technician. He said nothing in protest, though, nothing to provoke Halek into one of his rages. But he was worried, as he pulled a tool kit from the engineering locker. Why this particular assignment? Why now? Were they setting him up for something? A charge of sabotage?

Or maybe this was just a quick and dirty way to get rid of him. An "accident" when he was working inside the lock, and Bajoran space would swallow up one more Cardassian body.

The worst thing was knowing there wasn't anything that he could do to stop them, if that was what they meant to do. If he refused an order, they'd space him anyway. Only after he was hanged. It was a quick way to die, in comparison to some others he'd seen.

He double-timed it down to the airlock with Halek on his heels. Their boots rang on the bare metal deck plates. He passed a crew working on one of the massive power cables that fed the weapons systems, and they looked up to smirk at him, amused at the sight of someone being marched to a punishment detail. But there didn't seem to be anything wrong with the airlock when he got to the docking port and took a look at it. Maybe this was just routine maintenance.

Berat set to work, trying his best to ignore Halek, who stood over him with folded arms, giving unnecessary and contradictory orders and emphasizing them with an occasional kick or slap with his mesh-gloved hand.

"Lubricate those bearings.

37

"Well, it doesn't look aligned to me. Strip that farking seal off and set it again!"

"Do you call that track clean?"

Finally his tormentor took note of the time. "I'll be back at 0600 hours. You'd better have this back in working order by then."

Left alone, Berat leaned up against a wall. He was shaking with repressed tension and fatigue. He'd figured out their game on his first day on this ship. They wanted an excuse to bring him up on capital charges: refusal of a direct order, assaulting a superior officer. He wondered how long it would be until one of them provoked him past the breaking point.

Halek hadn't given him much time to finish, so Berat turned back to his task. Without interference, he reassembled the airlock mechanisms, making sure that the door rolled smoothly in its track, that the seals fit to the proper tolerances, that the air-pressure level was correct. The work, now that he had a chance to do it right, restored a little of his battered self-confidence. He was still a first-rate engineer, even if they had broken him to the lowest grade. No matter what else they'd done to him, they couldn't take that away. Only his rank, his career, and probably his life.

Halek returned finally, tested the airlock, and grudgingly acknowledged that the task had been completed to specifications. Berat noticed the deliberate way he checked off the job authorization on his data clip, and he felt that sense of dread again, that he was being set up somehow.

Released, he stumbled back to his bunk and fell into it, forgetting even that it wasn't safe to sleep.

It seemed like only minutes until alarms rang throughout the ship. The comm system blared: *"The ship will dock in thirty hours. All hands to duty stations!"*

Berat groaned. He dragged himself to his feet, swaying with exhaustion. How much longer could this go on? How much more could he stand? He knew they were going to break him, sooner or later. It was only a question of when.

CHAPTER
5

"COMMANDER SISKO, Gul Marak requests permission to meet with you at your earliest convenience."

Sisko acknowledged the message without surprise. He'd been expecting this, now that the *Swift Striker* had docked. It looked like this Gul Marak didn't plan to waste too much time, whatever he had planned. "Tell him I'll see him in my office whenever he comes on station."

He shifted impatiently in his chair. He never really did feel quite comfortable in this office, looking down from on high at the main Operations floor. But its design did provide some useful insight into the Cardassian mind-set. Gul Marak, like most who held that rank, doubtless considered himself a type of minor supreme being who expected his subordinates to jump at the snap of a finger and obey orders without question. Sisko had known others of the type.

Thinking of Cardassians, he activated his console and called up a view of pylon six, with the *Swift*

Striker now docked. He had observed the procedure from Ops. The Cardassian pilot had snugged the huge warship deftly into its berth with a minimum of thruster adjustment. The big winged ship fit there as if it and the station were made for each other. Which of course they had been. The *Swift Striker* might look rough and ungainly to Starfleet eyes, but seeing it docked now, Sisko was forcibly reminded that Deep Space Nine was Cardassian-built, that the very features he and his staff were constantly finding most irritating had been designed with a different utilitarian harmony in mind.

As a Starfleet officer, Benjamin Sisko was supposed to be free from xenophobia. Still, the Cardassians were everything he deplored, both personally and as an officer sworn to uphold the ideals of the Federation. Since taking over the station, he had often been sharply reminded of this contradiction within himself, especially here in Gul Dukat's office.

Marak burst through the door without knocking, a courtesy apparently not generally practiced by the officers of the Cardassian fleet. By now, Sisko was used to it.

"Gul Marak?" he inquired smoothly, letting a bland smile mask his irritation.

"And you're Sisko," Marak stated with an amiable sneer.

Sisko quelled his hostile reaction, but the smile faded. "I believe you asked to meet with me."

In response, Marak tossed a data clip onto the surface of his desk. "The Cardassian government has ordered me to communicate their demands to the United Federation of Planets. To you as their representative."

Sisko picked it up. "Sit down, Gul, while I read this."

"There's no need to read it. I can tell you what it says: My government demands that the Federation return the Cardassian station unlawfully possessed by you and currently designated DS-Nine. I'm authorized to assume command here at this time."

Oh, you are? Aloud, Sisko said only, "I'm aware that you've recently had a change of government."

Marak went on as if he hadn't spoken. "The Federation has no legitimate claim to this territory. It was relinquished by traitors falsely claiming to act in our name. If you wish, I can show you copies of their confessions. By all rights, this station is Cardassian domain."

"Gul Marak, I can't comment on charges of treason within the Cardassian government. But in any case, I'm not empowered to hand over command of DS-Nine. The station and the region it controls belong to the Bajorans. Perhaps you ought to deliver your *demands* to them."

Marak hissed in contempt. "Cardassians don't recognize Bajoran scum!"

"That's your problem, then! Because the former administration did turn over the station to Bajor." Sisko took a breath. "I will, of course, pass on your government's position to the proper authorities in the Federation. But until I see orders to the contrary, DS-Nine remains Bajoran territory, administered by the Federation at Bajor's request. And I'll retain command."

"I see." Marak's voice took on a menacing tone. "Then don't say you weren't warned."

"That's true on both sides, Gul. I hope we understand each other."

Marak nodded stiffly. "I assume that my ship is still free to dock here under your administration."

"Just the same as any other ship. Deep Space Nine is open to all. Even to Cardassians. Now, to other business. Do you intend to give your crew liberty during your stay here?"

"You have objections?"

"Not at all, as long as they're aware of our regulations. No weapons are allowed on the Promenade. No violence will be tolerated, or threats of violence, or forceful intimidation. This includes sexual encounters. If your crew has a complaint, they take it up with station security, they don't try to settle matters themselves.

"And—one other thing. We have a number of planetary delegations on the station. At the moment, our life-support capacity is near its limit. For that reason, I'll have to ask that you limit your liberty parties to no more than fifteen crew members at any one time."

"Is that all?"

"I'll have a complete set of current station regulations transmitted to your ship. Just so there won't be misunderstanding."

Marak bowed, machinelike in his stiffness. "Very well, Commander Sisko. You'll be hearing from me again."

"You know where to find me, Gul." Sisko couldn't have him off DS9 too soon. Again, briefly, he found himself with a strange sense of missing Gul Dukat.

As soon as Marak had left, he slapped his communicator. "This is Sisko. Get me Constable Odo right now. Then have all security personnel report for briefing. And notify Major Kira that I want to meet with her, but only when she reports back on duty. Don't wake her."

It was a good thing, he thought, that Kira had been

asleep in her quarters while Gul Marak was on the ship. He wouldn't have wanted to witness a confrontation between those two.

Kira simply couldn't sleep.

A human in her place might have taken a sleeping aid, but a Bajoran was different. Kira knew that her spiritual center was disturbed, misaligned. She had to set it right again, or she would never be able to rest in any meaningful sense.

The moment she stepped through the circular doorway into the temple's shadows, she could feel some of the tension leaving her. Candles made a soothing, flickering light, and from somewhere came the distant sound of a voice, softly chanting. Then her heart lifted when she saw a familiar, saffron-robed figure approaching from his place at the side of a small reflecting pool.

"Leiris! I hoped I'd find you here."

They touched hands, and the monk pressed his fingertips to the lobe of her ear, where a silver clasp dangled. "Kira Nerys, old comrade!" He drew her back to the edge of the pool, where they sat down together. "You're disturbed," he said. "I can feel it in you."

She sighed. "You can understand. Better than anyone."

He shook his head serenely. "We've all been scarred by our experiences. You aren't alone, Nerys."

She poured out her feelings. "I've sometimes felt like I'm alone. Here, on this station. When I first learned you were coming here, I realized just how much alone I've been, for so long. I avoided the temple for years, you know, during the war. I'd even stopped meditating. I was out of touch with myself.

But I think I had to be, to go on with the struggle. With what we had to do."

"Then perhaps the Prophets have sent me to help you."

She dropped her head into her hands. "I see the faces. When I shut my eyes. They won't let me rest."

"No, Nerys. You won't let yourself rest. The dead are at peace with themselves. You imagine their suffering, but you're only feeling your own loss."

"I remember what they suffered. So much, so long. How do you forget, Leiris? How did you manage to find peace, after everything?"

"I don't forget. But it's time to leave the past to itself. Time is a series of moments. At each point, it is always *now*. When we were oppressed, it was possible to find our center in the act of resistance. That is, some of us could. I'm sorry it was otherwise with you. But now, Nerys . . . you must look into yourself to find the center of your being. What pulls you into the past? What keeps you from finding your center, here, now?"

"Whenever I see a Cardassian, whenever I hear a Cardassian name."

"Ah, yes. The Cardassians. Tell me, if you had killed them all during the war, would you be at peace now?"

She said nothing, only exhaled.

"Nothing we do can harm the dead—or help them. We can only help ourselves. We can only live among the living. Come, we'll meditate together. Seek for your center, Nerys. Leave the dead to their rest. You are alive. Live *now.*"

Again, he touched the edge of her ear, pressed his fingertips against her temple. "Close your eyes, Nerys. Leave the past behind. Bid it farewell."

She exhaled, she shut her eyes, and in the inner vision saw the dead faces again, watched them fade.

"Look away from it. Turn away from the pain. Find your self, Nerys. Find the center of yourself."

Time seemed to suspend itself, or to cease altogether. Place faded away. There was only her self, the center that endured through all times, all events. She separated herself, from mere events, from the world, from its pain. Timeless, eternal . . .

When she emerged from the state of meditation, Kira didn't know how long it had been. She didn't want to check the time to find out, to reduce the experience to mere worldly dimensions, like minutes or hours.

She did think, when she finally left the temple, that sleep might have finally been possible—sleep without dreams. She was actually on her way back to her quarters when her communicator caught the announcement: "All security staff report for briefing."

"What the . . ." Suddenly, she was fully in the world again. Here, in the Promenade corridor, on Deep Space Nine. Where a Cardassian warship was docked. She slapped her comm badge. "Kira to Odo. What's going on?"

"Major, you're not supposed to be on duty."

"Odo, just answer the question. What's the emergency? Why are we still on Yellow Alert?"

"No emergency, Major. The meeting is merely a precaution with the Cardassian ship onstation. The commander wants to avoid provocations."

"What provocations?" she demanded, already on her way to the security office.

Sisko had clearly not expected to see her there. "Major, you're supposed to be off duty."

"Well, I'm here. What's this about Cardassian provocations?"

"The Cardassians have delivered a demand that the Federation turn the station back over to them."

Kira could feel her anger seething, the blood starting to heat. All her newly won spiritual balance deserted her. "They *demand!* Turn the station back over to them? They have the unmitigated—"

"Major!" At the tone in Sisko's voice, she caught her words. He went on, "This is probably just a *pro forma* display by the new government that took power recently. I suspect they're just going through the motions to satisfy the public at home. They deliver an ultimatum to me, I send it on to the Federation, and they've made their point.

"But, just in case it's something more than that, I've taken certain precautions. We'll remain on alert status. And I've limited the number of Cardassian crew members that can be on the station at any one time.

"But what we *don't need* right now is some Bajoran hothead deciding that this is the right time to look for a little personal vengeance for something that happened during the occupation. I don't think I have to remind you all that matters are at a very sensitive stage at the moment, with the ongoing negotiations. Ambassador Hnada has asked me to personally ensure that there are no incidents which might disturb the delegates.

"Clear? Everyone? Major?"

"Of course," she said stiffly. As much as she often disagreed with their decisions, Kira wore the uniform of the Bajoran provisional government. If they wanted these trade negotiations, it was her duty to support them—regardless of her personal feelings about Bajor joining the Federation.

"But Commander, one thing. I do know the Cardassians. It'll take more than just legal technicalities to satisfy them. They won't stop until they've seen blood."

Sisko grimly recalled the reports of the executions, the records of the confessions that Gul Marak had transmitted to him after he went back to his own ship. "I believe, Major, that they've seen plenty of blood already."

CHAPTER
6

ON THE grimly utilitarian decks of the *Swift Striker*, all the crew was in a state of knife-edged suspense, waiting for the Gul to return from the station, where he was delivering the official Cardassian demands to the Starfleet commander. Crewmen stood in clusters in the barracks, outside the heads, lining up for their meals in front of the galley, speculating as to what the outcome would be. Here and there officers ordered the groups to break up and get to work, but the excitement gripped the upper ranks, too. It was taken for granted that the Federation would refuse the Gul's demands. Then it would be war!

The more belligerent among the crew gleefully anticipated an order to stand away from Deep Space Nine and open fire with their whole array of phasers. But cooler heads argued against this probability. The space station, they pointed out, was the key to controlling the wormhole. They wanted to retake it, not destroy it.

All the talk was all conjecture, anyway. The Gul

certainly didn't make a practice of discussing his strategy down on the lower deck.

As for Berat, he was almost insensate with exhaustion. Orders had come down that the *Swift Striker* had to be in spotless order before it docked, everything scrubbed and polished as if the Fleet Admiral were waiting over there on DS-Nine, ready to conduct an inspection. The burden, of course, fell most heavily on maintenance and engineering staff. For once, Berat wasn't the only one working back-to-back shifts. But he still felt as if he had personally scraped the crud from every centimeter of hull and deck plating on the ship, polished every hand railing, every viewport. His only consolation was that the officers were too busy to single him out for particular abuse.

But the results of their work were plainly visible once the ship was docked. Next to the proudly gleaming *Swift Striker,* Deep Space Nine appeared battered and neglected, exactly what anyone would expect from Bajoran management, even with the Federation nominally in charge. The superiority of Cardassian discipline was clear to be seen by anyone.

Despite discipline, however, most of the crew was looking avidly forward to liberty on DS-Nine. Since several of them had been on the station before, they were well aware of the diversions and amusements to be found on the legendary Promenade level. Anarchy, after all, did have its advantages, compared with disciplined Cardassian austerity. Seated at the well-worn metal tables in the lower-deck galley, these veterans described the anticipated delights to their crewmates. On DS-Nine, there were exotic liquors strong enough to take off the top of a man's skull and leave him prostrate three days afterward. Games of chance, especially the Dabo tables presided over by exotic females in scanty, alluring attire. And holosuites that offered erotic fantasies beyond the possibilities of the average crewman's imagination. Berat was forced to endure overhearing lengthy recitations of exactly what his fellow crewmen intended to do in those holosuites.

There was a predictable reaction, then, when the Gul returned from the station with the announcement that liberty parties would be limited to fifteen members and for no longer than a duty shift.

As the men stood at attention, cursing under their breath, their commander's voice over the comm went on:

"There are ambassadors from a number of important governments on DS-Nine at this time. I want *no incidents* that would cast any discredit on Cardassian discipline. There will be *no weapons* taken aboard the station. There will be *no violence,* no assaults, no rapes, no confrontation with Federation personnel *or* natives. In short, there will be *no complaints* about any member of this crew. Any man who causes a problem onstation will spend a long, long time cursing his own mother for giving him birth."

The muttering among the crew mostly subsided to sullen looks. Gul Marak had not earned the reputation of a commander who made idle threats.

As for Berat, he hadn't expected liberty, anyway, and DS-Nine was the last place he would have wanted to spend it. But he wasn't immune to the consequences of the general dissatisfaction. As soon as he reported for his next duty shift, he caught the vengeful look in Subofficer Halek's eye.

Halek tapped his data clip meaningfully. "Well, *Technician* Berat, since you did such an excellent job with the main personnel airlock the other day, I think it'd be a good idea if you refitted the supply and emergency locks, too. *Get moving!*"

Berat groaned inwardly. As weary as he was, he felt a return of apprehension. He knew that the work had already been done in the general preparation for docking, but he said nothing. While he didn't know exactly what they were planning, he feared that working him to death wouldn't be enough for his enemies.

They went first to the airlock in supply hold C, a vast, stark metal cavern filled with the necessary supplies for a warship crewed by over seven hundred men. The lock, of course, was in perfect working order, but Halek ignored that detail and ordered Berat to work, keeping up a running stream of curses and abuse.

"This lock has a pressure leak. Take the whole thing down and reset the seals. No—did I tell you to check the pressure? I said to take down the farking door!"

Berat hesitated. The supply airlocks were oversized. Taking one of them down was a job meant for two men. But he had no choice. It was an order. He started to disengage the door from its tracks. But with the heavy circular panel half free and half still in the track, he felt his grip on it slipping. With a whispered curse, he tried to hang on, but his hands were slick with lubricant from the tracks, and the weight slipped again, pinning his fingers between the door and the bottom track.

The pain made white starbursts behind his eyes, and he gasped through clenched teeth. There would be no help from Halek, he knew that much. With a painful effort, he shifted the door with his good hand enough to free the other. Gingerly, he tried to flex the fingers. They didn't seem to be broken, but livid parallel welts were branded on them, and one had a bleeding gash across the knuckle.

A kick from the toe of Halek's boot struck him in

the ribs. "What the flakk are you waiting for? Get that door off! And I don't want to hear any excuses!"

From his knees, Berat silently cursed Halek, the door, the *Swift Striker,* and its commander—all his tormentors. Then he took the pry bar and levered the door up again, managed to get it disengaged and set aside. It was a simple matter to reset the seals. But then he had to lift the door up again and reengage it, all with no help from Halek but a constant flow of abusive orders and blows.

He finished, finally. Hit the control pad. The door hissed smoothly: open and shut again. He wanted to turn on Halek, say something like, "I did it. You thought it would break me, but you couldn't do it."

But he only looked down at the deck.

"All right! Let's go! Pick up your tools, Berat. There's the two emergency locks on this level we haven't checked yet. How much do you want to bet that they'll have pressure leaks, too? And don't think you're going to be off this shift until they're finished!"

"But . . . Sub. The airlock. The pressure check—"

"Did I tell you to check the pressure? You follow orders, Berat, or I'll have your hide hanging off you in strips! Now *move!"*

Berat picked up his tools, but he hesitated again. Regulations mandated a pressure check every time there was maintenance or repair to an airlock—it was a basic safety precaution, which Halek knew perfectly well. On the other hand, Halek had given him a direct order. He couldn't disobey. But if he followed the order, he knew who would take the blame for omitting the pressure check. And if something went wrong— Berat had a sudden sinking feeling that something was meant to go wrong.

Still, he protested again, "Sub, regulations—"

A mailed hand hit him in the mouth, and Berat tasted his own blood. Halek was grinning as he said, "So, Berat, you finally refuse a direct order? It's about time!" He pulled back his hand for another blow, and Berat broke, reacting without thought. With a desperate surge of strength, he flung the tool kit at Halek, striking him across the side of the face. As the subofficer staggered, Berat saw him groping for his phaser. Berat fell on him, grabbing the pry bar that he'd used to disengage the airlock door. The feel of the hard metal bar in his hand gave him a sudden surge of exhilaration. He hit hard, had the satisfaction of hearing bones crack as the phaser fell to the deck.

He snatched up the weapon, but standing there holding it, seeing Halek writhe in pain on the deck, Berat felt dread clutch at his belly. The image of his father's execution swam in front of his eyes. He knew that he was finished, now. Gul Marak had all the excuse he needed to hang him—and more. He had acted on desperate impulse, in self-defense, but that meant nothing. This was an assault on a superior officer: a capital offense. There would be no mercy from Gul Marak, no consideration of extenuating circumstances. This was what they'd been waiting for.

He looked down at his tormentor, and Halek stared back at the phaser aimed at him, suddenly still. So, Berat thought. This was the end. No way out. But it was an opportunity for vengeance, at least. An enemy life to set against his father's. If he was going to die, let him die for this, instead of on some petty, trumped-up charge.

But even as he gathered his resolve to fire, Berat paused. No way out? No escape? When only a few meters away, on the station, was Bajoran territory, beyond Gul Marak's long reach.

No. It was no good. But the surge of hope made him

look back again. There was more than one way off the ship. At least one of the emergency ports had to be connected to the station, he knew quite well, because this was a Cardassian ship and a Cardassian station, and that's how it was always done: a backup port was always engaged in case the main airlock malfunctioned. In case someone had forgotten to do a pressure check.

He looked at the phaser, back at Halek, then at the phaser again. If he was going to escape, he'd need time. He couldn't risk them coming after him.

He pressed the trigger, there was a brief burst of fire from the phaser, and Halek fell back onto the deck and lay motionless. Berat looked again at the weapon for an instant. It was the first time he'd actually fired on anyone. But there was no time to waste. He bent down to Halek and stripped the data clip from the sub's belt, thinking, It was him or me. He keyed in the job number, and there it was: authorization for the maintenance and repair of the supply hold and emergency airlocks. The pressure check of the lock in supply hold C, he noted, was not checked off as completed.

He attached the clip to his own tool belt, picked up the kit, started gathering the scattered tools. There was blood on the pry bar. Berat ripped off a scrap of Halek's shirt to wipe it clean. He deliberately didn't check the unconscious man's pulse or respiration. He didn't want to know.

He glanced for an instant at the airlock. That was one way to get rid of Halek. He shook his head reluctantly. It wouldn't do to have the body of a dead Cardassian officer floating outside the ship, not when he wanted to avoid drawing attention to his escape.

The *Swift Striker* had two emergency docking ports forward, one port and one starboard. With his tool belt and kit, no one challenged Berat as he made his way through the ship's crowded corridors. When he got to the portside access and found a guard stationed there, he knew he'd found the right one.

One hand reached inside the tool belt to the concealed phaser.

But the sentry had already spotted him. "No access," he snarled, raising his own weapon. "Gul's orders. Nobody gets onto the station this way."

Berat held up the data clip. "I've got orders, too. Maintenance. Got to check the airlock pressure."

The guard frowned dubiously. Berat held out the data clip with the authorization for repair and maintenance of the supply and emergency locks.

"Hmm." The guard was still doubtful. "I dunno about this. Three sorry scrags tried to sneak through on the last shift. Wanted to get onto that Promenade. I hear the Gul's still got'm hanging."

Berat swallowed in sympathy, but he managed to say, "Well, Sub Halek will hang me if I don't get these jobs finished. I don't know what's going on, I've just got my orders. Look at this—I almost lost a finger on the last job, I'm supposed to be off shift already, and I've still got the starboard lock to check out after this one. I shouldn't even still have to *be* on duty, with this hand!"

The familiar sound of griping allayed the sentry's misgivings. "Well, I suppose. You got your orders, I guess." He stepped aside to let Berat at the airlock, watched as he set down the heavy tool kit, got out the pressure gauge.

Berat could feel the eyes on the back of his neck, the guard watching. What was he going to do now? "Flakk it!" he swore feelingly, imitating the language of the lower deck, "Not another leak! That's the second one today! Now I'll have to replace the seals! I'm gonna be on duty till next year with all these farking airlocks to work on!"

He continued to complain as he unpacked his kit, hoping the sentry wouldn't notice when he turned casually to the security access panel.

But the guard didn't back out of his way. "Say, don't I know you? Aren't you—"

As if he were reaching for a tool in his belt, Berat pulled out the phaser, turned and fired before the guard's suspicions could fully materialize. The man crumpled to the deck. Time was crucial now. Cursing his injured hand, Berat put the phaser back in his belt before he got the panel open and switched off the security alarm.

Then he hit the control pad, and the door rolled open. Inside the chamber, it seemed like a full minute before the pressure sensors flashed the stationside light and he could activate the other door. He was just about to hit the control to open it when he remembered—there was a security alarm on the station side, too!

Fighting panic, he told himself, Stop. Think. But any minute now, someone could come by and look down the access corridor. See him getting away. And the sentry—when was he going to wake up? In five minutes? Ten?

The sentry was the most immediate problem. He was alive and breathing strongly. Berat opened the shipside door and dragged the guard inside the lock with him, then, deliberately, took out the phaser and stunned him again, making sure he wasn't going to be able to interfere. Next, he wedged the pry bar into the track to block the door if anyone tried to open it.

Now, if he was lucky, he'd bought himself enough time. He peered through the stationside door into the corridor. There, only a meter away, was the security panel with the switch to shut off the emergency alarm. But it might as well have been on the other side of the docking ring for all the good it did him here, on this side of the lock.

No, he had to do it the hard way. Working quickly, ignoring the pain in his bleeding hand, Berat removed the door's control pad to get access to the circuitry. The alarm was set to go off whenever the door was activated. The two lines were linked: he could sever the circuit, but then the door wouldn't open. Even worse, cutting that circuit would set off a malfunction alarm that would instantly alert the station's maintenance crew.

He studied the complex branching network for a moment, to make sure of what he was doing. It wasn't such a difficult job, but only if you knew which circuit was which. For obvious security reasons, none of them were marked. Cutting the wrong one, even touching it with his probe, would set off the very alarm he was trying to silence.

His hands were sweaty. He wiped them on his greasy fatigues. Then he severed the circuits, to the maintenance alarm first and then the security line. The door control had to be reconnected, next, bypassing the other circuits, directly from the power node.

Automatically, when he was finished, he replaced the access panel. Then he took a breath, hit the control pad. The stationside door rolled open with a faint hiss.

Berat looked out into the corridor. It was empty. In fact, it looked like it had been deserted. Most of the lights were off-line, panels were missing, and there were black stains on the walls and ceilings that looked like smoke. There'd been rumors that when the occupation troops pulled out of DS-Nine, they'd trashed the station, wrecked it. Now it looked like the rumors had been true.

But no guards. Only the sensor mounted at the top of one wall, which would let station security track him wherever he went. But—he paused. With the condition the rest of the hall was in, these monitors might not even be functioning.

Berat hadn't given much thought, in his panic, to what he was going to do when he was on the other side of the airlock. Where he was going to go, how he was going to hide—a Cardassian on a station full of Bajorans! He couldn't go back to face Gul Marak's mercy, not now. But for the first time, he realized that he might have stepped into something even worse. He'd heard what the terrorists did to Cardassians. He might end up begging Gul Marak to hang him.

He glanced nervously back at the shipside door, at the sentry who might start stirring soon. No, he couldn't go back, no matter what, and he was almost out of time.

Grabbing his tool kit, he stepped out of the lock into the station corridor. The security sensor was his first priority. Quickly, he pulled out his diagnostic probe and discovered it was, in fact, nonfunctional. Relief almost made him dizzy. For once, luck was going his way!

Now if it would only last. One thing was clear. He couldn't stay in this section, not where the *Swift Striker* was docked. As soon as he was reported missing, as soon as the sentry woke up, the Gul would have guards out after him—

He ran.

When he reached the first branch corridor, Berat glanced back the way he'd come, listening for the sounds of pursuit, but he heard nothing. No guards, no one chasing him. Not Marak's deck patrol or station security.

He started to wonder. What if the deck patrol ran into station security? Into a Bajoran security force? That might be his best chance! And this corridor looked like it was in even worse repair than the other. Certainly ships hadn't been docking regularly at this pylon!

He could hide here. Not only was the place deserted, there were cargo bays, lifts, access shafts—just like there'd been on Farside Station. Where he knew every kilometer of them. All Cardassian space stations were built on the same general plans.

Cautiously, apprehension making his hands tingle, he probed the nearest security sensor. This one wasn't working, either. A circuit burned out. Just a basic repair job. And he had the tools with him, here on his belt.

He popped off the panel, started to probe. There it was. The whole junction node burned out. Well, he could fix that, too. A new unit, a few connections, and that was it. He could have done the job in half the time, if he hadn't constantly been stopping to listen to the sound of imaginary footsteps in pursuit. A quick check with the probe, and, yes, the monitor was working again!

Now when the Gul sent the deck patrol after him they might run into something!

Then Berat ducked into a deserted cargo bay and into the power-conduit shaft he knew would be there. He started to crawl, to find some place where he could hide. And rest.

Finally, to get some rest.

CHAPTER
7

IN THE DS-NINE SECURITY OFFICE, Constable Odo sat at a desk surrounded by banks of surveillance monitors, some of them lit up with schematic displays, some of them blank. At the moment, he was staring at one particular display. Now, *that* was peculiar! Sensors in a whole section down on pylon six had just come back on-line. How had that happened?

Under ordinary circumstances, he would have simply made a note to have the anomaly checked out by maintenance. But these were hardly ordinary circumstances, not with the recent bombing incident. And pylon six was currently where the Cardassian warship was berthed.

Immediately, Odo made an urgent call to Major Kira. Alone in his office, his attention engaged on his work, the shape-shifter had slowly allowed his features to blur until his appearance was only generally humanoid, although it retained all functional aspects of the form. By the time Kira answered, he had resumed his usual aspect, close enough to Bajoran to pass at first glance.

"Major, there's an anomaly in section nine, pylon six."

Kira was on duty in Ops. The place had been quiet, with technicians working at their stations. But hearing Odo, she started, and her hand made an instinctive move toward her phaser. Pylon six: that was the Cardassian ship! With an effort, she controlled her reaction. If Odo had said "anomaly," he didn't mean a riot or a Cardassian invasion.

The constable went on. "Sensors in the section have all been burned out since the Cardassians wrecked the place. Now they're functioning again. And I don't think there's a repair crew scheduled to be in that section."

Kira shrugged. "Call Chief O'Brien and make sure about the maintenance schedule. Then get down there and check it out," she ordered. "I'll meet you."

She was just starting toward the transporter pad when the communications tech called out, "Major! There's an urgent message from the *Swift Striker*. Gul Marak is demanding to talk to the commander."

Kira paused. With Sisko off duty, she, as the ranking officer in Ops, would normally handle such communications. Of course, in an emergency, Sisko could be paged, but no one had said anything about this situation being an emergency. And why should that Cardassian be making demands, anyway?

With an unmistakable set to her jaw, Kira said quickly, "I'll take it," as she strode over to the master console.

The furious face of Gul Marak was immediately displayed on the main viewscreen. As he saw who was facing him, his thin lips drew back from his teeth with distaste. "I *said* I wanted to speak to the Federation commander."

Kira concealed her own loathing only a little more effectively. She snapped stiffly, "I'm Major Kira, first officer on this station. Commander Sisko isn't available."

Marak's nostrils flared as he took a breath. Reluctantly, he said, "A deserter has just escaped from my ship onto the station, through the emergency airlock. I insist that you return the criminal *immediately."*

Kira felt a warm vengeful glow in being able to say with absolute truth, "We have no report of a Cardassian deserter on this station."

"This man is a traitor and a murderer! He's armed and dangerous. He's brutally murdered his superior officer and assaulted a sentry."

"I'll inform our security office about the situation," Kira replied shortly, conceding nothing. "We will, of course, investigate your charges."

Marak looked as if he was going to say something intemperate, but his image abruptly disappeared from the screen.

Kira still felt the warmth of satisfaction as she signed off and logged in the exchange. Thwarting Marak had given her more pleasure than anything since the time she held off three Cardassian warships with not much more than hand phasers and bluff.

A *murderer. You're a murderer, Marak. All your breed are murderers.* Nevertheless, she had to admit that having a rogue Cardassian armed and at large on DS9 was a dangerous situation. If Marak's story was true. But she had reason to believe it might well be. More than that, she was willing to bet that it might have something to do with Odo's report of an "anomaly" in section nine on pylon six. The emergency airlock to the Cardassian ship was on section eight, just one level above. But of course she had said nothing about any of this to Marak. He had no need to know about security arrangements on DS9. And there was no real evidence to connect the two incidents. Other than coincidence.

"Inform the security office about the report of a Cardassian deserter," she told the comm tech as she went quickly to the transporter pad. Then, "Beam me down to section nine, pylon six."

Odo was waiting for her. "Did you contact O'Brien?" she asked.

"He said the only repair teams he had down here were to check out the airlock systems and the turbolifts. That work was already completed before the ship docked."

"Well, this whole situation may be more complicated. Gul Marak claims an armed Cardassian deserter has come onto the station through the emergency airlock on section eight. He may be hiding somewhere around here."

Odo's expression managed to show concern. "Armed?"

"Marak claims the man murdered his superior and assaulted a guard, then escaped through the lock."

"But . . . there was no alarm!"

"Another malfunction?" Kira speculated.

"This is my fault!" Odo exclaimed through clenched teeth. "I take full responsibility. When the ship docked here, I forgot about the emergency lock! Most of the ships that come here aren't configured to use it."

"So it wasn't guarded?"

"No. And the sensor array in that section wasn't even working!"

Kira glanced at the monitors overhead. "But now *these* sensors are working? What about the monitor at the emergency airlock?"

Odo quickly checked his security padd. "No sensor function."

Kira shook her head. "This just doesn't make sense. Have you checked these sensors out? Do we know why they just came back on-line?"

"My probe reveals normal functioning, that's all. I've asked Chief O'Brien to come and look at them. Maybe he can tell if there's been any tampering."

"Good. But first, we'd better take a look at this emergency airlock," Kira said grimly.

But nothing in the lower corridor seemed wrong or out of place. Kira stared at the closed airlock door. Just on the other side of that lock was the Cardassian ship. So close. She had to shut her eyes for a moment.

"Major?"

She opened them again. "Sorry."

She looked at the wall panel. "You say the security alarm didn't go off. Was it set? Is it broken?"

But a quick look inside the panel showed the alarm switch was properly set. If someone had gone through the lock, it should have gone off. "You can't switch it off from inside the lock. So how did he get through?" Kira demanded, frustrated.

"Unless the deserter had someone on the station helping him. To switch the alarm off from this side."

Kira scowled at the thought of a conspiracy between a Cardassian and someone on the station.

"Or unless . . ." Odo flipped on his probe, then hissed through his teeth. "It's not functioning, either! But—if the alarm isn't working, then the door shouldn't open, either. At least, it's not supposed to. So no one should have been able to come out this way."

"Maybe they didn't. Maybe this is all some trick of Marak's," Kira said slowly.

They stared at each other. There was one way to find out. Kira took a breath, then hit the airlock control pad. But the door remained closed, and instead of the security alarm, she heard the louder buzz of the hazard warning, and the door panel flashed red in Cardassian script that both Kira and Odo could read:

PRESSURIZATION FAILURE
AIRLOCK INACTIVATED

They looked at each other again. This situation was getting harder and harder to make any sense of.

"We could override it," Odo suggested unenthusiastically, but neither of them wanted to make the attempt. Pressurization failure was no trivial matter on a space station.

What was going on? The airlock malfunctioning, no alarm, broken sensors suddenly working again.

"Do you think, somehow, that you could be getting false readings?" Kira asked Odo.

He checked his probe again. "I don't see how. But, I suppose it's possible. In this situation, anything seems possible."

Kira inhaled with a sharp hiss of frustration. Where was O'Brien? She hit her communicator. "Kira to O'Brien. Have you checked those security monitors in section nine?"

The ensign's good-humored voice came over the link. "I'm here right now. It looks like someone's been repairing our security sensor grid."

"Are you sure?"

"Oh, absolutely. I can see where one of the nodes had been fried. Somebody's fixed it, put in a nice new unit. Not a bad job, either. Wish I knew who it was—I could use the help around here."

Sometimes Kira could find O'Brien's cheerful manner irritating. But she only said, "Could you come down to section eight, to the emergency airlock? Something strange is going on here."

"I'll be right there."

O'Brien came up via the turbolift a few minutes later. He stared at the hazard warning, still flashing, then took out his engineering tricorder to probe the situation. After a moment: "Well, it seems that we may have a leaky seal somewhere, but no major depressurization. I think we can take a look." He keyed in the sequence to override, and the warning light stopped flashing.

"What about the security alarm?" Kira asked him. "Odo's probe says it's not functioning."

O'Brien went to the panel. "He's right, it's not. Now, that's damned odd." He turned to the door control pad, swept it with his tricorder. *"Damned* odd."

"What do you mean?"

"These are on the same circuit. That control pad shouldn't be working. You shouldn't even have gotten that warning. Hell of a way to set up a system, if you ask me, but that's the way the Cardies wanted it to work."

He went back to the panel, opened it up, and probed around inside for a few minutes. "Everything normal here."

Kira frowned in thought. "Could someone have tampered with the circuits from the other side? From inside the lock?"

O'Brien looked blank. "Why, I don't know. I'd have to take a look. It could be possible, I suppose."

He cautiously touched the control pad, and the door

rolled open normally. They stepped into the lock, still nervous about the depressurization warning. But what they found in the lock was the shipside door half-dismantled, with a Cardassian maintenance crew hastily working to repair it, and a Glin who shouted for them to halt where they stood, enforcing his order with a drawn phaser.

"No one is allowed through here!"

Kira bristled, although she resisted the urge to pull out her own weapon. Beside her, Odo and O'Brien were tense and alert. She knew she could count on both men to back her up. Neither of them trusted Cardassians.

In common law, the interior of an airlock between station and ship was station territory that ended only at the shipside door. Kira informed the Glin of this fact in unambiguous language, but he kept his weapon pointed at them. "I have my orders."

Kira refused to back down to the Cardassian. "And I'm investigating a threat to the integrity of the security systems on this station." Then she had a truly malicious inspiration. "Or do I have to inform your Gul that his subordinate is impeding the search for the deserter he claims to be at large on Deep Space Nine?"

The Glin's face paled, and he took an uncertain step backward. "I'm not to allow anyone through this airlock," he insisted again, though less confidently.

"Fine," Kira snapped. "We have no intention of setting foot onto your ship." To Odo, under her breath, "Keep an eye on him."

And aloud, "Chief O'Brien, please carry on."

While the two security contingents faced each other in an uneasy confrontation, O'Brien proceeded to inspect the airlock's interior controls. On the Cardassian side, the maintenance crew also began to carry on with their work of remounting the shipside door.

Kira couldn't help wondering what had happened to it, but she had no intention of asking the Glin.

"Ah!" O'Brien exclaimed a moment later.

"What?"

"See what he's done? He's shut off the exit alarm from inside here, then reconnected the circuitry to bypass it so the door control would work. Neat job!"

Kira might have wished he weren't quite so cheerful about the discovery. "You can fix it?"

"Oh, no problem." O'Brien glanced back at the dismantled door on the ship side of the lock, and his tone was less light as he said, "Now I suppose we know why that depressurization warning went off."

"Yes, but I'd like to know what happened there," Odo said, also stealing a look at the Cardassians.

In only a short time, O'Brien had restored the original circuitry and tested it.

"Well," asked Kira from the station side of the lock when he was done, "what are we supposed to make of this? A Cardassian crewman kills his superior, breaks down the shipside airlock door, bypasses the station-side security system, then escapes onto DS-Nine?"

"And fixes the monitors in the next section, while he's at it," O'Brien added. "I think our boy's some kind of technician."

"But why fix the security system?" Odo asked, still frustrated. "I suppose I can understand why he'd want to dismantle them if he could do it, but why stop and make repairs?"

Kira was just beginning to think she might know the answer to that one, when suddenly, in the empty, half-wrecked corridor, the stationwide comm startled them all: *"Full station alert! All Security to the Prom-*

enade. Civilians, evacuate levels nine through eleven. Medical, report to the Promenade."

In the distance, they could hear the alarms.

Kira reacted instantly, full of certain dread. She and Odo looked at each other, back at the airlock leading to the Cardassian ship. Whatever had happened here, it would have to wait.

Kira hit her comm badge. "This is Kira and Odo. Beam us up to the Promenade!"

CHAPTER
8

KIRA AND ODO materialized into a scene that was all
too familiar to someone who had grown up in the
midst of wars and refugee camps: people screaming,
running blindly, the sound of alarms blaring, the
unmistakable scents of smoke and fire. A child was
crying in terror and pain, bleeding from a cut on her
arm. Kira picked her up, looking around for help. Her
first reaction had been *Cardassian attack,* but now her
anger found a different target: terrorists! Another
Prophet-cursed bomb! And this time on the crowded
Promenade, with civilians present, with *children.*

She spotted a medic, handed over the child. There
were other, more serious casualties. She could see the
medical team working over them on the deck. Dr.
Bashir was working on—Kira almost stopped and
drew her phaser for an instant before she recognized
the Cardassian, Garak, who ran the clothing shop.
Another innocent civilian, she reminded herself. It
was too easy to forget that Cardassians could be
innocent, too.

Garak seemed to be in shock. His face was bloody from what looked like a dozen tiny sharp fragments. He kept saying, "I only stepped out for a minute. Just one minute. I was going right back inside. Just one minute. I would have been in there."

"It'll be all right." Bashir tried to quiet him. "Just hold still."

Kira looked past them to the door of Garak's shop—to where the door of his shop had been. Nothing there now but shards and wreckage and smoke still slowly billowing out.

"I want this area cordoned off!" Odo shouted, striding quickly toward the scene. "No one touches a thing until we go through this mess!"

From what Kira could tell, the explosion had been directed inward, containing the evidence in a reasonable area instead of blowing it halfway across the Promenade. Oh, she hoped this time they'd manage to nail whoever was doing this!

"I want the names of everyone who was in this area! Every possible witness," Odo was ordering the security forces as the converged on the disaster scene.

A familiar voice broke in. "What's happened here?"

Kira looked up to see Sisko. His rage was obviously under tight control. She told him, "It looks like another bomb. Planted at Garak's. We're having the place cordoned off till we can sort out all the evidence. Whether or not it's the same type as the last one, we can't tell yet until we do a forensics test."

Bashir was coming toward them now. The front of his uniform was smeared with blood. "No fatalities," he reported. "Six injury cases, primarily from flying shards from the window. The most serious case could lose the sight in one eye." Then he was off toward the infirmary, following in the wake of the stretcher cases being carried there by volunteers.

"Major," said Sisko tightly, "I *want* whoever's responsible for this."

"Major, Commander, you'd better came over here and take a look." It was Odo, calling them from the side wall of Garak's shop, where security forces were setting up a barrier.

Kira felt broken shards crack under her feet as she followed behind Sisko's longer strides. There was a paper stuck to the wall—a crudely made poster. The words had been written in obvious haste:

DIE, CARDASSIANS!

And it was signed, *Kohn Ma*.

Kira swore: "May their souls wander in the darkness until the end of the last eternity!" For a Bajoran, this was almost an unthinkable curse, and some of the onlookers gathered on the other side of the barrier made signs for averting it, but others nodded in angry agreement. Children had been hurt here, Bajoran children. They could have been killed.

Now, adding to the confusion, a group of monks was approaching from the direction of the temple, intoning chants in the traditional Bajoran mode. "We're going to need to get all these people out of here," Sisko said. "To close down this section of the Promenade so we can investigate. We can't really do much here now."

"I'm getting the names of witnesses now," Odo told him.

Kira looked dubiously at the approaching procession. She knew it wouldn't be easy to get the monks to leave, and the crowd might not like the idea of interrupting the chant. There were times when she wondered about her own people.

Then, among the monks, she caught sight of one

familiar face. "Excuse me, there's someone I need to question right away."

She touched Leiris on the sleeve of his robe. "Old friend, I need to talk to you. Now. Is it possible?"

"Of course, Nerys." He brushed her earlobe with his fingertips. "I can see that you're disturbed."

Kira let him lead her back into the temple, to the side of the reflecting pool where they had talked before. The contrast of this peace and serenity with the chaos outside almost made her feel as if she had entered another plane of existence. It was strange— no matter how long it had been since she'd been inside the temple, the minute she set foot in it again, she couldn't understand why she'd stayed away for so long. It was, she supposed, just part of being Bajoran.

"Now, tell me what troubles you. It has to do with these bombings, doesn't it?"

"This is Bajoran territory they're attacking. Bajoran civilians, children . . ." Her eyes went to a stain on her sleeve. "Bajoran blood—the blood of Bajoran children. There's been too much of it spilled. I'm going to find them, Leiris. I'm going to stop them. I've sworn a vow. No matter what they are. No matter *who* they are. No matter if I have to—"

"Betray a former comrade?"

She looked down at her hands. "If that's what it comes to, yes."

"I see. This is a grave burden on your soul, Nerys. You have knowledge that many others do not, knowledge imparted to you in confidence."

She nodded. "I know names, I know methods. These are people I fought next to, side by side. We suffered together, we bled together. For the same cause."

"You know who they are, then? You have . . . evidence?"

"Not yet. But I will. Sooner or later. Because they're not going to stop. After today, I'm sure of it."

"I see. And you suspect some particular group?"

She shook her head. "Not yet. So far, we don't have much evidence to go on. Only today, there was a note left near the scene. It said, 'Die, Cardassians.' And it was signed, Kohn Ma. That's why I need to talk to you. Do you have *any* possible leads to whoever could have done this thing?"

"You believe it was Kohn Ma?"

She shook her head. "I don't know. It could have been. But the Kohn Ma has always tended to the more . . . extreme solutions. I am sure these bombings are politically motivated, but they don't seem to be meant to kill Cardassians or destroy the station."

"What would be their purpose, then?"

Kira ran her hand back through her hair. "They could want anything. To provoke the Cardassians. To disrupt the trade negotiations. To keep Bajor out of the Federation. And they've never hesitated at violence. But this—is terrorism directed against Bajorans!

"That's why I have to ask you, with your connections—do you *know?* Is there anything you can tell me?"

"I'm sorry, Nerys." Leiris put his hands together in a posture of meditation. "You know, long ago, when we were both young and fought together for the freedom of our world, they called us terrorists, too. And sometimes, yes, innocents were harmed. Even our own people."

"This isn't the same!" Kira said passionately.

"There are those who might say otherwise. That we've only replaced the Cardassians with the Federa-

tion. These terrorists you've vowed to apprehend—
are they any different from what we were?"

"Yes!" she cried passionately. "You tell me to let the
past die. But this is about the future. Bajor's future.
Right now, docked at pylon six is a Cardassian
warship. There's only one thing that keeps them from
attacking, and that's the presence of Starfleet personnel. I admit I don't like it, I'd rather see Bajor capable
of defending itself, but we're not, Leiris! The Federation is the only thing standing between us and the
Cardassians or any other power that wants to take
over the wormhole. It's the isolationists like the Kohn
Ma who'd leave us in the hands of our enemies. I can't
let past loyalties tie my hands. For Bajor's sake, I
can't."

"I see. Yes, this is your path, Nerys. But I think it
will be a hard one."

"They'll think I've betrayed them. I know."

"But you must follow your path. Away from your
past. Yes. Let us meditate together, Nerys. Let us look
forward down the paths we must take."

But she shook her head, regretfully pushed his hand
away. She couldn't afford right now to slip away into
the no-time, no-place state of meditative peace, assuming she could manage to achieve it. "I don't have
time, not now. I have to get back there."

"I will pray for you, Nerys."

"Thank you." She hurried away, out of the temple
and back to the scene of disaster.

CHAPTER
9

IT HARDLY CAME as a surprise to Commander Ben Sisko that after the worst of the mess from the bombing was cleared away, he found every diplomat on the station clamoring to see him, "with the greatest urgency"; "with extreme urgency"; "with the utmost urgency."

After one brief, futile attempt to sort the messages into some order of priority, he finally took Hnada first, on the ground that the Bajoran ambassador had called three times already since he'd come through the door of his office.

Hnada was in a state of acute crisis, which Sisko might have called hysteria if he were feeling uncharitable. "Commander Sisko! You're here! Finally! You have to tell them . . . assure them, we had nothing whatsoever to do with this, not Bajor, not the government! These are outlaws, criminals! Unsanctioned terrorism! They don't represent the Bajoran people! Whoever's responsible for these attacks will be prosecuted to the full extent of the law! Bajorans were injured here! You must make this clear!"

"Ambassador . . . Ambassador Hnada . . . if you'd let me . . ." Sisko finally broke through her protests. "I *assure* you, Ambassador, that I'll do everything possible to make your position clear to the various delegations . . . Yes, I understand. . . . We *are* investigating. . . . I'll certainly stress that point with the representatives." Finally, "Ambassador, the representatives are waiting for me to contact them now."

Then, with a sense of inevitable dread, he took the next call. The Nev'turian representative appeared on his viewscreen, his fangs fully bared in outrage. Without initial courtesies, he launched into his complaint: "I was told these Bajorans were civilized people, a *spiritual* people! I was told that these charges of terrorism were unfounded! Now I find them setting explosives in a contained environment, endangering everyone! How can you expect me to negotiate in good faith with such a race? How can you conceivably expect such a world to be admitted to the Federation?"

It didn't get better. The Agguggt! ambassador had no expression that Sisko could make out, being in appearance little more than a mass of greenish bubbles writhing inside a translucent sac, but its voice came through the translator in sharp-edged, angry tones. "We cannot remain in this place. Our safety is clearly compromised. We have been *damaged,* Commander, by a shard of sharp material. You see?" It rippled vigorously to demonstrate the extent of its injury, which Sisko was unable to discern. "Damaged! Punctured! We were assured that this was a secure location. Assured by the Federation. This is a serious grievance. We intend to file a complaint. Once we are

gone from this place. There will have to be restitution.
We will insist!"

One by one, Sisko attempted to mollify the ambassadors, deny the obvious falsehoods, squelch the
rumors, and salvage the battered reputation of the
Bajoran provisional government. No, he assured
them, the Bajorans did not condone the terrorism, no
one had been killed, the station was not about to be
evacuated. Yes, the bombings were under investigation, security personnel were on duty, the safety of the
delegates was being given the highest priority.

No, the negotiations had not been canceled. He had
no expectation of their being canceled. No, he would
not advise breaking off all relations with Bajor.

In the middle of the calls, a disturbance broke out
on the floor of Ops, and he had to rush down the stairs
to intervene in what was almost becoming a duel
between the Klingon and the Aresai ambassadors,
disputing the issue of who had precedence when it
came to taking a sword to the terrorists—whenever
they were identified. It was a matter, they both
insisted, of honor.

In the meantime, the Vnartia representative, whom
he'd had to leave on hold, was swollen purple with
indignation by the time he got back, declaring that she
had never been subjected to such an insult before, and
if Sisko had any sense of shame, he would cut off one
of his right hands immediately. She was not pleased to
be reminded that human limbs didn't regenerate, and
didn't really think that was a very good excuse for
avoiding obligations of honor. "I intend to inform
your superiors about this lapse, Commander. I intend
to inform your grandparents!"

By the time Gul Marak's enraged face appeared on
Sisko's screen, it seemed almost indistinguishable

from the rest of the diplomatic horde. "Sisko, do you know how long I've been kept waiting? No, I don't care about the delegations you've got on your hands! What about the fact that Cardassians are being attacked on the decks of your station! A Cardassian has been injured by one of these filthy terrorists! For all I know, they're planning to attack my ship next! What are you doing about all this, Sisko? When are you going to put an end to these constant attacks on Cardassians, on Cardassian property?"

Sisko clenched his jaw so tightly it hurt, trying not to damn the Bajorans. As much as he hated to admit it, especially as much as he hated to admit it to Marak, the Cardassian commander had a legitimate point.

"What are you going to do about it, Sisko?" Marak asked again. "This Bajoran terrorism has gone on long enough! Even after we've withdrawn from their filthy dirtball of a planet, even after the traitors have turned over this *Cardassian station* to these scum, even now they refuse to observe the terms of the truce!

"This shows you how much the Bajorans value peace! All their drivel about spiritual harmony— excrement! We should have exterminated them when we had the chance, before Starfleet got around to meddling in our affairs. We should have wiped them out, scattered their ashes into space where they couldn't breed, poisoned the water and soil so nothing would ever take root on Bajor again!

"I'm telling you now, Sisko! I'm not going to leave this station until I see these terrorists hanging! Even if I have to come onto this station and string them up myself! I'm not going to stand by, not with Cardassian lives at risk! If you can't or *won't* take care of these terrorist scum, I'll do your job for you!"

"Gul Marak!" Sisko finally interrupted the Cardassian diatribe. For at least the dozenth time he

repeated his lines: "I do not condone terrorism, on DS-Nine or anywhere else. The legitimate Bajoran government deplores this violence. Our security team is investigating the latest crime with all the resources at our command. We do *not* need Cardassian interference. When the perpetrators are caught, they'll be prosecuted to the full extent of the law."

"The law!" Marak snorted with furious derision. "You mean *Bajoran* law? You expect Bajoran filth to punish terrorist acts against Cardassians! They'd be more likely to give the murderers a medal, call them heroes, call them freedom fighters—or saints! They'll put up a statue with a bomb in its hand and a halo on its head!

"I want *retribution,* Sisko! I want them to hang, I want them to suffer for their crimes! Oh, I know your Starfleet directives! Pusillanimous Federation rules! It's all sewer gas! You'll always treat Cardassians as your enemies. You couldn't defeat us in straightforward battle, so now you work behind our backs, using traitors and terrorists to do your dirty work for you!

"And don't tell me about your security forces! I've seen your security at work! Your *Bajoran* major! Tell me, Sisko, are you in collusion with them, or are you just blind? Just why do you have terrorists running around free on your station? And traitors, deserters, murderers?

"I'm warning you again, I'll take matters into my own hands. I should have sent my deck patrolmen onto your station to drag him back on the spot, but no, *I* respected our agreement! I trusted the word of a Starfleet officer! Well, not again! You want to see a show of force, well, you'll see one! I'll take this station apart piece by piece if I have to."

"Is that a threat, Marak?"

"If you don't like it, then you know what to do,

Sisko. I'm telling you, I want those terrorists, I want that deserter back—"

"*What* deserter? What in . . . hell are you talking about, Marak?"

"Don't pretend you don't know!"

Sisko was now speaking through clenched teeth. "Marak, there's just been a bombing on my station. Before that, I was off duty in my quarters, trying to sleep. I've just spent the last two hours trying to explain the situation to a flock of panicky diplomats, and now I've got you ranting in my face. I tell you again, I don't know anything about a deserter!"

Marak's face lit with malign triumph. "Then maybe you'd better ask your *Bajoran* first officer! Maybe there are a few more things she hasn't told you about, like the names of her terrorist friends!

"This is your last warning. Or you can call it a threat if you want. I want that traitor back. I want those terrorists hanging. Or you're going to be hearing from me again. Soon, Sisko. Soon."

The screen blanked. Sisko took several long, deep breaths to calm himself. He was becoming all too familiar with Cardassian lies and Cardassian bluff, but Marak's passionate ravings about a deserter had the ring of genuine, enraged sincerity. And what was this about Major Kira? However much he trusted Kira, however much she'd proved herself, it was hard to entirely forget her past.

Remembering Marak's voice sneering, "Your *Bajoran* first officer," Sisko scrolled back anxiously through the station log for the time he'd been off duty. It was there, all in order, with Kira's personal authorization: Gul Marak's call, her response. All right. Time to get to the bottom of this, *now!*

"Major Kira, to the commander's office. At once!"

Communications broke in before he could sign off.

"Commander Sisko, a message from the Kovassii ambassador." Sisko took another breath. "His ship will be undocking within thirty minutes. They're leaving DS-Nine."

Sisko exhaled. *Another one leaving.* He thought for an instant of trying to dissuade the Kovassii, but second thoughts convinced him it would do no good.

"You wanted to see me, Commander?"

Kira. "Come in. Close the door." He pointedly did not ask her to sit down.

"I've had a complaint, Major. From Gul Marak. He claims we're harboring a Cardassian deserter on DS-Nine. He wants the man returned to face charges. Now, don't you think this is the kind of situation the station's commander ought to be aware of?"

Kira looked surprised and, possibly, guilty? Or was that just his imagination?

But her expression went stiff and neutral again immediately. "The communication from Gul Marak was recorded in the station log. With my reply."

"Yes, I checked the log. And you didn't see the need to inform me about this communication?"

"You were off duty at the time. As first officer, I was on deck in Ops. It was standard procedure for me to take the call. Unless, of course, it was an emergency. I didn't judge it to be so."

"I see." Sisko suppressed a frown. She was, of course, quite correct about the letter of the regulations. As for her interpretation of the situation, he wasn't so sure.

Kira went on. "Gul Marak informed me that he suspected one of his crew had deserted the ship onto the station. I told him we had no information about a Cardassian deserter. I told him we would investigate. We did."

This time Sisko found it harder to keep the disapproval from his expression. Again, Kira's account was, taken literally, quite correct. Except that it left out the bitter tones of mutual animosity in the exchange: Marak's threats, Kira's fierce, vengeful defiance.

"And you didn't consider the situation an emergency?"

"No, I didn't. There was no evidence of a threat to the station. At that time."

"Well? What about now? Do we have this Cardassian deserter on the station or not?"

Now she did look slightly uncomfortable, but her voice didn't betray it. "I did investigate, immediately. Odo had just reported an . . . anomaly in the security system in pylon six, and I thought there might be a connection. We discovered that the airlock to the Cardassian ship's emergency docking port had been sabotaged."

"Sabotaged? How?"

"The exit alarm had been bypassed. And someone had been tampering with the security sensors in the vicinity of the airlock. So it does seem likely that a Cardassian deserter did come off that ship. Chief O'Brien thinks he's probably some kind of technician."

"That's it?"

"We were still in the middle of the investigation when the emergency alarms went off. I assumed that the bombing took priority over this other matter."

"Yes, of course." Sisko groaned inwardly. This *wasn't* what he needed now, with diplomats deserting the station and terrorists trying to blow it up. Marak had claimed the deserter was armed and dangerous. And there was Kira standing on the other side of his desk, lips pressed tightly together, black eyes staring down at him with more than a slight trace of the same defiance she'd shown Marak during their exchange.

He wished he could order her to avoid contact with the Cardassian commander, but that was impossible. He knew she was right; as first officer, it was her job to take over when the station commander wasn't available. To suggest otherwise would be as much as a public declaration that her position carried no real authority. He couldn't do that to Kira, not when DS9 was supposed to be a Bajoran station.

But, dammit, couldn't she at least try not to be so *provoking* whenever she dealt with the Cardassians?

Marak, he had to admit, didn't make matters much easier.

"All right," he finally decided. "If these bombings aren't stopped, we might as well toss Bajor's hopes for a trade agreement into the waste recyclers. So: Stopping the terrorists has got to be our first priority. No question. And you're still in charge of that investigation.

"But this business of a Cardassian deserter isn't something we can just brush aside and ignore. Gul Marak does have a legitimate claim here. And if, as he says, this man is a murderer, then he could pose a significant danger to the station. I'm going to ask Odo to take charge of the situation.

"And, Major? Let's *try* to have a little bit more communication, all right? I don't want any more of these surprises. Clear?"

"Clear, Commander."

CHAPTER
10

THE TWO BOYS crouched low behind a barrier, back where the lights had been blown out by the bomb blast. Out on the main deck of the Promenade, security teams were herding the last lingering civilians away from the scene. The wounded had long since been taken to the infirmary, and the immediate area of Garak's shop was cordoned off.

"What a mess!" Jake Sisko whispered uneasily. Scenes like this always reminded him of that time on board the *Saratoga,* when it was hit by the Borg ship. *When Mom died.* His memories of the event weren't entirely clear, but certain sounds, certain smells always brought it back: women screaming, the acrid, choking scent of smoke.

Now that he was on DS-Nine, though, disaster was almost becoming an everyday affair. Assessing the current situation, he decided that he'd seen worse, though there was going to be one huge job cleaning all this up. "This station is always a wreck, anyway," he pronounced finally.

"You can say that again," Nog agreed. The Ferengi boy was much shorter than Jake, with the oversized, sensitive ears of his race. The primary thing the two of them had in common was their mutual wish to be anywhere else in the galaxy besides DS-Nine. And knowing that in both their cases there was nothing they could do about it. Jake's father was the station commander, Nog's uncle Quark owned a prospering casino on the Promenade.

Nog's avid little eyes kept flickering back and forth, from the smashed storefront to the figure of Constable Odo working with the security team to clear the area. "Why did *he* have to show up?" he muttered.

It was Odo's well-known belief that all the Ferengi were thieves or worse. He distrusted Quark most of all, but the feeling extended strongly to Quark's nephew Nog. And it was just as strongly reciprocated on Nog's part.

Jake wasn't quite sure why Nog was insisting on hanging around here, now that the excitement of the bombing was over. They were going to get in trouble, he *knew* it. Dad didn't like him spending too much time with Nog, anyway. But Dad wasn't around right now. Some kind of urgent message had called him back to his office, and it didn't seem likely that he'd be home again for a while, either.

But now Odo was talking with someone on his communicator. And now he was heading away toward the security office.

Nog inhaled with a sharp hiss of satisfaction. "All right! Let's go!"

"Go where?"

"I know a way we can get in from the back."

"But . . ." Jake stared in dismay at the security barriers set up in front of the store. "You can't do that!"

Nog sneered. "I *told* you, I can get in from the back. I know the way."

"No," Jake argued desperately. He knew that appeals to stupid human notions like right and wrong meant nothing to Nog. "I mean, well—what about Garak?"

"What about him? He's still in the infirmary."

"No, I mean—"

"If he's smart, he has in*shoor*ance. Right? And if he's not—"

But just then, without warning, the lights overhead suddenly came on again, Jake yelped in startled surprise, and a voice yelled out, "You! Come out of there! This is a restricted area!"

While Jake hesitated in guilty indecision, Nog took the opportunity to bolt. The Ferengi boy was quick and experienced at the game of escape, but this time he wasn't lucky. A few minutes later, he was being dragged back by the constable, who had a painfully firm grip on an ear ridge. "You, too, Mr. Sisko," Odo ordered, and Jake slowly stood up from his hiding place, miserable and ashamed.

"We weren't *doing* anything! We just wanted to watch," he pleaded desperately.

"Empty your pockets," Odo ordered sternly, utterly without mercy or sympathy.

The prisoners complied, Nog sullenly and Jake in mounting dread that the constable would call his father, or take him to detention. He couldn't stand it if Dad had to come and bail him out of detention. *If I get out of this, I'll never do anything again, I promise, please.*

Odo inspected the contents of the pockets, making a more thorough search of Nog's, but apparently he found nothing he could classify as contraband or evidence of any crime. This seemed to disappoint him. "I'm going to let you go this time," he said finally, "but I don't want to find either of you around here again. This area is restricted until further notice. Unauthorized persons in a restricted area are subject to detention *indefinitely* during a state of emergency."

They were released and personally escorted by Odo from the Promenade.

"I knew we were going to get caught," Jake moaned.

"I could have gotten in, if *you* hadn't made so much noise," Nog snapped. "Next time, I go by myself!" The little Ferengi stomped away.

"All right, then! Go by yourself! Get thrown in the brig again!" Jake yelled back. "See if I care!" Nog was nothing but trouble, he seethed. Maybe Dad was right about him.

Jake stood alone, abandoned in the corridor. "I *hate* this place," he muttered to himself.

The sirens and alarms had stopped sounding a long time ago. Berat checked his chrono again. Hours ago.

They hadn't caught him yet. At first, when the alert went off and he knew they were after him, Berat almost gave in to panic. Crouched in his hiding place, a supply closet down in an abandoned-looking section of the lower core, he'd held on to his stolen phaser as his only salvation, not quite sure if, in the end, he was going to turn it on his pursuers or himself.

But they hadn't found him. He hadn't even heard the sounds of pursuit.

It was dead dark in the closet, except for the faint momentary glow of his chrono when he checked the time. Silent and dark. Berat couldn't keep his eyes open any longer, but he could hear himself breathing, his own heartbeat pulsing, accelerated by fright. And if he held his breath, he could hear the station, the creaky hiss of the ventilation system, the fitful suck and choke of the hydraulics.

They were familiar, soothing noises, although DS-Nine didn't have the sound of a healthy station. Berat had never seen a Cardassian facility in this kind of condition. Whole sections down in the docking pylon seemed deserted. Sections of the power plant, too. The signs of wreckage and wholesale destruction were everywhere, although attempts had obviously been made at some point to clean up the worst of the mess.

But no one chasing after him, despite the alarms. That was the main thing. He was safe in this place, in part because it was half-wrecked.

Berat's head fell forward. Still keeping his grip on the phaser, he finally slept.

In his dream, Sub Halek was kicking on his bunk. *"Berat! Wake up! On your feet! I've got a job for you, scrag! Today you're going to hang!"*

Berat's eyes flew open in panic, he started up, and banged his head on a wall before he remembered where he was. And why: what he'd done.

For a moment, he was reliving the scene: Halek's angry face, the blow, the slashing pain. Reaching for the pry bar. The sensation of the impact with Halek's skull, the sound of bone cracking . . .

Berat gingerly touched his face, felt the bruises throb. But he ached everywhere, worse than ever, crammed into this closet.

Well, so he'd been an idiot, played right into the hands of his enemies. They had every excuse now to do what they wanted to him. Once they caught up with him.

But at least he had options now. Some room to breathe. And on DS-Nine there were ships coming in and out all the time. A way out. Off the station. Out of Cardassian space altogether. His experience was more on stations than ships, but certainly he could find a ship that could use another engineering technician. After what Halek had put him through on the *Swift Striker,* he wouldn't consider any job beneath him, ever again.

He was wondering whether it might be better to try to stow away or openly ask for a berth, when a pang hit his gut and he started to figure how long it had been since he'd been able to eat. He paused in the dark, listening. No one out in the corridor that he could hear.

All right. Here he was, somewhere in the lower core, maybe level thirty-one or -two. Near the reactors. In some section that *seemed* to be deserted. So where was the closest food replicator going to be? What was the best way to get there without being seen? Mentally, as if he were back on Farside Station, he traced a path of utility shafts, maintenance accesses, conduits, ducts—hard to squeeze through, some of those places. But working under Sub Halek hadn't let him put on a lot of extra weight. A good thing for him now.

He cracked open the door. The whole section was dark, either from neglect or because it was on power-save, only a few dim safety lights glowing. Even fewer of those than there should have been, in fact. More malfunctions. Thinking of malfunctions, and food replicators, he went back to the closet and strapped on his tool belt.

He opened a panel, crawled inside a maintenance tunnel, and shut the hatch behind him. Now he was safe from discovery, safe enough, anyway. Massive power conduits ran through the tunnel, but they were lifeless. Berat followed them, wondering how the station managed to function at all with so much capacity shut down. Was there something wrong with the reactors? How could this place defend itself against attack?

Whatever was wrong, though, it was lucky for him. If no one ever came into these sections, maybe he could hide out here indefinitely. As long as he could find food. Feeling slightly more hopeful about his prospects for survival, he headed through a shaft up to one of the cargo levels. After prowling around the corridors for a while, he found a deserted workers' lounge with a replicator against one wall. He approached it cautiously. Someone had kicked in the front panel. Probably the same someone who'd smashed the chairs and tables, broken the lights, and thrown something disgusting against the far wall. Malicious, systematic destruction.

Berat shuddered. This place was *too* empty, too long deserted. It was almost like being on a ghost station. Maybe none of the stories were actually true, but ghost stations, ghost ships were a staple of spacefaring myth:

Something got onto a station. Sometimes, no one even ever saw what it was, until it was too late, and everyone was dead, and the station drifted, drifted through space as its systems shut down, one by one. Other, more violent versions had pirates attacking, or unknown alien ships.

This place looked more like the work of pirates. Which maybe wasn't all too much different from what he knew to be the truth, that the damage had been done by Cardassian troops, enraged at having to retreat and abandon the station to the conquered race they despised, determined to leave them as little as possible to enjoy.

Such as a functioning food synthesizer. With weary resignation, Berat pulled off the broken panel and started to probe the replicator's interior. On all his previous assignments, up to thirty percent of station malfunctions had involved the replicator systems, and half of those had been the fault of the matrix grid. There was something not quite right about the basic design, although the procurement department would deny it to their graves.

But this time, it was a ruptured power-flux modulator, doubtless broken by someone's big, armored boot kicking through the front panel. On Farside, he'd have just plugged in a replacement, but he wasn't on Farside now, and he didn't have a replacement modulator in his tool kit.

But that didn't matter. There were tricks you learned when you'd served on stations and ships for a while, tricks that didn't come out of the book and you didn't want the inspectors to see—ever. And in a lounge like this, there was always a head for the workers to use to relieve themselves.

While everyone pretended to ignore the fact, food supply and waste disposal were just opposite sides of the same basic process. And so . . . here . . . in the disposal unit, you needed a flux modulator, just like you did in the replicator. And though it was true that this model operated at a different modulation rate, if you adjusted the resistors on the replicator to compensate . . . like that . . . as far down as they could go, then plugged the other module in . . . there, it would work, as the saying went, as long as it worked.

Holding his breath, Berat programmed the replicator for something simple: one of the hot meat rolls that were a favorite of the Cardassian troops on Farside Station. There was a pause, a humming sound as the power faltered; then the roll materialized on the replicator tray, steaming and redolent with familiar spices that made Berat's eyes water gratefully.

He took a bite. Oh, that was good! He almost laughed aloud in relief.

Maybe, just maybe, he was going to be all right here on this miserable wreck of a station. For a while. Until he found a ship and could get away.

CHAPTER
11

KIRA HESITATED at the door of station detention. She was dreading this interview. She thought that maybe she ought to take a few moments to meditate before she went in to see the prisoner. But that would just be putting off the moment.

They finally had a suspect in the bombings.

Working for hours without sleep, Kira had gone through the computer profiles of every station resident, relying not only on the computer's files but her own memories of the resistance years. It had been a long, painful process, reviving that past, recalling so many names and faces that had been lost. Names of friends, faces of lovers: their dead, accusing eyes.

But finally, from the records, she'd assembled profiles of all the people on the station with a known or suspected connection to any of the resistance groups, including herself and four of the monks serving in the temple. While the computer worked to track the known whereabouts of each back to before the time of the first bomb incident, security officers had been busy questioning everyone known to have been on the Promenade before the attack on Garak's shop. Someone had put that poster on the wall just before the bomb went off. That person might have been seen by the witnesses that Constable Odo had located in his search.

At the same time, Lieutenant Dax had been working with the poster itself, using a new, submolecular chromatography procedure capable of isolating and identifying the DNA markers from a sample smaller than a single cell. In the last few hours, their work had all come together. Two persons, both Bajoran females, had been identified by Dax as having contact with the poster. The same two persons had been recognized by the witnesses. Kira was one of them. The other was a cargo handler named Gelia Torly, whose whereabouts were unknown at the time of the bombings.

Now Gelia was in detention, and it was Kira's job to interrogate her. There was no use putting it off. It wasn't going to get any easier.

She hit the control pad and the door slid up. Deep Space Nine had been built by the Cardassians, which meant there were plenty of cells in detention. Most of them had been occupied throughout the station's history by Bajoran prisoners awaiting interrogation and execution by their oppressors, an irony that Kira felt acutely as she faced Gelia in her cell now. They had both been in the resistance, both fighting for the same goals. There was a bond between them that someone like Commander Sisko or even Odo could never share.

The Bajoran prisoner stood defiantly and shook back her long hair. She was wearing the wrinkled, grease-stained coveralls of a dockworker, and a simple silver clasp on her ear. "So. I should've known it'd be you. Major Kira Collaborator. Nice uniform you have on, there."

Kira's lips pressed thinly together, but her only other reaction was a slight stiffening of her back. "Gelia Torly, this conversation is being monitored and recorded. You've been identified and placed under arrest in connection with the bombing of a clothing store owned by the Cardassian Garak. DNA tracing has linked you with an inflammatory poster left at the scene, and witnesses have placed you there, as well. Can you account for your whereabouts and activity at the time of the bombing?"

Gelia put her hands on her hips. "I was at work."

Kira shook her head. "According to computer records, you left your job three hours before your scheduled shift ended."

"Then maybe I was having a drink at Quark's."

"Maybe you were—a full hour before witnesses claim they saw a person resembling you put that poster up on Garak's wall. Do you have anything else to say?"

"What if I don't? Are you going to bring out the pain inducers? Or do you like to conduct your interrogations the old-fashioned way, with whips and thumbscrews? Maybe you picked up some tips from the Cardassians, did you?"

A flush of anger colored Kira's face, but her voice was controlled with an effort. "You don't have to say anything now. That's your legal right. On the other hand, you're a known associate of the Kohn Ma, and at the moment the only suspect connected with two terrorist attacks on this station. You know as well as I do that the provisional government has declared terrorism a crime, regardless of motive. The Kohn Ma is an illegal organization. Think about it, Gelia.

Cooperate with us now, and save yourself a lot of trouble."

Gelia's face twisted in a look of contempt. There was a scar across one cheekbone, Kira noticed. An old scar, faded white by now. "Oh, I've already thought long and hard about it, *Major*. Just the way I thought ten years ago, when it was a Cardassian cell I was in." She paused in mock surprise and looked around her. "Oh, I forgot, this still *is* a Cardassian cell!" Then her voice went hard again as she snarled at Kira, "And I still don't betray my comrades! Some of us haven't forgotten the meaning of loyalty!"

Now Kira didn't care anymore. Her hard-won composure had evaporated. Her voice rose in pitch. "Loyalty to what? Not to Bajor! Not when you try to blow up a Bajoran station! Not when you try to ruin relations with the Federation—the only force that's keeping a Cardassian war fleet off our throats!"

But Gelia shouted back, "A Bajoran station? That Cardassian warship you're talking about is docked here right now! We've got Cardassians right on the Promenade! This isn't what I spent fifteen years fighting for! And what about you—is this what you call freedom? Independence? Oh, I know who you are, *Major* Kira! We both came from the camps. But now look at the two of us: there you stand outside the cell with the Feds and the Cardassians, and here I am. On this side of the cell. Where *true* Bajorans always stand."

"It wasn't the Cardassians who killed Bajoran babies this time. It was Bajorans who can't stop fighting even when the war's over."

"No babies got killed!"

"And I suppose you knew there wouldn't be any children in the way when you planted your bomb? Oh, but I forgot! Real freedom fighters can't let the lives of a few babies stand in the way of their cause! Real freedom fighters know we have to make these kind of sacrifices for the greater good!"

The two of them faced each other with open hostility, separated only by the invisible force field at the front of the cell. In the back of her mind, Kira kept thinking, She could be me. I could be her. If only . . .

But in the end, it was Gelia whose eyes broke contact first. "I was only following orders. You know how it is. You don't ask questions."

Kira tried to keep her voice even. "Then you had orders to plant the bomb. Orders from whom?"

But Gelia shook her head, slightly subdued. "No. I didn't plant it. I didn't have anything to do with a bomb, I didn't even know that's what it was about. I mean, I guessed, but—anyway, you know how this kind of thing works. I got a message. It had the right code phrase. It told me to make a poster and leave it in a certain place. I did that."

Kira nodded, all too well aware of the methods used by the resistance. Still, she had to ask. "Your orders told you to make this poster. The exact wording?"

"Right. 'Die, Cardassians!' And signed, Kohn Ma."

"What was the code phrase?"

"Whirlwind of the Prophets." Gelia shot Kira a challenging look. "Why, is that one familiar?"

Kira shook her head. It was a slogan, like so many others the freedom fighters used. Each code phrase was good only among the same three people. She'd used over a dozen, herself, but never that particular phrase, for which she was intensely grateful now. During the resistance, it could be dangerous to know the names and identities of the people you worked with. She'd been dreading the possibility that Gelia might have been one of her own operatives, or even a superior, unknown all this time.

"And the message? What did you do with it?"

"I flashed it. Of course."

Of course. Leaving no evidence. This was getting nowhere. "Are you a member of Kohn Ma?"

Gelia crossed her arms over her chest and laughed. "You don't think I'd admit it, if I were?"

Kira sighed. "You realize that so far, you're the only suspect in all of this. We have only your word that you had nothing to do with the bomb itself, just the poster."

"I stand by my statement. You can truth-test me if you want."

"Oh, don't worry. We will. And even so, there's still the conspiracy charge. Membership in a terrorist organization. You're in serious trouble, Gelia, facing a prison term. A little cooperation at this time could only help you."

But Gelia's arms folded even more tightly across her chest, and Kira recognized that expression on her face: Gelia was ready to become a martyr for her cause.

Martyrs were Bajor's most popular export, Kira thought ruefully. Sometimes I think it's about all we're good for.

But there was no use talking to Gelia any longer. She wasn't going to learn anything more from her. It was part of the code of the resistance: Better to die than to talk.

Odo was sitting at the monitor when Kira came back out from the cells. "I take it you believe her story?"

Kira nodded. "I'm afraid so. That's the way the resistance worked. You didn't know the name of the person you took your orders from so you couldn't spill it in case you were interrogated."

"So essentially, we're back to nothing."

"That's right. If Gelia didn't set the bomb, then we're still looking for whoever did, plus whoever sent her that order, if they aren't the same person."

She glanced down at the monitor, saw Gelia's image. The suspect was seated on the edge of her bunk in a posture of meditation. "You know, I've been thinking. This business with the poster is crude. Signing it Kohn Ma. It's too . . . obvious. I wonder if Gelia wasn't set up."

"I have to agree," said Odo. "It could well be the real terrorist trying to divert attention to a more obvious suspect. We'd be investigating the Kohn Ma connections anyway."

"Right." Kira deliberately looked away from the monitor. "But now look what everyone sees: random bombings. Hate-crimes against Cardassians. A known Bajoran terrorist captured on the station. I tell you, it's political! This whole conspiracy is aimed at sabotaging the negotiations. To keep Bajor out of the Federation. Odo, sometimes I think Bajorans are worse enemies to themselves than the Cardassians ever were."

To which he had no immediate reply.

She shook her head furiously, making her silver earring jingle. "In fact, if I hadn't just heard Gelia's confession, I'd almost suspect it was the Cardassians behind all this!" But then she remembered Garak on the Promenade deck, bleeding. No, maybe not.

"Is there any evidence from the bomb site?" she asked finally.

"Nothing. I'm going to have to reopen the Promenade. It's not an out-of-the-way docking pylon that we can keep shut down indefinitely."

"No," Kira agreed, sighing. "So, have you found your Cardassian deserter? Or at least any more suspicious anomalies?"

"According to Chief O'Brien, this entire station is an anomaly," Odo said glumly. "But, no, whoever our deserter is, he's hiding his tracks very well. Even with a reward out for him. I still don't like it, someone tampering with our security sensor grid that way."

"I don't suppose," Kira frowned, "that this deserter affair could be some kind of Cardassian trick? A way to infiltrate DS-Nine?"

"Infiltrate? Major, look at this." Odo turned to his monitor and brought up an image of part of the Promenade that hadn't been shut down. A Cardassian military policeman in his black uniform stood looking up and down the corridor while traffic detoured around him. A few meters farther down the corridor, a figure in the uniform of Starfleet security stood casually keeping an eye on the Cardassian.

"There are at least four more like that, all with liberty passes from the *Swift Striker*."

"Looking for the deserter?"

"It's Cardassians they're watching. Poor Garak has been stopped so many times he finally complained to Gul Marak. We're keeping close watch on them, as you can see. Officially, they're crewmen on liberty. And so far, they're staying out of the restricted areas of the station."

"And they're not armed."

"Not armed," Odo acknowledged.

"I still don't like it. Our security is supposed to be handling the matter."

"I know. But it's the commander's orders. As long as they're not armed, as long as they don't cause any disturbance, they're free to come and go like any other visitors to the station. He doesn't want any provocations—on either side."

Kira heard the warning in Odo's voice. She glanced back at the monitor. "Sisko's crazy if he thinks this isn't going to lead to more trouble."

Once again, Odo had no comment.

CHAPTER
12

To CELEBRATE THE REOPENING of the Promenade and his casino, Quark had hung colored banners over the doorway and announced new prices for all imported drinks. The Ferengi gambler stood proudly in the doorway of his brightly lit establishment, effusively inviting all passersby to step in, enjoy themselves. Quark was small in stature, as all Ferengi were, but his instincts for profit were limitless. To those few veteran customers who pointed out that his new prices were higher than what he'd charged before the place was closed, Quark apologized with an obsequious, sharp-toothed grin and reduced the amount, blaming his bartender for the error.

Inside, the casino's decor was riotous with flashing red and yellow lights and a great deal of sparkling surface. The long gleaming bar invited customers to sit and have a drink, scantily dressed Dabo girls smiled and invited them to come up to the gaming tables and lose their money, but it was not a particularly festive crowd that gathered to drink or gamble away their cares. People would wonder aloud where the next bomb was going to go off, looking nervously around behind them. Others complained that they couldn't get any business done with all the security uniforms watching over their shoulders every minute. Why didn't they go somewhere else and arrest more terrorists, let honest traders alone?

At a corner table, a group of a half-dozen crewmen off the *Swift Striker* were keeping a waiter running back and forth with full pitchers of synthale. It was the cheapest drink they could buy at Quark's, but they were making up for it in volume.

The Cardassians had serious grievances.

"Eight hours' liberty! Do you know, they've got holosuites upstairs that'll keep you going for eight hours straight?"

"Yeah, when I was here before, I ran this one: there were these two Bajorans, see . . ."

"I tore off all her clothes . . ."

"And then she got on her knees . . ."

"So I took this whip . . ."

"And she was begging me . . ."

Inspired by their reminiscences, the crewmen stared longingly at the door to the holosuites, but their passes expired in less than an hour, and they had barely enough time left to get seriously drunk before it was time to check back in at the ship. Being late was something none of them wanted to risk. "Hey!" they yelled for the waiter. "We're *dry* here! More synthale!"

A passing couple of Bajoran miners gave them a look of loathing and contempt. One of the Cardassians saw it, started to stagger up from his seat, snarling, "I'll show those farking scum they can't look at *me* that way! What do they think they are?"

But his companions were sober enough to pull him

back down. "Kulat! Remember the Gul's orders, no fighting! Not even if they start it."

"Yeah, think about what he did to poor Lok!"

Kulat subsided and sullenly drained another mug of ale. "Lok still hanging, is he?"

The others nodded. One said, "Yeah. You shoulda heard him this morning. I took a couple whacks at him—not much, just to see him kick a little. He could barely squeal."

They all laughed at the image of their suffering crewmate, except for Kulat, who poured the rest of his synthale down his thickly corded throat and yelled for more. "Can't do anything around this place," he muttered. "Deck police all over the place."

One of his companions agreed. "Looking for that traitor, Berat. I want to be there when the Gul hangs *him,* that's for sure!"

"I'd like a cut of that reward," another crewman added.

"Too much farking security," Kulat muttered. "And Bajorans! Bajoran security! And farking Starfleet. Man comes to a station, he wants some liberty, hang it! One shift. Eight hours! Can't even get drunk in eight hours."

Suddenly the rest of the Cardassian crew sat bolt upright, frightened into near-sobriety. Only Kulat, whose back was to the door, kept up his litany of complaints as a smiling Gul Marak walked into the gambling hall accompanied by the Klystron ambassador.

Quark hurried in the Gul's wake, drawn by his unerring instinct for profit and advantage. "Your Excellencies! Ambassador! Gul! Welcome to Quark's! How can my modest establishment serve you?"

Marak held up a gold piece between two fingers.

"We'd like a private suite. Where we can talk undisturbed. And a new bottle of your best imported Rigellian brandy. None of your local swill."

Quark's eyes glinted, and he executed a low bow. "My establishment can accommodate Your Excellencies. I can tell that you are both persons of taste and discrimination. Please come with me. I'll escort you to our most discreet private accommodation. And when you've finished your discussion, if you'd like more entertainment—"

"Just bring the brandy and get out," snapped Marak.

"Of course. Right away. Our very best Rigellian brandy." Hurrying to the bar, Quark hissed at his nephew Nog, who was serving as a waiter, "That table in the corner, they want more synthale!"

But the *Swift Striker*'s crewmen were already on the way back to their ship, dragging the reluctant Kulat, every other man thanking his own patron diety that the Gul hadn't spotted them in Quark's Place.

Once Quark had left the brandy with them and shut the door of the suite behind him, Marak sat down on one of the couches and cracked the seal on the bottle. "I hope this is drinkable," he told the Klystron ambassador. "As you can see, standards in this part of space have declined." He took a sip. "Not too bad, actually."

The Klystron took a sip of his own drink. "Well, you wished a private conversation, and they tell me this is as private a place as exists on the station."

Marak nodded briskly. "You've seen enough of conditions here to know what I'm talking about. This is what things are like under Bajoran control. When DS-Nine was a Cardassian station, let me tell you, we had *order*. Systems functioned properly, people knew their place, and commerce and trade thrived. As it will thrive again, when the right people are back in charge."

"Meaning Cardassians, I suppose." The Klystron sipped his brandy speculatively. "No, you haven't made a secret of your intentions."

"And why should we? This region of space is ours by right. We occupied it for years, and we only lost it through treachery."

"According to your government, that is."

"According to the *legitimate* government," Marak corrected him grimly. "The traitors have been eliminated."

"Indeed, so I understand. But the Federation has upheld Bajor's claim."

Marak ignored that. "Tell me, do you really want to do business with the Bajorans? Look around you! Look how they've let this station deteriorate. Nothing functions, from the docking systems down to the food replicators. And look how they welcome the ambassadors who've come in good faith to negotiate. With sabotage and terrorism."

"I understand that they already have the suspect in that bombing locked up in detention. The Bajoran representatives have been at great pains to assure us that they don't sanction any kind of terrorist activity."

Marak snorted in contempt. "Bajoran representatives! They were all terrorists themselves! And this first officer, this Kira female—she was known to our intelligence as a member of one of the most notorious organizations: a group called Shazaan or something. I wish we'd been able to get our hands on her then. But now—she's practically in command of this station. *That's* who's investigating this bombing! A former terrorist. That's the kind of commitment you can expect from a Bajoran government.

"No, if you want to know about Bajoran treachery, ask a Cardassian. Ask that innocent merchant whose shop was bombed the other day, who was almost killed."

The ambassador stared thoughtfully into his brandy. "One does hear that there were Cardassian . . . excesses during your occupation."

"Sewer gas! Rumors! Lies! Cardassian rule was *firm*. The Bajorans needed a firm hand over them to keep them in order. Look at them now: factions fighting constantly, fighting each other. Setting bombs on their own station. *They* can't even agree on trade with the Gamma Quadrant! It seems it might violate their religion or some such stupidity."

"This is certainly true. I've sat through a few sessions with them already. But, of course, one does have to point out, Bajor is their homeworld. They might have had cause to object to Cardassian occupation."

Marak waved his hand dismissingly. "As far as I'm concerned, the Bajorans can keep their filthy planet. If you'd ever seen the place, you'd understand why. But this space station and the territory it controls—we'll never renounce our right to it!"

"And to the wormhole."

"The wormhole is in Cardassian territory. Naturally we insist on controlling it."

The Klystron contemplated the color of his brandy again. "If," he said finally, "one were to—hypothetically—accept that your position with respect to the wormhole is valid, how would Klystron benefit from Cardassian control of this territory?" He looked directly at Marak. "Why should we prefer you to the Bajorans?"

Marak poured more brandy, now that they had finally broken through to the point. "With Cardassian control, you have order, stability. Your traders will be able to dock at DS-Nine knowing there won't be a fanatic setting off a bomb in the airlock. And, of course, you'd have the most favorable terms possible in such matters as duties, tariffs, exchange rates, station charges and fees."

The ambassador leaned forward toward him very slightly. "Exactly . . . *how* favorable?"

"Ah. If an influential world like Klystron, for example, were to openly repudiate this spurious Bajoran claim to the territory in question, were to abandon the trade negotiations now, then I think the Cardassian government could guarantee very attractive terms indeed. Certainly more favorable than anything Bajor might offer."

"What an interesting notion," the ambassador said softly. "Tell me, Gul—hypothetically, of course— what sort of guarantee did you have in mind?"

In his private office, Quark moaned in excitement as he bent closely over his monitor. There was a sheen of sweat on his bulbous brow, and his eyes glittered with an avarice close to lust. To watch a deal like this being negotiated was better than any sex holo ever made!

To his customers, Quark guaranteed that his private holosex suites were free from any surveillance by station security. They could feel free to indulge their most depraved fantasies without fear of condemnation or arrest. Naturally, it was common for people to take advantage of this privacy for other purposes, such as sensitive discussions like this one.

And also naturally, Quark carefully recorded everything that went on in the suites, in case he might be able to turn the information to some personal advantage. Information, the Ferengi well knew, was often more valuable than gold—and easier to transport.

Now he watched the performance between the Cardassian and the Klystron with an acute appreciation for the nuances of the negotiating art: the lies and half-lies, the rare moments of candor, the careful use of the hypothetical. Treachery, self-interest and greed: it took a Ferengi to appreciate moments like this. And Quark had it all recorded.

Just in case.

But the matter under discussion was of immediate concern. To have the Cardassians back in charge of the station—where did Quark's interests lie? The Bajorans and the Federation or Gul Marak's government? Which side to choose?

He had prospered under the previous Cardassian rule. All this talk about enforcing order and stability applied to the subject Bajorans, not an independent businessman. Cardassians were enthusiastic customers for drinking and gambling, when their officers allowed it, as Gul Dukat had. Quark had a large, expensive inventory of holo programs that catered to their peculiar tastes in entertainment, and there was much less demand for it these days. In fact, Sisko had once threatened to confiscate and destroy some of the more extreme examples.

Quark bared his small, sharp teeth at the thought of the current station commander. Now, Gul Dukat, when he was in charge of DS-Nine, had been a different type. Dukat had always been willing to see Quark's point of view, when it was presented the right way—accompanied by appropriate amounts of gold-pressed latinum. Sisko, on the other hand—it still rankled, the way Sisko had used young Nog the way he had, threatening to keep the boy in detention unless his uncle cooperated. Yet it was true that business under the new administration hadn't been as bad as Quark had first expected.

Then there was the matter of the bombings. Politics didn't make for good business, and the Bajorans were political to a fault—to more than one fault. How could he turn a profit if the Bajoran terrorists were always going to be blowing up the Promenade, getting it shut down by security?

And thinking of security, there was the insufferable Constable Odo. A real thorn sticking in his side. It was true that Odo had also been in office under Gul Dukat, but he was even a worse nuisance these days, with Sisko's encouragement. And now working so closely with that Major Kira.

Quark's tongue flicked lasciviously against his lips as he thought of Kira. No one else seemed to appreciate the major's female attributes. But Gul Marak seemed to particularly dislike the Bajoran major. There might be an advantage there. Perhaps Gul Marak could be persuaded that Odo had been entirely too closely connected with Kira. With the Bajorans. Unreliable. Yes.

At the thought of a Cardassian-run station without Odo, Quark began to grin. He left his office and shouted for his nephew to take another bottle of Rigellian brandy, with his compliments, to that noble Cardassian commander, Gul Marak.

CHAPTER
13

NOG KNEW he was taking a big chance, sneaking out of Quark's while there were customers waiting. He rubbed his upper ear ridge, which was still stinging from contact with the back of Rom's hand. He knew he'd get another slap just like it from Rom or Quark if he came back empty-handed. But then, Nog didn't intend to show up again until he had something to show his impatient elders. And besides, waiting tables on drunken Cardassians wasn't work for an ambitious young Ferengi entrepreneur.

No one knew DS-Nine like Nog did. At least, no one but maybe that Constable Odo. Nog's opinion of Odo was even more unfavorable than Quark's. But even Odo had to rest sometime. Nog knew that Odo turned into some kind of liquid puddle when he slept. Nog thought he'd really like to see that someday. In fact, he thought it would really be great to be a shape-changer like Odo. Too many people on the station could recognize his face. Ferengis weren't all that common on DS-Nine. But if he could change what he looked like, anytime he wanted, then no one would ever be able to identify him. The vendors on the Promenade wouldn't always guard their stuff whenever they saw him coming. And if they were chasing him, he could just turn into a liquid, slip through some crack, and get away.

Although Odo was just about the only one who could catch him now. Nog just wished his uncle and father appreciated his abilities.

The humiliation of getting caught in front of Garak's place was still festering. And it was all that human boy's fault. That Jake. Why did he have to jump and yell so loud when the lights went on?

Sometimes Nog thought Jake was a pain. All right, so they were friends and sometimes they could have a good time, but whenever something really important came up, some real opportunity for acquisition, Jake was always wanting to tail along, then pulling back when it came to a good opportunity for profit—like looting Garak's shop. Nog had no patience for human scruples. And he particularly didn't plan on cutting Jake in on his latest enterprise. Nog aimed at no less than cornering the stationwide market in spare parts.

The scheme was brilliant in its simplicity. DS-Nine had been constructed by Cardassians, all its systems were Cardassian. But there were no available spare parts for any of them. And no way to get spare parts from the Cardassians, with the political situation the way it was. They would sooner cut off their own lobes than trade with Bajorans. The Starfleet engineer, O'Brien, was complaining about the problem all the time.

But Nog had come up with the solution: Steal components out of the deserted regions of the station and sell them to people who needed their systems repaired!

He took the turboshaft down to the lower core, where he knew there were whole sections deserted and unused. He was imagining himself old and immensely rich, like Quark, reminiscing to a large gang of sons and nephews about his youth on DS9: how he'd hidden, terrified, as the rampaging Cardassian troops systematically demolished the station, destroying everything of value they could find. But he, Nog, had succeeded in turning disaster into profit!

The only drawback to the scheme, he thought, was the problem of how to market his wares without attracting the bothersome attention of the authorities. But as he began to prowl through the lower cargo sections, a few further complications began to present themselves. Such as the fact that the more deserted regions of the station tended to be the ones where the fewest parts had been left intact. And that he apparently wasn't the first brilliant mind to have had this same inspiration. Most of the systems that weren't wrecked had already been gutted or stolen outright. Control pads: broken. Power-junction nodes: burned out. Even most of the lights were broken or missing.

Several hours later, a weary, hungry Nog had only half a sackful of spare parts, and he wasn't sure how many of those would actually work. His brilliantly imagined future had begun to tarnish, and he could almost hear Quark's acid voice berating him about the way he was wasting his time, the sharp slap of Rom's palm against the sensitive upper ridge of his ear. He sighed with a distinct whining tone. Nothing ever went right in this place!

So when he peered into the wreckage of a workers' lounge, the sight of a food replicator that was still mostly intact didn't raise his spirits much. Even in the habitat ring, the replicators only worked right half of the time. The front panel of this one was off, lying on the floor, shattered. Nog gave it a halfhearted kick. Stupid replicators—

Suddenly his little eyes widened and his jaw dropped, his attention attracted by the sight of half a meat roll sitting on the tray: it was spiced ground meat wrapped in pastry, a quick, nutritious snack food that most Cardassians were fond of. He hadn't seen one of them around the station since the Bajorans had taken over. But this one—it looked, it even smelled . . . fresh? Nog prodded the crust, and a crisp flake broke away. It was even—he picked it up—still warm!

He spun around, still holding the roll, but there was no one in the lounge. Then he stared at the replicator again, burning with new visions of wealth. It worked! He could sell it! If only he could find some way to transport it back to Quark's with no one spotting him.

But as he considered the unit in frustration, he started to wonder: Whose meal was this—and where were they now? How could anyone, even in this abandoned section of the station, have overlooked a functioning replicator? Someone knew about it, someone had just programmed it to deliver this meat roll. Someone who liked Cardassian food.

Berat pressed himself back against the wall of the head, next to the door, trying not to breathe. He held the phaser ready, in case they came bursting inside to arrest him. Who was out there? Was it station security? Or worse: Cardassian MPs, searching for him?

He had just gotten a fresh hot meat roll out of the replicator when he heard the footsteps out in the corridor. He instantly dashed into the closest hiding place, the head.

Now he cursed his stupid panic. He'd trapped himself in this place, trapped with no chance of escape. He looked desperately around the room for a way out, but the ventilation ducts were too small, no way he could squeeze through. No way to escape, no way to hide, either. Any minute now, they'd break through the door. . . .

But out in the lounge it was too quiet. So it couldn't be Marak's deck patrol. They would have been kicking the furniture around, breaking down this door by now. The thought reassured him slightly. Maybe it wasn't even station security, maybe no one was after him at all. Maybe life as a fugitive was starting to drive him crazy. It could just be a maintenance worker out there, coming to clean this place up. Or a scavenger, or a casual passerby. Maybe all he had to do was keep still inside here until whoever it was went away.

The notion reassured him, gave him hope—until he remembered, and the panic started to squeeze his throat and chest again. The replicator. The meat roll. *I left the meatroll out there, still on the replicator tray!*

Even as he tried to make up his mind what to do, he heard footsteps approaching the door to the head, saw the handle ease back—*why didn't I lock it?*

Because that would have told them for sure that somebody was inside. They would have broken it down, then, anyway.

Again, gripping the phaser, he held his breath, until his temples throbbed and his lungs ached for air, while the door pushed open—very slowly. One more centimeter, one more, and he would fire. Even if it wasn't security, he couldn't afford to be identified. If there were too many more of them, then he was dead for sure, but he had a chance if it was only one or two. It was either fight, or turn the phaser up to lethal and use it on himself. Better than letting them take him back to the ship, to Marak's version of justice.

But the door seemed to pause for a long moment, and then, just as slowly, it began to slide closed.

Disbelieving, Berat released his breath, an involuntary gasp. They were *going away*. It had to be a trick, a trap. He knew it. But there was nothing he could hear out there, nothing. Not even footsteps. And after a while, standing with the phaser ready, waiting . . . waiting, he finally realized he couldn't stay inside here forever.

Just as slowly as the unknown intruder, he slid the door open, still holding the phaser ready. But the lounge was empty. The meat roll was still on the replicator tray where he'd left it.

For a brief instant he shivered with the impossible thought: A ghost? A haunted station? He almost wanted to call out to see if anyone would answer. Now, that *would* prove he was going crazy!

Nog's senses were all hyper alert as he slowly slid open the bathroom door. His most basic instincts were screaming, *Danger, run away!* But maybe whoever had just used that replicator was in there—in there hiding. But why was he hiding?

Just as he was about to take a first step through the door, just as Berat, behind it, was beginning to press his finger against the firing trigger, Nog hesitated. There was a familiar scent, close enough that he could almost feel the body heat generating it. Catching his breath, glancing down, he could just see in the room's darkness the toe-tip of a heavy dark boot. A Cardassian boot.

Nog had grown up surrounded by Cardassians. He knew how they smelled, what they wore, what they liked to drink and eat. Here was a Cardassian. Hiding from him. And he would have had to be blind and deaf, with all the commotion the last few days up on the Promenade, not to know there was supposed to be

a Cardassian deserter, armed and dangerous, somewhere on the station.

With a reward on his head.

But not just somewhere. Here. He was right here
behind this door! Nog was sure of it. Trying not to
make a sound, he slowly let the door slide shut again.
He backed away in silence, ready to run if the deserter
came bursting out after him.

A reward. Gold-pressed latinum. Nog's avaricious
little soul yearned for it. But they said the deserter was
a murderer! And how could he capture a murderer
himself, single-handed, unarmed?

He crept soft-footed to the comm node, but hissed a
curse as he discovered it smashed, the transceiver unit
missing. Now what?

And there stood the replicator. The *working*
replicator. The meat roll still on it. The warm, flaky
crust, done just right.

Nog started to think. He thought of how much
money he could get for the replicator. He thought of
the reward. It occurred to him that the replicator was
probably worth a lot more than the Cardassian deserter. But if it was working, and producing meat rolls,
then who had made it work? Who else but the
Cardassian? And—an inspiration came to him, the
most brilliant he'd ever had—if the Cardassian could
fix one replicator, why not another? Why not *all the
broken replicators on the entire station?*

Stricken by the scope, the audacious grandeur of his
notion, Nog bared his teeth in a hiss of indecision,
weighing the immediate short-term gain against the
possibilities of larger long-term profits. And the practical difficulties of the scheme.

A short way down the corridor, a wall panel had
been kicked out. Nog hurried to it, wedged his small

body into the recess. Fortunately, most of the lights in the hall didn't work. It would be too dark to see him crouched in there. Nog hoped.

He waited in the shallow space, seething with doubts and misgivings. Maybe this wasn't a good idea. Maybe he should get out, run, while he still could. But what if he ran into the deserter then?

He might get hurt. He might even get killed!

There! Someone was coming out of the lounge! Nog held his breath and squeezed his eyes shut, so no one could see him. Then he forced himself to look. Yes, it was obviously a Cardassian. A Cardassian, and armed, yes—carrying a phaser like he was ready to use it. Nog tried not to whimper. But the Cardassian, though he looked hard up and down the corridor, didn't appear to see him. Instead, he moved off in the opposite direction.

Nog took a deep breath. He was safe. But the deserter was getting away!

After a moment's hesitation, he crept out of his hiding place and scuttled down the corridor after the Cardassian, just in time to see his feet disappearing into an uncovered access duct. Nog snorted indignantly. No one could move through the station's tunnels and ducts like he could—most especially not an oversized Cardassian!

Quickly, he slid into the opening after his quarry.

Someone was after him!

Berat could hear the hollow scrape of a body moving through the duct behind him. He would have run, but he could barely squeeze forward through the tight, confining space. His knees and elbows were already scraped raw, and his tool belt was constantly hanging him up on some seam or protrusion. Worst of all, there was no room for him to turn back and fire on whoever it was.

There was probably only one of them. The thought gave him enough hope to keep going. It was clear to him by now that no one did regular maintenance in these tunnels. If he could just go on, he could find a space large enough to turn and fire and leave his pursuer's body behind where it wouldn't be found, maybe for weeks. It was hope enough that he un-hooked the tool belt and dropped it; he crept on without its awkward weight encumbering him. He could come back for it later, if he got away.

He paused, hearing his breathing echo loudly in the darkness. There was nothing else but silence, but it was the silence of someone else holding their own breath, waiting for him to move. He cursed his indecision back at the lounge. Someone had spotted him back there, whoever had started to open that door. And now they were after him. For whatever reason. He wondered if the Gul had offered some kind of reward for turning him in.

He knew now that he should have fired when he had the chance. He was sure now that it couldn't have been the *Swift Striker*'s deck patrolmen. No Cardassian could crawl through this narrow space so easily, so quietly. If he hadn't been half-starved lately, he wasn't sure he'd have been able to make it through himself.

But the duct was long and dark, and he'd lost track of how many meters he must have crawled. He was heading downward—he thought he was—toward the level of the fusion reactors. But there should have been an outlet, some way to escape by now. Instead, the air seemed to be getting close and warm, too warm. Hard to breathe.

His hand, groping in front of him, hit something solid. There was—a wall? Frantically, his hands searched for an opening, a turning, another way to go, but the duct simply ended. A dead end! Someone had sealed this section off! He was trapped!

There was a microlaser torch in his tool belt; maybe he could cut his way through. But when Berat reached for it he remembered—somewhere back there he'd taken off the belt and left it behind. All he had left was the phaser.

In despair, he closed his hand tightly around the weapon. He closed his eyes. At least they wouldn't be able to take him alive. . . .

"Cardassian!"

Berat froze at the sound of the whisper in the dark. No Cardassian had a voice like that. There was a slight hiss to it: *"Cardassian!"*

Nog paused in the dark. His acute hearing picked up the sound of the Cardassian's fists pounding on the ductwork, the frantic gasping of his breath. Luck was with him. The deserter had run into one of the sealed-off reactor sections. He had nowhere now to turn.

"Cardassian!" he whispered out loud.

Finally there was a response. "What do you want?"

There was a desperate, strained tone to the voice. Nog knew he'd better not forget—the deserter was still armed. Dangerous.

"We can make a deal!"

A pause. "What do you mean? What kind of a deal? Who *are* you?"

"I *know* who *you* are! The Cardassian deserter. Your captain, Gul Marak, has a reward out for you."

"You'll never get it! Not if he wants me alive!"

He was desperate, yes. But Nog figured he could use

that to his advantage. "I can hide you!" A longer pause. Nog went on, using the convincing tone he'd learned at his uncle Quark's knee, "I can. Nobody knows this station like I do. All the best places to hide, places where the Gul won't ever find you, not even if he tears the place apart looking."

Finally, "Why would you bother to hide me?"

"Are these your tools that you dropped?"

"Suppose they are?"

"Did you fix that replicator back in the lounge?"

"What if I did?"

"You're some kind of maintenance techie, aren't you? Well, if you can fix the systems on this station, then we can make a deal. I'll hide you. You can repair things."

"You want me to . . . *fix* things?"

The Cardassian sounded slow, or something. "Hey, you've seen what things are like around this place? Everything's trashed, wrecked! Nothing works right around here since Gul Dukat pulled out. Especially the food replicators."

"You have a hiding place?"

"Dozens of them!" Nog replied with confidence. "I tell you, I *know* this station like the palm of my own hand! How else do you think I found you? You come with me, and you'll be safe as a snug in its shell." He was about to add the additional inducement that they'd split the considerable profits he was anticipating, but just in time he recalled one of Quark's Rules of Acquisition for dealing with employees: that the less they knew about the cash flow, the smaller the share they could demand.

Trapped in the confined dead-end space of the duct, Berat considered his dwindling options. He had the phaser, he could still shoot whoever this was and make his escape. Until the next person discovered him. And then he might not be so lucky. Next time, it might be Marak's deck patrol.

But . . . "How do I know you won't turn me in for the reward?"

"If I was going to do that, security'd be here right now," Nog lied glibly. "All I'd have to do is make one call on my comm unit here. . . ."

"All right," Berat said at last, surrendering to fate. "I'll come with you."

It came down to this: He had nowhere else better to go, and no one else he could trust more than this unknown voice behind him in the dark.

CHAPTER
14

BEN SISKO was not enjoying this session of the trade negotiations. He had only reluctantly agreed to serve as a mediator. This, after a memorable meeting with Ambassador Hnada and other distraught representatives of the provisional Bajoran government, who had flown up to the station for the purpose of insisting that he do something to convince the Klystron and Orion ambassadors to change their minds about supporting Bajoran membership in the Federation.

Sisko pointed out, repeatedly, that these negotiations were intended to work out trade agreements, not Federation membership for Bajor, but he could hardly deny that some Federation governments seemed to regard the current sessions as a kind of preliminary step in the process. He declined to raise the point that the Bajoran government hadn't even decided whether to apply for membership yet.

"This is all the Cardassians' fault!" Hnada had charged passionately. "Cardassian subversion! Why aren't you doing something to stop it?"

Although it was painfully obvious to all parties that Cardassian influence had been involved in the decisions of some worlds to withdraw from the negotiations, Sisko had to insist that under present circumstances there was nothing he could do. The Federation was no longer actively at war with the Cardassians, and they had the same diplomatic rights as the Bajorans. He couldn't stop them from talking with the representatives or even trying to bribe them, if that was in fact what was going on. And he certainly couldn't order them off the station, just for that.

But nothing he could say had been able to satisfy the Bajorans, owing partly to the fact that the Bajorans themselves weren't sure what they wanted to do about the situation. A few intemperate voices had been raised to suggest an attack on the *Swift Striker* or Cardassian personnel, and at that, tempers had erupted completely, with delegates accusing each other of terrorism and appeasement, respectively.

At the moment, Sisko wasn't quite sure whether he was supposed to be mediating between the Bajorans and the other worlds, or between the Bajoran factions themselves. He shifted restlessly in his seat.

On the floor, a Qismilian representative was protesting the presence of the wormhole creators. "Our religion states clearly: 'Thou shalt not listen to foreign gods.' Now, these wormhole beings are the gods of the Bajorans, are they not? I demand that they be enjoined from contacting our ships as they pass through to the Gamma Quadrant."

"You speak disrespectfully of the Prophets!" several Bajorans shouted, and a minor theological dispute broke out in the far corner of the room.

The Z'ood ambassador rose so quickly that it forgot its height and scraped its horns against the ceiling. The Qismilian shrieked, "Unfair! I protest! The

126

thirty-third article states clearly: 'No being shall speak from a higher stature than any other'!"

When the general security alert came through on his communicator, Sisko jumped to his feet with profound relief. He would much rather deal with Gul Marak than the ambassadors. At least there was only one of Marak.

"Excuse me, Ambassadors, Excellencies. An emergency on the station. Please, continue without me."

The Cardassian deck patrol had deployed onto the Promenade in groups of three and four. They were careful to maintain a casual appearance, and if their expressions looked particularly grim, most of the passersby would have told themselves that these were, after all, Cardassians and not some other, more lighthearted species.

Even Constable Odo found nothing in particular to rouse his suspicions as he saw them emerging onto the Promenade deck. They weren't visibly carrying arms, and liberty parties from the *Swift Striker*'s crew had been coming onto the station for some time with even less than the usual level of trouble. Although Odo loved law and order for its own sake, he was wise enough to recognize that there was a certain inevitable level of disorder on a station that served spacers from a multitude of races.

There was, of course, the problem of the Cardassian deserter, which was a matter of no little concern to the constable: not just the presence of a reputed murderer on his station but the fact that he was apparently capable of disabling his security array. And besides the fugitive, there were the military police who'd been strolling the decks obviously watching for him. But they were unarmed and officially on liberty, the same as the rest of the crew. As long as they didn't cause trouble, Commander Sisko was letting the situation stand. Odo even supposed that the presence of the deck patrol accounted for the better-than-normal behavior of the rest of the ship's crew, which was a kind of unlooked-for benefit.

As the Cardassian party split up, one group headed toward Quark's Place, another to a nearby importer who specialized in exotic luxury goods, another to a warehouse/storage operation. In the security office, Odo paused to watch the Cardassians on the monitors, saw nothing to indicate incipient trouble, then moved on to scan the rest of the Promenade.

The luxury importer was a Bajoran merchant who stiffened in reflexive fear as he saw three Cardassians come into his shop. A subofficer stepped up to him, uncomfortably close. "We're here to search these premises for an escaped criminal. Cooperate, and we won't give you any trouble." He turned to one of the others. "Show the Bajoran what kind of trouble we won't give him."

Grinning, the other patrolman tipped over a shelf of harmonic fronds, which shattered on the floor with a discordant jangle of sound.

As the merchant moved reflexively to save his goods, the Cardassian noncom struck him across the side of the face with a hand encased in a mail glove. The Bajoran fell against another counter, but the deck patrolman pulled him back up. "All right. We know he's been spotted around here somewhere." To his men: "Start searching in the back. Be *real careful* not to overlook anything." And to the merchant again: "Are you sure you don't have anything to say?"

"I don't know!" gasped the bleeding Bajoran. "I don't know anything!"

"Sure you don't. Your kind never do. Not until after

a little *persuasion.*" He grabbed the man's elbow and twisted until he cried out in pain.

Elsewhere on the Promenade there were similar scenes as the search got underway. But in Quark's Place, the customers were less inclined to submit to the invasion.

A table of asteroid miners from Port Horrtha ignored the Cardassian Glin's profane order to get "On your feet, you scum! Hands on your heads and get over against the wall!"

Nostrils flaring at this display of defiance, the Glin stepped closer and repeated his demand. This time, the miners raised their eyes to take a hard look at what had interrupted their dedicated gambling. Then the closest one swept up a chair and brought it down across the officer's head.

Taking his cue from the miner, Quark's huge B'kaazi henchman, Jas-qal, lifted up an entire Dabo table and flung it in the direction of two Cardassians next to the bar. As the table exploded into splinters, other customers whooped with pleasure and seized the nearest pieces of furniture, ready to do battle.

But the furious Glin pulled out his concealed phaser and fired a burst that felled Jas-qal in midroar. As the Cardassian staggered back to his feet, bleeding, his men pulled their own weapons, and the heart went out of the other combatants. Sullenly, they lined up against the far wall of the casino.

Quark took quick note of the invaders' firepower. "What is this?" he demanded with a genuine tremor of indignation in his voice. "This is a respectable establishment! We don't harbor criminals here! I'll have you know that Gul Marak himself is a patron of mine. A very special patron. I'd like to know what he'll say when he learns his men have come barging in here this way, making a disturbance, disrupting my business, roughing up my customers!"

But at the same time, he was pressing a button hidden behind the bar, summoning DS-Nine security. Although Quark had a dim view of security officers in general, particularly when they tended to interfere in his private business dealings, he had no objection to taking advantage of their protection when it seemed necessary. As it certainly did at the moment.

Odo's monitor in the security office flashed, and he switched to the scene: armed Cardassians holding phasers on the occupants of the gambling hall. Immediately, he recalled the rest of the crewmen in the apparent liberty party, splitting up into groups, and he upgraded the status of the alert to the highest priority before running out onto the main corridor of the Promenade.

Kira's communicator shrilled: *"All available security to the Promenade! Armed Cardassian intruders on level eleven!"*

A red rage washed over her, and she was instantly running toward the nearest transporter unit, phaser already drawn, imagining the very worst possibilities: a takeover of the station, a new invasion of Bajor, another war.

Although one corner of her mind was relieved that at least this time the alert wasn't for another terrorist bombing.

What she encountered was less than total war, but it was close enough to many other scenes she'd witnessed during the occupation of her homeworld. Kira pushed through the crowd surrounding an import office to find an implacable Constable Odo, backed up by a pair of station security officers, facing a pack of armed Cardassian military police. Broken merchandise littered the floor, and the Bajoran businessman who owned the shop stood slightly behind Odo, holding a red-stained cloth to the side of his head.

"What's going on?" she demanded furiously.

The Cardassian subofficer turned from Odo to Kira with a slight alteration of his sneer. "We're searching these premises for an escaped criminal. I'm warning you, Bajoran, don't interfere."

The hand holding her phaser twitched slightly as she restrained the almost irresistible impulse to blast him with the weapon's full power, to wipe all the features off that arrogant face. But then Odo also answered her question. "These Cardassians are under arrest. They've brought unauthorized arms onto the Promenade. They're also charged with destruction of property and aggravated bodily assault."

The Bajoran merchant took the cloth away from his head to display his wounds. "Three of them came bursting in here, knocked over that shelf of fronds, then they said they were going to search the back rooms. When I tried to stop them—"

Other voices shouted to be heard:

"They came into my place, too!"

"They kicked out all my customers!"

"I want compensation for this!"

The Cardassian noncom laughed scornfully. "You have to be joking! Arrest us? I don't surrender to *Bajorans!* Or"—glancing at Odo—"whatever *that* is!"

Kira's jaw tightened. "This station is sovereign Bajoran territory. Hand over your weapons or face further charges of resisting lawful authority."

The Cardassian grinned unpleasantly as he raised his phaser. "Authority? Lawful? Get out of my way, *Bajoran!*"

Odo's hand moved with a speed too quick for

merely human eyes to catch, his arm stretching half again its usual length, and his hand closed around his target's wrist. As the Cardassian gasped in pained surprise, Kira pressed her own phaser against the side of his head. To the rest of them, she said, "Drop the weapons! Now!"

Slowly, they lowered their phasers to the deck as the station's security moved in to pick them up and place the men under arrest. "Lock them up," Kira ordered. "And charge *this* motherless spawn with resisting arrest!"

When security had led them out, she turned to Odo. "Are there any more?"

"I think this accounts for all of them. There were a dozen who came onto the station. We didn't have much trouble with the bunch in Quark's Place. As soon as our security team showed up, the customers jumped on them. In fact, I think their Glin will need medical attention."

Kira nodded. When the miners were on station, a brawl was almost part of the regular entertainment at the casino. If Quark thought about it, he might even decide to charge them for the privilege. As the crowd parted reluctantly to let someone through, both Kira and Odo looked around to see Commander Sisko. "What's happened here?" he demanded, looking from Kira to Odo. "I just passed Quark's Place, and it was a wreck!"

"Cardassian patrolmen searching for that deserter. They were armed," Odo said with grim disapproval. "They're in detention, charged with bringing weapons onto the station, assault, endangerment, property destruction, and resisting arrest."

Kira added, "These other people are demanding compensation for property damage and physical injuries."

Sisko's face reminded her of a thundercloud. "They can get their compensation from Gul Marak!" Then his frown turned on Odo. "Constable, I want to see you in my office as soon as possible!"

As he strode away, Kira started to clear the crowd. "All right, it's over now, everyone go home. Anyone with a claim can file it in the station's legal office tomorrow." She paused to summon medical aid for the injured merchant, then told Odo, "As soon as this place is cleared, I'll go down to detention and help book the prisoners."

That was a job she was going to enjoy. A lot more than having to face Sisko when he was in one of those moods. She was glad she wasn't in Odo's position right now.

As soon as Sisko had checked out the damage to the station and was back in his office, he called up the Cardassian ship. "Marak! What in hell are you doing —sending armed men onto this station?"

The Gul's face appeared immediately on the screen. He'd clearly been expecting this call. "I told you, Sisko! I warned you! I mean to have that deserter back, one way or the other!"

"And I warned you, Marak. A stowaway on DS-Nine is a matter for DS-Nine security. I thought I'd made that clear! Instead, your deck patrolmen smuggle weapons onto the station and terrorize innocent civilians!"

"Well, this shows you what I think of your security! That traitor is hiding on your station! He's been spotted near the Promenade! I have witnesses! And your *security* does nothing! Nothing! I have a right to arrest that man, Sisko! He's mine!"

"The only people under arrest right now are your

thugs, Marak. They're being processed in station detention this minute."

The pupils of the Gul's eyes expanded rapidly. His nostrils flared. "You've dared arrest *my* patrolmen? When they were doing their duty?"

"Your deck patrolmen have no jurisdiction on DS-Nine. They're facing serious charges. A citizen was injured."

"A citizen? A *Bajoran?* You've thrown my patrolmen in jail for roughing up a Bajoran?"

"And several more merchants are demanding compensation for the damages they caused."

Gul Marak leaned forward toward the screen with his white-knuckled hands clenched over the edge of his desk. "Now you're showing your true colors, aren't you, Sisko? Bajoran-lover! You and your Bajoran friends are openly harboring a known traitor to the Cardassian state. A man who's committed the most despicable crimes: murder, mutiny, sabotage. *Berat* is running free on your station and you arrest *my military police,* who were only following legitimate orders to apprehend this *criminal!*"

The Cardassian had to stop to take a breath. Then, in a lower, threatening tone, "I want them released, Sisko. I want them back now, unless you want to see this station reduced to something even the waste reclamators wouldn't bother with!"

Sisko's brows lowered. "I don't think so, Gul. Oh, I don't believe you'd hesitate to fire on a few hundred unarmed civilians. I know Cardassians too well to think you'd worry about something like the loss of innocent lives. But you wouldn't want to fire on your own men, too?

"Or maybe you would. But you'd also be endangering the ambassadors. I doubt if your government would be happy to hear that you'd started a war with the Klingons and the Andorians at the same time."

Marak's expression was murderous. "You'll regret this, Sisko."

"That may be. But at the moment, it's your deck patrolmen regretting things. I suggest, if you want to see them again sometime before the next ten years are up, that you pay close attention to the claims for compensation you ought to be receiving tomorrow. In the meantime, this station is off-limits to *all* Cardassian personnel."

"You can't do this, Sisko! I'm warning you!"

Sisko cut the contact, feeling no little satisfaction at the outcome. It was almost as good as the time he'd decked that insufferable, interfering Q.

"Commander? You wanted to see me?"

Sisko sobered as Constable Odo entered the office. "Ah, yes, Constable."

In his years with Starfleet, Ben Sisko had served with a number of different nonhuman species, but he was always slightly off-base in dealing with the station's shape-shifter security chief. The constable was indefinably different, somehow. Possibly because even Odo didn't know what he was.

"I want to commend you for the way you dealt with the Cardassian deck patrol. However . . ." Sisko paused, took a breath, then continued. "However, we still have the problem of this deserter that Gul Marak claims to be on the station. Is there any doubt at all about this? Marak claims he has witnesses who've spotted the man near the Promenade."

Odo didn't look happy. "Commander, I'd like to say that if there were a fugitive hiding on my station, I'd know about it. But . . . I'm just not sure. Something is going on. Someone did tamper with the security systems, someone who knew what they were doing. A Cardassian technician, Chief O'Brien thinks. But is he a deserter? Or one of Gul Marak's agents? And is he connected to the terrorist attacks? That, I just don't know."

Sisko's brows drew together. "What about these witnesses, then?"

"Or alleged witnesses? We know that Gul Marak has offered a reward for information. It wouldn't surprise me if someone had tried to collect it."

Sisko sighed. As much as he hated to admit it, "The fact remains, Constable, I did assure the Gul that our security would take charge of finding this fugitive. If we had him in custody by now, none of this could have happened. On the other hand, if all this is just some Cardassian hoax, then what is it leading to? Why would Marak send armed men onto the station?

"I need to get to the bottom of this. You've got to find this damnable deserter, Constable. Or whatever he is. And if he's connected to our bomber, I'll send him back to Marak in pieces."

CHAPTER
15

QUARK CAME OUT of the DS-Nine legal office smug with satisfaction, having just filed a compensation claim for an amount ten times the value of the damages his gambling hall had actually sustained in the Cardassian takeover. For that kind of profit, he'd have been willing to let them break up the place every day.

He supposed they must really want that deserter, to go after him that way. But obviously someone must have informed. For the reward.

Quark paused and frowned. Wait a minute. Now that he thought about it, something wasn't quite right. It didn't add up. What made Gul Marak's patrolmen decide to search his casino? It was crazy to think he'd harbor a Cardassian fugitive, even one without a reward on his head. Where was the profit in doing that?

Maybe he had an enemy he didn't know about. Maybe somebody wanted to see his place wrecked. A Cardassian who wanted to open his own casino after

Gul Marak took over, and didn't want the competition.

The first thing Quark did when he got back to his place was to curse and shout for his nephew Nog. Where *was* that infernal boy? All the broken furniture and glassware was supposed to be swept up and replaced by now.

"He said something about getting the ale synthesizer fixed," said Rom from behind the bar.

"The synthesizer was broken? When did that happen?" Quark demanded in a panic, rushing behind the bar to see for himself. He groaned. Indeed, the unit was gone.

This was a real crisis. Quark imagined a mob of unhappy, thirsty gamblers, pounding on the bar, demanding synthale he couldn't supply. Chairs and glassware could be replaced with no trouble. But he could hardly open the doors for business without a functioning ale synthesizer, no matter how much compensation money he got out of the Cardassians. As fritzed-up as his old synthesizer had been, the thing at least could produce a drinkable ale.

Rom scratched his head. "Y'know, that's funny, I didn't know it was broken, either. At least, I didn't *think* it was. The boy just said, Was it worth three hundred credits to get it fixed by tonight, and I told him, Sure, because we can't open up this place if we can't serve ale." He paused. "Say, you don't suppose . . ."

Quark scowled. He wasn't sure what he supposed, but something was going on, he knew that much. "If that boy thinks he can cheat his own uncle . . ." He supposed he ought to be pleased that Nog was finally showing initiative and ambition, but this was sure an inconvenient time for him to start.

His good mood having evaporated, Quark joined

his brother in stocking the shelves with cheap new glassware and setting up the place for business again. Assuming they could open tonight. Assuming Nog could bring the ale synthesizer back in any kind of working order.

That boy's ears were going to be sore for a *long* time if it wasn't.

After several hours' more work, the gambling hall was restored to a rough semblance of order, the bar was restocked, and potential customers could be seen passing by with a glance at the closed doors. "Where *is* that boy?" Quark demanded for the hundredth time, seething as he watched his profits walk away.

From behind him came the sound of a door opening, and Quark turned around to see Nog emerging from the back room with the synthesizer unit in his arms. He cried aloud in relief and seized it from his troublesome nephew. "Is it fixed? Does it work?"

"Don't forget," Nog reminded his father as they worked quickly to reinstall the unit, "my money. You said you'd pay to have it fixed. That was our deal."

Quark reached out to grab the little wretch by the earlobe and pull him closer, yelping. "That's quite a deal, Nog. Charging to fix a synthesizer that *wasn't broken in the first place!* And in the meantime, while we're waiting for you to bring it back, I've had to keep the place closed with the customers waiting outside the doors—"

"No!" Nog insisted, squirming in the vise of his uncle's grip. "It's fixed! It really is! Try it! You'll see!"

Quark's reply was interrupted by a firm knocking on the door. "We're closed!" he yelled, but the knocking persisted, louder.

"Um, Quark. It's that constable. Odo," Rom said nervously.

Quark released his nephew. "What does *he* want?

Don't I have enough problems right now?" Greatly annoyed, he went to the door. "Can't you see we're busy right now, Constable? It seems that while your security force was off meditating in their temple or something, a mob of Cardassians trashed my place. We're *trying* to get it back into order so we can open again before I have to declare bankruptcy."

"Before you do," said Odo smoothly, stepping inside, "I'd just like to take a look around. As you may know, there's a fugitive hiding somewhere on the station. It seems that the Cardassians, at least, had reason to believe he might be somewhere here on the Promenade. I'm sure you won't mind if I search the place."

"I'm sure that won't be necessary," Quark said, taking a step to block his way.

Odo made an approximation of a frown. "This fugitive is supposed to be armed and dangerous. I know you're concerned for the safety of your partrons."

Quark laughed nervously, being in fact concerned about certain items of contraband not declared on any customs manifest. And as a matter of general principle, the presence of security prowling through his back rooms was to be avoided. "Come on, Constable! Don't you think I'd know if there was a Cardassian hiding around here? Those deck patrolmen already tore up my storage space looking for this deserter, and Rom and I have been back there all day, trying to straighten the mess. Believe me, if I'd spotted him, I'd have already turned him in for the reward Gul Marak offered, just to pay for the damages!"

"Claims for damages can be filed with the station's legal office."

"Well," said Quark lightly, "you can file a claim,

but who knows if the Cardassians will ever pay? And in the meantime, I have a business to run, customers waiting, this synthesizer to hook up. . . ."

Odo was not to be moved. "I still have to investigate these rumors. Someone did report seeing this deserter—"

"Oh, it was probably just Garak!" Nog interrupted nervously.

Odo looked dubious. "What about Garak?"

"Well, I mean . . . he's a Cardassian. And I've heard he was complaining about the patrolmen, you know, always stopping him? Looking for this deserter, see. And he was in here a couple of nights ago, wasn't he? I'll bet somebody thought he was that deserter, and told the Cardassians—you know, for the reward? That's what I would have done."

Odo regarded the boy with unconcealed distaste while Quark frowned at his nephew. What was that boy up to?

"All right," Odo finally agreed, "I'll go talk with Garak, see what he has to say. But I'm warning you, I intend to find this man. I don't like the idea of unauthorized persons on my station."

There was visible relief in Nog's eyes as he watched the constable leave.

"Quark?"

"What?" he snapped at his brother.

"Taste this." Rom held out a glass full of a dark, creamy-topped brew.

"Not now!"

"Quark, I think you should taste this."

"What? What is that stuff, anyway? You know the dark ales out of that synthesizer always taste like sewer sludge."

"I know. That's why you should taste it."

With a sudden surmise, Quark took a sip, then a long, satisfied swallow. "Mavarian stout! I haven't tasted that since . . ."

Then his eyes widened to stare at Nog, who crowed nervously, "See? I told you! And we had a deal, right? Now do I get my credits?"

"Never mind that! I want to know what's going on and I want it now!"

Nog backed away, bringing up a hand to protect his tender earlobe. "Nothing!" he protested. "I said I could get the synthesizer fixed, and I did! That's all!"

Rom moved to cut off his son's retreat. "Since the first day I came to this place, that synthesizer couldn't produce a decent Mavarian stout."

"And what were you doing bringing it out of the back room? Either you've got a secret transporter hidden back there, or . . ." Quark finally added it up. "Or a Cardassian technician!"

The look on Nog's face was as good as a signed confession. Rom, slower to comprehend than his brother, said, "What? You mean he's got that . . . got that deserter hidden *here?* When there's a *reward?"*

"But . . . but *look!* See how he fixed the synthesizer! He's an engineer! He can fix *anything* on this station! I've seen him! He fixed a replicator, but I couldn't move it by myself, and——"

"Wait a minute! Just wait a minute!" Quark was thinking. The boy might actually be right. For once. If this Cardassian really was an engineer, if he could fix replicators . . . "Where'd you find him, anyway?"

"Down in the lower core, in a lounge near some deserted cargo bays. There was this replicator, see, and it was *working.* Anyway, he's really scared the Cardassians will catch him and take him back to his ship, so I said we could make a deal, that I could hide him if he'd fix stuff. Like the synthesizer. And he did it, see?"

"Odo said he was armed and dangerous," Rom said doubtfully. "Maybe we should just turn him in for the reward and forget this other business."

"No! *I* found him!"

"What kind of a deal did you make with him?" Quark wondered.

"I just said we'd split the profits. I didn't say *how* we'd split them, though." Nog grinned.

"How did you get him up here?"

"Through the maintenance tunnels and cargo shafts, mostly. He's too big to crawl through the ventilator ducts."

"But somebody must have seen you with him, right?"

"I was careful!"

"But not careful enough, it looks like. And so Gul Marak sent his strong-arm gang of deck patrolmen to tear the Promenade apart to find him. It looks like your little project has caused a lot of trouble, nephew."

Nog whined sulkily, "It *could* have been Garak. They look alike. Sort of."

Quark ignored him. "I think we'd better go visit this Cardassian of yours. Where is he?"

"In the back storeroom?"

Quark snorted. "That's no place to keep something valuable. I thought I'd taught you better than that." He aimed a swat at Nog, who cringed and ducked, but not far enough to avoid a grip on the edge of his ear.

With Nog held tight, Quark took him back behind the bar to the storage rooms. Rom followed, grumbling. Quark prodded his nephew. "Call him."

"Berat? It's me, Nog."

"What's wrong? Didn't it work? Did you link up the lines the way I showed you?" Then the Cardassian came into view from the dark corner of the room, and caught sight of Quark and Rom behind Nog. He gasped and pulled out a phaser from his belt as Quark ducked down and Nog cried out, "No! Berat! It's all right! This is just Quark! My uncle. He owns this place! And my father."

"More Ferengis?" the Cardassian demanded suspiciously from behind the weapon.

Quark knew he had to be cautious. This was a Cardassian, after all, and there was a wary, desperate look in his eyes. But Quark knew how to use desperation to his advantage.

"Nog's uncle," he said in soothing tones. "You don't have to worry, the boy didn't turn you in. But I'm afraid there's been a lot of interest in you lately. Yesterday, patrolmen from Gul Marak's ship raided our place, did a lot of damage. And just now the head of station security came by. He wanted to search the back rooms."

The fugitive Cardassian looked wildly behind them, and Quark could see how his grip tightened on his phaser. "Security? Here? Now?"

"Fortunately, we managed to send him elsewhere. For the moment. But he's a tenacious type, to say the least. You can bet on it—he'll be back, maybe even tonight."

"They won't take me," the Cardassian muttered, holding his phaser tightly.

This *was* a desperate case, Quark thought to himself. And quite possibly not entirely sane. He lowered his own voice. "What you need is a better place to hide. Someplace even security doesn't know about. You're lucky that my nephew came to me. Quark's discretion is renowned throughout the entire quadrant. You'd be surprised at the secrets I've known, the items that have passed through my hands. Yes, you're safe with Quark.

"Now, Berat? Is that your name? My nephew tells me that you're an engineer. You have an arrangement with him? Nog's a bright boy, he always knows a good opportunity when he sees it. I must say, that synthesizer you repaired has never worked so well, not in all the years since I bought it. If that's a sample of your work, then I think we can do business together. Now, about your share of the net proceeds—"

Berat broke in, "I don't care about any profits. All I want is someplace to hide until that ship pulls out of here. And then passage *off* this place."

"Passage? To where?"

"Anywhere that's outside Cardassian space," Berat said bitterly.

"Well, I think we can arrange that," Quark temporized, having no real intention of letting the Cardassian go if he proved to be as valuable as he promised. "But we can worry about the business details later. First, let's get you to someplace really safe."

"This was *my* deal!" Nog started to complain, but a gesture of Rom's shut him up, and they followed Quark and Berat to a hidden room beneath the holosuites, next to Quark's own private office.

"I'm afraid you'll have to stay locked in here," Quark explained apologetically, while Rom hurried to remove certain valuable and illegal items to Quark's office. "But I promise, security will never find this room, not if they peel the station apart like a matushki fruit. We can fix up a place for you to sleep and to work. Those are your tools? Good. Excellent!"

Quark rubbed his hands together. "Nog, you can help our new guest get settled in. He's probably hungry, isn't he? I apologize for being so hasty, but I have an establishment to run." He paused to grin reassuringly back at Berat. "Don't worry. You're in good hands with Quark."

CHAPTER 16

"Kᴇɪᴋᴏ? Have you noticed anything strange around the station lately? I mean, things working differently?"

"Why, no. Everything seems to be just fine."

"But . . ." *But that's just what I mean.* O'Brien started to explain, then changed his mind. He kissed his wife and daughter good-bye.

"Oh, Miles, could you stop at Garak's and pick up Molly's new jumpsuit? He said he'd have it finished by today."

"Sure. But—"

"What? Is something wrong?"

"Uh, no. Never mind. It's no trouble."

O'Brien got off the lift tube at the Promenade. Most of the strangeness seemed to be turning up here, in the domain of private enterprise. Quark's casino was crowded, even at this early hour, and there was a line outside the Replimat, but the people seemed full of cheerful anticipation, not irritated at having to wait.

He went into Garak's shop. The Cardassian tailor's

face still showed the healing scars. "Morning, Garak. I see your shop repairs are all finished. My wife said you have her order ready—a child's jumpsuit?"

Garak gave him that slightly too familiar smile. "Of course, Chief, it's all finished. I'll bring it out. Just wait right here."

In a moment he was back with the garment. "There it is. I think your little girl is going to just love it!"

"Mmm. Garak? I thought your patternfitter was broken in the explosion, isn't that right?"

"Oh, yes, it was. But I got it fixed."

"Fixed?"

"Well, I couldn't do any work without it. I am a clothier, you know, Chief."

"Right, of course." In point of fact, as O'Brien was well aware, Garak was perhaps rather more than just a clothier. He was generally believed to be in the business of receiving, or passing on, information—to the Cardassians, possibly to some other governments.

But none of that was quite relevant to O'Brien at the moment. "Um, could I see it? Just—you know— professional curiosity?"

"Why, do you know how to fix a patternfitter, Chief? If I'd known that . . . ."

"Well," O'Brien laughed, slightly uncomfortable, "not that I've ever had a chance to work on one, you understand. But on a starship, if you can't fix it, it doesn't get fixed, you know. And how complicated can a patternfitter be, after all?"

Garak gave him a raised eyebrow, but led him to the piece of equipment, and O'Brien examined it, saw how it had been broken and reassembled, the painstaking welds—a careful, meticulous job. "It works just as well as it used to?"

"Better. The calibration is more even now. The cut

is more precise. You should appreciate the difference on your daughter's jumpsuit."

"Ah, right. Well, that's good to hear." O'Brien left the shop, scratching his head. No doubt about it. There was something peculiar about this situation. Damned peculiar.

But he didn't have time to think about it right now. Too much work to do.

"O'Brien to Odo. How's your picture now?"

"Coming in clear."

"That's as well as we can fix it now, with the parts we've got here."

"I appreciate it, Chief."

Miles O'Brien gave his Bajoran technician a friendly thump on the shoulder. "Good work, Jattera. That's the last of them."

At Odo's insistence, seconded by Commander Sisko, the job of restoring DS-Nine's security sensor grid to full operational status had been given top priority. O'Brien had done his best, despite the pilferage that was one of his biggest problems on the station—people lifting usable components from one unit to repair another. He'd done enough of this himself to understand the temptation.

But there were a few cases, obvious to his trained engineer's eye, in which the security system had been deliberately, skillfully sabotaged. This was an unsettling thing to see on a station where a terrorist bomber was on the loose. Especially unsettling to a man with his wife and daughter living here.

"Do you think this 'deserter' might have something to do with the bombings?" he'd asked Odo. "Could it be the Cardies trying to sabotage the station?"

"So you think so, too?" the security chief said

testily. "I don't know if there really is a deserter or not. Major Kira was asking that same question, but remember, the first bombing took place before the Cardassian ship even arrived in the system. The only thing I'm sure of is that *someone's* been tampering with my security system!"

"I'm afraid that's true," O'Brien said. "Um, you know, Odo, about those 'anomaly' things you were talking about?"

"What anomalies?"

"Um, never mind. It was just a random thought." O'Brien supposed that maybe he ought to leave actual security matters to the security people and just concentrate on repairing their sensor array. But there *was* something unusual going on around the station.

The technician Jattera had packed up his tools. "Care to get something to eat up in the Promenade?" O'Brien suggested.

The Bajoran paused. "All right."

Seated in the Replimat, Jattera chose the first thing on the menu, a fish-and-dumpling stew, while O'Brien ordered grilled mutton chops and fried potatoes. "And two tall, cold synthales," he added with a sense of cheerful anticipation. Miles O'Brien loved his wife, he really did, but sometimes the things that Keiko could put on the table—kelp and plankton and . . .

Well, sometimes a man just needed to tuck into a good, hearty meal. "What I wouldn't give," he sighed wistfully, "for a good Irish ale right about now."

"Irish?" Jattera asked in pardonable confusion.

"A nation on Earth. My homeworld. My ancestors were Irish. Ah, I can almost taste it, that ale, washing down those mutton chops."

The waiter had been in earshot. "You'd like an Irish ale, sir?"

"What? You're serious? The real stuff? Imported from Ireland? From Earth?"

"Well, no, not imported. But our synthesizer can provide whatever type of beer or ale you can name," the waiter said proudly.

"We'll see about that," O'Brien declared. But when the glass was brought to the table, he took a hard look at the color, the creamy texture of the head, the size of the bubbles streaming up the side of the glass. He frowned. He took a sip, and his eyes went suddenly closed, while a blissful expression played across his face. "Faith! It's the real thing! I'd swear it!" he exclaimed, opening his eyes.

The waiter looked smug.

"What about kanar?" Jattera asked tentatively. "Do you have that?"

"Coming right up!"

"Kanar?" O'Brien asked. "You drink that stuff?" It was a favorite drink of Cardassians, and he was surprised to find a Bajoran ordering it.

Jattera shrugged apologetically. "I guess I got used to the taste. During . . . you know. It's been hard to find around here, these days."

A few moments later, the waiter brought their orders, with Jattera's kanar and another Irish ale for O'Brien. The mutton chops were thick, browned, savory, and edged with a crisp border of fat. Juices flowed as O'Brien cut into the meat. "Oh," he moaned in pleasure, chewing. "Oh, my sainted mother, this could have come right off the top of her stove!"

The waiter hurried off in satisfaction to take another table's order. "How's yours?" O'Brien asked Jattera after a few more blissful bites.

"Good. Um, surprisingly good, in fact."

O'Brien nodded agreement, his mouth full. But

about the time he was soaking up the last mutton juices with a slice of potato, he was starting to wonder: Was he really in the Replimat on DS-Nine? It hardly seemed possible. Since when did things work so well around here?

"Back again, Chief? Was there something wrong with the jumpsuit? Didn't it fit?"

"Ah, no. I mean, I haven't had time to take it home yet. You know, Garak, I'd like to know just who fixed that patternfitter of yours. They did a good job." He laughed. "If they're not already working for Operations, I'd like to recruit them!"

Garak's expression blanked slightly. He looked down to adjust a display of tunics, evading O'Brien's eyes. "Well . . . I'm not sure who did the work, exactly. It was picked up and delivered back here when it was fixed."

"Oh? And who picked it up?"

"The Ferengi boy."

"Nog?" This was crazier and crazier! O'Brien supposed there must be some capable engineers and technicians among that race, but the only Ferengi he knew of on DS-Nine were Quark and his crew of quick-change artists. And he'd have bet against any odds that the Ferengi boy, Nog, was no technician. A pickpocket, maybe, but that was about the extent of his visible skills. O'Brien had heard more than enough about Nog from his Keiko, who kept trying to interest the boy and his father in the value of an education.

But Garak said uneasily, "I understand he's working for someone who's just starting up a business in repairing equipment. About time, too," he added, "the way so many things have been allowed to deteriorate around here."

O'Brien ignored the slighting reference to his department's efficiency. "Someone?"

"That's right," Garak answered evasively.

"About when did they start this sideline? Whoever they are."

"Mmm, well, I guess I heard about it three days ago. I couldn't do any work without that patternfitter, you know. He said they'd give it *priority* attention."

"For an extra fee, I suppose."

"Well, yes. But I needed it fixed. Is that a problem, Chief?" He leaned slightly closer across the counter.

"No!" O'Brien assured him quickly, backing away. "Not at all."

It was just bloody strange, that's all.

CHAPTER
17

JAKE SISKO made his way listlessly through the Promenade. There were big crowds around Quark's Place and the Replimat. He was aware that his dad didn't want him on this level of the station because of the terrorist threat, but Dad never seemed to stop and think that there was nothing else for a kid to do. Except for school. Which was over for the day. And schoolwork. Which Jake didn't feel like doing. Once he started his homework, the day might as well be over.

Nog didn't have to go to school all the time. Jake hadn't seen him since the day Garak's shop had been bombed. In fact, he was almost sure Nog was avoiding him. Remembering that particular incident made Jake uneasy, though. He was sure that Nog had been actually going to loot the shop. There were times when Jake thought his dad might be right about the Ferengi, but, Nog was the only thing like a friend he had on this whole station!

He stopped to buy a glopstick from a vendor, took a

few licks, and tossed the rest into the nearest recycler. He never could make himself like that stuff. It was Nog's favorite. Actually, it had never tasted as good as that one time he and Nog had snatched the sticks and run with them.

That had been wrong, of course, as his dad had made painfully clear at the time. Jake knew it. But, it had been *fun,* too, in a way. Exciting. Nog sure had a way of stirring up excitement. Jake could use a little excitement. For a station full of alien diplomats, terrorists, smugglers, stowaways and Cardassian soldiers in uniform, DS9 could sure be a dull place. If you were a kid.

Thinking of Nog, he slipped through a door marked OFF-LIMITS TO UNAUTHORIZED PERSONNEL, down a corridor, and into the freight conduit that ran behind the shops on this side of the Promenade. Nog liked to prowl these back alleys of the station in search of what he called opportunities, but which Jake's dad called trouble.

A pair of workers saw him and said, "Say, you're not supposed to be back here," but they did nothing to chase him out. Then Jake spotted a familiar short figure coming out of the back of the mineral-assay office. "Nog!" he yelled out, hoping to stop his friend.

The Ferengi boy paused and turned back to look at who was calling him, and then his neck seemed to hunch down into his shoulders. "Nog!" Jake called again. "Wait for me!"

Nog slowly turned around. He was holding a carry-all that seemed heavy. "Where have you been?" Jake asked him eagerly. "I haven't seen you—anywhere! What've you been doing?"

"I've been busy. With important business. I don't have time to *play.*"

He tried to leave, but Jake followed him. "Well, what kind of business? Is that it, there?" He looked eagerly at the carryall in Nog's hands.

Holding it tight against his chest, Nog said irritably, "It's confidential. You know, a *secret.*"

"Well, you can tell me. I know how to keep a secret."

Nog looked dubious.

"Is it another one of your uncle's special holosuite programs? Come *on,* Nog!" Jake, being at a vulnerable point in his adolescence, was as eager to see another one of Quark's special sex programs as he was afraid of his father's reaction should he ever find out his son even *knew* about them.

"It's something else," Nog snapped. "This is *my* business, not Quark's!" Even though Quark had all but taken it over, ever since the night that Odo came into the gambling hall. It wasn't fair. Nog was the one who'd found Berat in the first place, he was the one who had the idea to start the repair business, he was the one who should have had the profits! Instead, he was just Quark's errand boy again. Fetching and carrying. Doing all the dirty work.

"So what's in there?" Jake asked again. "I'll bet you stole something, didn't you?"

Nog was about to protest when a Starfleet security officer materialized in the corridor ahead of them. "Hold it, you two!"

Jake froze as the officer activated her comm badge: "Security, this is Occino, I've found them." Then she turned to the boys. "Someone reported unauthorized persons in the cargo passages. Don't you boys know you're not supposed to be back here? These conduits can be dangerous, even when we don't have terrorists and whatever running around the station."

She scowled at Nog, obviously aware of the Ferengi reputation. "What's that you've got there, anyway?"

One instant Nog looked like he was about to bolt, then he clutched onto his carryall protectively, as if he didn't dare drop it to run. And Jake was seized by inspiration. "It's schoolwork," he said earnestly. "Our science project. We're supposed to be working on it together."

The security woman looked doubtful. "Aren't you Commander Sisko's son?"

"Yes, I'm Jake Sisko. We're just on our way back from school."

"Well, this is no shortcut for kids." She escorted them back to the public deck of the Promenade with the warning to go straight home and stay out of trouble.

"That was quick thinking. For a human," said Nog, visibly relieved. "Good thing it wasn't Odo."

"Well, now you can tell me what's in there," Jake insisted.

"I told you, it's private business."

"C'mon, Nog, I saved your tail just now. Doesn't that count for anything with you?"

"Maybe. If you swear to keep it a secret." Nog was well aware that humans, like Klingons, were peculiar about this business of their personal honor.

"I swear! I won't say a word!"

"Even to your father?"

Jake hesitated. "This isn't something *illegal,* is it?"

"Not according to Federation law," Nog declared, though he was slightly vague on exactly what constituted Federation law in this case.

"Well, all right, then. I swear. I won't tell anyone."

"On your honor?"

"I *said* so, didn't I?"

"All right. Come with me." The two conspirators made their way with the carryall to another access door, this one closer to Quark's Place. "Quiet," Nog warned as they slipped in the back way, although the warning seemed unnecessary.

The gambling hall was full, with an especially large crowd around the bar. Beings of two dozen different species—although no Cardassians—were loudly and cheerfully wagering away their gold and other precious assets. Lines of them were going up and down the stairs to the holosuites, the site of Jake's most guilty adolescent fantasies.

Nog led him through a narrow hall to a room that Jake thought was just a storeroom, full of crates and boxes. But at the back was another door, and another hall behind it.

Nog turned to him. "Better not say anything about your father, all right?"

Jake nodded, tingling with excitement.

Nog pressed a certain place on the wall, and the section slid aside, revealing a hidden room. "Hey, Berat. I brought some more stuff for you to fix! Priority!"

Jake stared at the man who was sitting at the table. A Cardassian!

And the Cardassian, seeing someone else with Nog, nervously reached for a phaser lying on the table close at hand. "Who's that?"

"Just my friend Jake. He won't say anything. He's sworn an oath on his personal honor."

"A human?"

"A friend of mine. His father works around the station. You know, with the diplomats."

"Diplomats? Then he knows someone who could maybe get me onto a ship?" There was sudden hope in Berat's voice.

"That's right! Maybe. Isn't that right, Jake?" Nog said pointedly.

"Uh, yeah. Sure. Maybe."

"I *have* to get a ship off this place," Berat said desperately, to himself as much as anyone else.

"I'm working on that. Aren't I, Jake? See? But look, right now here's the gemological analysis unit from the assay office. Harilo says it fritzed up two days ago, and now the display doesn't display. I told him I'd give it the highest priority. Can you do anything about it?"

"You tell them all they have the highest priority, Ferengi. There's only one of me, and machines like this aren't my speciality."

"I know. But you can at least take a look, can't you?"

"I can take a look," Berat said wearily, pulling the unit over to him.

The table was covered with all kinds of devices, some intact, some just heaps of parts. By now Jake was almost seething with excitement. He was just sure this Cardassian, Berat, was the deserter the whole station was looking for. Dad had really been steamed about the *Swift Striker*'s MPs coming onto the Promenade to search for him. And Nog had been hiding him all this time, right below Quark's holosuites! He could hardly believe it. Rumor was, this Cardassian was wanted for murder!

Jake bit on his lip. Maybe he should tell Dad, after all. But he'd promised Nog not to. He'd sworn not to tell anyone. And besides, the Cardassian, despite the phaser he kept right there on the table next to him, didn't look all that much like a murderer. He looked like a Cardassian, of course. But mostly he looked tired and hungry. And nervous.

Berat looked up from the gemanalysis unit. "I can't

159

fix this unless you can find a new chromatospectric crystal. This one is cracked along the axis. I suspect it wasn't calibrated right to begin with, or someone tried to make illicit adjustments. This kind of crystal is very sensitive."

Nog looked disappointed. "What about these jobs?" he asked, pointing at some other equipment piled at the other end of the table.

"Those two are finished. This other I may be able to have done by tomorrow. *If* you bring me those parts I asked for."

"It's all in here," Nog told him, handing him the carryall.

Berat spilled the contents onto the table and sorted through the miscellaneous bits and pieces. "Yes, I guess that should do."

Then he looked up at Jake. "You can get me a ship, human? Off this station?"

"Um . . ." Jake saw Nog's face take on a pained expression, as if he were urgently trying to tell him something. "What kind of ship?" he temporized. "And to where?"

"Anywhere! Anywhere outside Cardassian space! A freighter, I suppose. I wouldn't be dead weight! You can tell them that. I'm a qualified engineer. I might not know everything about starship drives, I mostly specialized in station operations, but I'll do anything. Maintenance, cleanup—anything."

Nog interrupted. "I told you, it's too dangerous to move right now. Gul Marak hasn't gone away, and station security is still looking for you. We were stopped by security on the way here. Weren't we, Jake?"

"Uh, yeah. We were."

"If it weren't for Jake, here, they would have found

all that stuff." Nog was pulling on Jake's arm. "C'mon, time to go. I got to bring Berat his meal."

But for some reason, Jake didn't want to leave yet. Berat fascinated him. He'd never met a real Cardassian—in uniform. Only Garak, and Garak was just a tailor. You could hardly imagine him doing . . . all those things Cardassians were supposed to do. "Look, can't you go get it? While I wait here?"

Nog scowled, "I don't think that's a good idea. I don't think Quark would like it."

"Oh, c'mon, Nog! You said this was your business, not Quark's."

And Berat added, "Let the human stay, Ferengi. It might bring you back faster with the food for once."

With bad grace, Nog gave in, although warning, "I'll have to lock the door again. In case anyone comes down here while I'm gone."

Jake belatedly realized as the door hissed shut that he was now locked inside this room with a maybe-murderer. He felt for a moment like yelling for Nog to come back. Nervously, he glanced at the clutter on the table, the tools, the pieces of equipment. "You can fix all these things?"

Berat shrugged. "Most of them. If I have the right parts." He shook his head. "This station hasn't been well maintained."

"My father says, uh, he says the Cardassians wrecked DS-Nine on purpose when they pulled out, just to keep the Bajorans from having it. I remember, when we first got here, you could find broken stuff everywhere." Jake paused. He pulled a couple of items from his pockets. "I found these. . . ."

Berat took them, shrugged. "This is a chronometer. It would probably run if you had the right power cell. This one's a personal communicator." He pried off the access panel.

"You can fix it?"

"Possibly."

Suddenly Berat looked up from the unit and asked him desperately, "Is it true? What the Ferengi says? About the station security? I can't believe I'm trusting my life to a Ferengi."

Jake nodded, feeling guilty for hiding at least part of the truth. "They really are looking for you. I've heard Gul Marak has even put up a reward. Not that anybody from Starfleet would take it."

Berat's shoulder slumped. "So I'm trapped here." He picked up a tool and started to probe the inside of the comm unit.

Jake dared, "Um, they say you deserted from the Cardassian ship? They say you . . . murdered someone."

Berat's head lifted. "Killed, not murdered. He was my enemy. He meant to kill me. You have that concept in your law, human?"

"Uh, you mean self-defense? Well, yes, I suppose." Jake thought a moment. "But, if that's true, you could turn yourself in—"

"No!" Berat's hands shot out and seized hold of Jake's arms, hard. "You don't understand! I can't let them find me! I was assigned to Marak's ship so they could have me out of the way, kill me where no one would see or care. My only hope is escape! They've killed my father, two of my uncles, my brother. They won't rest until they're rid of me, too."

"Killed them? What for?"

Berat released him with a sigh. "For being on the wrong side. My family was in the previous government. My father was on the cabinet. He knew the war was costing our homeworld too much. Bajor's resources were depleted, the terrorist activity was only growing worse, the Federation was threatening to intervene—it made no sense to hold on to it any longer. He had *no idea* about the wormhole. No one did!

"But they made him confess to lies. They hanged him as a traitor. His brothers and son next to him. They forced me to watch. . . ."

Jake was horrified and fascinated at the same time. "They *hanged* them?"

Berat shuddered, remembering. "In the public square of our capital. They were strong men. It took a long time for them to die. The new government made a spectacle of the event. They didn't begin the stoning until the third day."

"Stoning? You mean . . . the third day *after* they hanged them? They were still *alive?*" Jake stared at the massive musculature of Berat's neck, the armored tendons, and slowly began to understand that hanging might be different for a Cardassian.

"They made me watch all that time. Then, when the stoning began . . . In a way, it was a relief. To have it over."

He snapped the panel back onto the communicator. "Here. This should work now."

Jake took it numbly. "Thanks."

"Just find me a ship, human. Some way out of here."

Jake nodded, feeling terrible about Nog's lie and his complicity in it. But maybe he *could* do something. He could try, anyway.

Behind them, the door slid open, and Nog came into the room with a tray holding a plate of drolis and a pitcher of beer. He glared suspiciously at Jake and Berat. "Here. Dinner." And to Jake, impatient, "Are you ready to go, yet? I have work to do, you know.

And so does he. Some of these repairs are priority orders."

Jake stood up. "It was good to meet you," he told Berat. He would have held out his hand, but the Cardassian's bleak expression stopped him.

All he could think of to say was good-bye.

CHAPTER
18

THERE WAS A NEAR-RIOT outside the DS-Nine security office as the Cardassian deck patrolmen were finally being released from detention. Security officers were forced to intervene between the sullen ex-prisoners and the jeering, mocking crowd of Bajorans that clearly meant to escort them all the way to the airlock, and possibly out of it the hard way.

O'Brien managed to slip inside to wait until Odo had finished processing the releases. He found Major Kira monitoring the situation.

"So, I see Gul Marak finally paid up."

Kira said irritably, "Bloody Cardassians come onto this station with their weapons, flout our regulations, abuse our citizens. Then they think they can just pay a fine and walk away."

O'Brien blinked, a little taken aback by her tone. "I thought it was Commander Sisko who imposed the fines."

Kira sighed and ran her fingers back through her

hair, standing it on end. "Sorry I snapped, Chief. It hasn't really been a good day."

"Not another bomb?"

She shook her head. "Posters."

"Posters? You mean, like the one on Garak's shop?"

"Exactly. On the Promenade, near the VIP quarters, in the turbolifts." She punched a display into her padd and showed it to him. He read:

BAJORAN BLOOD, BAJORAN SPACE.
WHERE WAS THE FEDERATION WHEN WE WERE DYING?
ALIENS OFF BAJOR!
YOU HAVE BEEN WARNED!

"Bloody hell!" he murmured. "You've got to trace these?"

Kira frowned at the hint of pity in his voice. "It's my job." She glanced at the monitor again, then got to her feet. "Well, it looks like the show's over. The Cardassians are back on their ship, and the merchants have their money in their pockets." She looked at O'Brien again. "Did you want to see me about something?"

"Actually, I was waiting to talk to Odo. But maybe I'll come back later."

Ben Sisko had been expecting the call from the *Swift Striker,* ever since he authorized the release of the Cardassians from detention.

"Yes, Gul Marak? What is it?"

"All right, Sisko! I've paid your blood money! Now, what are you going to do about it?"

"What do you mean, Marak? Your men have been released already."

"I *mean,* when are you going to start allowing Cardassians back on DS-Nine?"

"I plan to discuss that question with my security officers later today. I'm afraid there's a great deal of tension on the station since that incident. I don't want any violence."

Marak leaned forward with a menacing expression. "Are you telling me that I'm not going to be able to come onto the station? I have legitimate business with several ambassadors here, Sisko. Am I going to have to tell them the Starfleet commander won't *allow* them to speak with me?"

Sisko sighed. "I'll inform security that you and your aides are permitted onto the station. As for liberty for your men—we'll see about that."

"Fine!" the Cardassian commander snapped. "Now, what about that deserter? You *assured* me that your security would be taking care of the matter. So, what have they done about it? Where is he?"

"I've assigned my chief of security to investigate the matter, personally. He's found nothing, not a trace. *You* claim you have witnesses who've seen him, but who are they? What did they say?"

Marak bared his teeth. "What kind of farking limp excuses are you trying to hand me now? Maybe you need a new security chief! Maybe this station needs a new commander! What good are any of you, if you can't find a fugitive stowaway after all this time. Well, I'm warning you, I won't just let this matter drop! If you can't do the job, I will!"

"You know, Gul, you seem to be awfully eager to have your men come onto this station. I wonder why that is?"

"What in the last cold hell are you talking about, Sisko?"

"I mean, maybe this is just an excuse to get more of your men onto DS-Nine. For whatever reason."

Marak's gloved fist hit his console with such an impact that Sisko distinctly heard the shattering of components. The Cardassian's face had turned an alarming shade, and the veins in his neck pulsed visibly with rage. "I've *told* you—this man is a *traitor!* If you're behind this—"

"I'm not behind anything, Marak!"

"Do you want to see the body of the officer he killed? Or the sentry he assaulted? Would that satisfy you? Look, Sisko, I'm warning you for the last time—"

"Don't threaten me, Marak!"

The two commanders were both standing, glaring at each other's image. But it was Sisko, this time, who finally backed down. "All right, I'm doing everything I can to find your fugitive. After all, I don't want a murderer at large on my station. But if you really want him apprehended, it might help if you gave us a little bit more information."

"What kind of information?"

"About these witnesses, for one thing."

"That report is confidential."

"And more details about this man. His background. Dammit, we don't even know what he's supposed to look like! Send us his personnel records, and we might have something to go on!"

"Cardassian service files are restricted."

"In other words, you refuse to cooperate. And we're still expected to believe you?"

"Just let my men search that station, and *we'll* find him, I guarantee that."

"Out of the question," Sisko snapped. "Now, if you don't have anything else—"

But Gul Marak's image abruptly winked off the screen.

Sisko dropped back into his chair. "Dammit" was all he said.

"Well, Chief O'Brien! Are you feeling lucky today?"

The engineer dropped into a seat at the bar. "No thanks, Quark. Just feeling thirsty. How about a cold synthale?"

"Any special kind?" the Ferengi asked smugly. "Name your favorite poison, Chief!"

"How about an Irish ale?"

"Coming right up, one Irish ale! Straight from Old Ireland on Earth—or as close as you can't tell the difference!"

O'Brien sipped the brew when Quark brought it, and praised the quality as it deserved. In fact, it was at least as good as the glass he'd had in the Replimat. Which was just one more piece of evidence . . . for what, he wasn't quite sure.

"Your nephew doesn't happen to be working around here today, does he?"

"Nog? Ah, no, he's somewhere else at the moment. Why?"

"Oh, I'd just like to talk to him for a minute."

Quark was unenthusiastic. "Well, Chief, I don't know, I haven't seen him for the last few hours. You know how boys are." He laughed insincerely.

"I know. But my wife made me promise I'd try to get him back to school."

"School. That might be all very well for your kids, Chief, but the things Nog needs to learn are right here."

"That could be," O'Brien admitted reluctantly, "but I did promise Keiko."

"Ah, the lovely Keiko," Quark murmured with a lascivious glint in his eye, but quickly, under her husband's glare, he amended his remark. "And a fine teacher, I'm sure. Just what Nog needs. When I see him, I'll tell him what you said, all right?"

O'Brien sipped his ale. That boy Nog had something to do with whatever was going on. And Quark was hiding something. He knew it. But—what?

CHAPTER
19

ODO LOOKED UP from his desk to see the chief of operations come into the security office. "Chief O'Brien. Major Kira said you were looking for me a little while ago."

"I was, yes. Um, Constable, this may be a little far-fetched, but I think I've been running into some more of your anomalies."

Odo was immediately attentive. "What do you mean?"

"Well, you remember when we first found those security sensors fixed down in docking pylon six? The alarm bypassed on that airlock? And how I said at the time, Here's someone who knows what he's doing? Probably a technician? Now, lately, someone seems to be fixing things all over the Promenade. And doing a bloody good job of it, too. Now, I've been doing a little checking, a little asking around, you know?"

"Yes? And?"

"Well, I think that Ferengi boy Nog is involved somehow. I know, it doesn't make a lot of sense, but people are saying that he's involved in a repair business somewhere on the station. He picks up equipment and brings it back—working better than ever. Now, if there was someone on this place who could do that, I'd know about it. Unless—"

"Unless it's somehow connected with our deserter," Odo completed the thought.

"Most of this is Cardassian equipment," O'Brien added.

"Thank you, Chief," Odo said briskly. "I think you might have something. Let's try to find out." He turned to his console. "Computer, connect me with Gul Marak on the *Swift Striker*."

A Cardassian face appeared on his screen. "Gul Marak can't talk to you now, he's busy."

"I'll just bet he is," muttered O'Brien under his breath, recalling the cheerless expressions of the Cardassians as they were being released back onto their ship. If he'd been one of them, he wouldn't have liked to be going back to face Gul Marak's temper, not by a long way.

But Odo addressed the screen. "I'm chief of DS-Nine security, calling with regard to the matter of the Cardassian deserter."

"I'll . . . see if the Gul has a moment," said the face on the screen.

A moment later, he was seeing Gul Marak's image. "You have him? You've got him under arrest?"

"I have a lead. A possible lead."

"You called me out of . . . you called me because you have a *lead?*"

"Gul, I was told you wanted progress on this case. Well, I'll be able to make more progress if I have information. Now, just what was this deserter's function on board your ship? Did he have any particular technical skills?"

"Berat? He was a maintenance scrag. The lowest grade. He scrubbed the floors, he mopped out the heads."

"Then he wouldn't be especially skilled at systems operations, maintenance, repairs? We have reason to believe our suspect may be a technician."

Reluctantly, Marak admitted, "I suppose you could call him a technician. He previously served on the systems-operation staff of one of our space stations. But he was demoted for gross neglect of duty and incompetence."

"I see. It would be helpful if I could see his personnel file."

"I already told Sisko, those records are restricted information!"

"That's unfortunate. However, even with this limited amount of information we may be able to make some progress."

"Just make sure you catch him," the Gul snarled, and cut the connection.

Odo exhaled. "You know, hard as it might be to believe, at times like this I really miss Gul Dukat. He was treachery to the bone, but at least you could carry on a conversation with him."

Miles O'Brien stared at the empty screen. "Actually, I don't find it hard to believe at all."

"Back again, Chief?"

"Just for a couple of minutes, Quark. Long enough to put away another one of those Irish ales!"

"Well, coming right up, then!" Quark said cheerfully, going to the synthesizer. "One Irish ale for Chief O'Brien!"

The operations chief swallowed deeply. "This is the real thing, all right! Tell me, Quark, what is it? Did you have a new synthesizer installed?"

"Now, don't tell me you're planning to start up your own business, are you, Chief? I can hardly give away all my secrets to the competition!"

"I suppose not. Well, whatever you did, I like the results." He took another, smaller drink. "Um, I don't suppose Nog has been around?"

Quark's small eyes shifted slightly to glance around the room. "Uh, no, I don't think so. I'll have to have a talk with that boy, running all over the Promenade the way he does."

"Mm," O'Brien answered, lifting his glass. He turned his attention to the glass, and Quark moved away to importune another customer. O'Brien sipped his drink slowly, taking his time, glancing around the casino. The place was starting to fill up now, as duty shifts let off and people were looking for entertainment. Quark was soon too busy at the tables to pay much notice to him watching quietly at the bar.

Sure enough, he spotted Nog, coming out of a back room—a small, furtive figure. O'Brien stood up from his seat. "Say, Nog!" he called out, but the boy stiffened slightly, then turned and headed back the way he had come.

O'Brien went after him, winding his way past the crowds gathered at the gaming tables.

Nog had only left the back corridor a few minutes ago, but now he came slipping back inside, looking around as if someone might be following him. He failed to notice that one of the crates in the hall hadn't been there before.

The crate, in fact, was Constable Odo, who had been making his own inquiries on the Promenade and come to the same conclusion as O'Brien, that the Ferengi were involved in the mysterious repair of

174

equipment around the station. Odo's disapproval of the Ferengi was no secret, and he had never quite reconciled himself to Commander Sisko's plan to retain Quark on the station. Odo himself would have packed the gambler and all his relatives into the first freighter heading out of Bajoran space.

The secret rooms Quark had hidden beneath the holosuites were a long-standing annoyance. No one, in Odo's opinion, needed such privacy unless they meant to evade the notice of the law. Now, finally, he had the excuse he had always wanted to find out just what was going on back here.

Quark's secret rooms were well hidden, but Odo wasn't discouraged. There had to be some kind of ventilation, and that meant there was a way inside for Odo, who could slip through the slightest crack or fissure. He had just been about to probe the walls when Nog came back in from the main room of the casino.

The Ferengi boy looked behind him again, visibly nervous and, in Odo's eyes, guilty. Then he slid up to the seemingly blank wall, looked around one more time, and pressed his palm to a certain panel. As the door slid open, he called out softly, "Berat! Cardassian!"

That was all Odo needed to hear. In mere instants his body had flowed and re-formed into his usual humanoid shape to follow Nog into the room. There, he announced to the startled Cardassian seated at a worktable: "You're under arrest for unauthorized entry onto this station!"

At the sight of the constable, Berat reacted violently, snatched up his phaser with one hand and with the other grabbed Nog by the collar and dragged the boy, kicking and squealing in terror, across the table.

Pressing his weapon to Nog's head, he held him as a shield in front of him, warning, "I'll kill him before I let you take me back there!"

Odo hesitated, recognizing the level of desperation in the fugitive's voice. *Armed and dangerous,* Gul Marak had called him, and right now it looked like Marak was right. Nog was hissing and squealing in real pain at the grip on his throat. He might be a Ferengi and a cheat and a thief, but he didn't deserve to be killed this way, and by all known accounts, this Cardassian was a killer. Odo knew he was going to have to time his move very carefully.

Berat was moving away from him, holding his struggling hostage, backing up to the wall, edging in the direction of the door. Odo moved to block his way, but just then Berat suddenly gave Nog a powerful shove in his direction. Odo staggered off balance with the boy clutching his legs and screeching in fear.

Berat ran past them, out into the corridor, looking around wildly for a way to escape. After days closed into that single room, he wasn't exactly sure where he was, how to get out of here. There was noise and laughter echoing in the corridor, a few good-hearted oaths: *Frakk it! Red again! I just can't win tonight!*

He was in the casino, just behind it. That was the only way out.

Berat headed for the door, but just then a man in Starfleet uniform came into the corridor, started on seeing him, brought up his hand to reach for some kind of weapon—or was it a weapon? Berat had no time to wait and find out. The man was in his way, blocking his escape, his only chance.

He fired the phaser.

The Starfleet man crumpled and fell, and Berat ran over the inert body, out into the main room of the casino. He stumbled, half-blinded by the bright, flashing lights. So crowded in here, the noise, so many people. Those lights, they hurt his eyes. Where was the way out? The door? People were yelling at him, crowding in his direction, but he aimed the phaser, and the customers parted, got quickly out of his way.

Berat ran for the door.

It took a few moments for Odo to untangle himself from the shrieking Nog. He ran out into the hallway just in time to see O'Brien crumple and fall to the floor and the Cardassian escaping into the casino. He chased after him, shouting at his comm badge: "Security and medical to the Promenade! Emergency! Quark's Place! Fugitive is armed and dangerous!"

Berat ran for the door, out into the open main level of the Promenade, but the station's alarms were blaring now, and the people were running from him, they were screaming. A security officer materialized just in front of him, another one off to his left, both of them armed. Phasers aimed at him. Berat spun around, disoriented, isolated in the center of the Promenade, the two-tiered walls closing him in, the size of the crowd. Too many of them. No one close enough to grab to use as a hostage this time.

A voice shouted, "Halt! Throw down your weapon!"

Berat's breath was coming hard. They had him surrounded. Trapped. No way to escape. Nowhere to run.

His hand tightened on his phaser. Never. They'd never take him. Not alive.

It had finally come to this. To his last, most desperate option. The only choice he had left.

He raised the phaser slowly. With his thumb, he

flipped the setting higher, to the lethal range. Held it against the side of his own head, to his temple. Someone cried *"No!"* but it was too late. Too late. No other way out, now. He closed his eyes.

Pressed the trigger. The shock struck with a jolt that ran through his whole nervous system, then faded instantly into dark. He let go of his last breath. Then no more feeling, nothing.

Odo ran up, pushing his way through the crowd as the security people tried to get them to disperse. He halted at the sight of the Cardassian's inert body lying on the deck. A woman in Starfleet security uniform was kneeling over him, compressing his chest in an effort to induce breathing.

She looked up at Odo. "I tried to stun him, but I think I was too late. He fired that thing. On lethal."

Odo shuddered, hating weapons. These species were all so fragile, died so easily.

He hit his comm badge. "Medical to the Promenade! Emergency! Hurry!"

CHAPTER
20

THE FURIOUS FACE of Gul Marak glared out from the viewscreen. "I said I wanted to talk to *Sisko,* or that security constable, whatever he is."

Kira glared back, but her voice was chilly and expressionless. "Commander Sisko is in conference off the station. Constable Odo is presently unavailable." Odo was in fact in his native liquid state, regenerating his energies after a hard day's work.

After a moment Marak's breath exploded impatiently. "All right! I understand you have my deserter under arrest. Is it true?"

"We have a suspect in detention."

"Suspect! Detention! Look, Major Bajoran, I don't want to hear any of your slimy excuses. That traitor is *mine!* I want him!"

Kira ground her teeth together. It took all her effort to keep from yelling back at Marak, to tell him to take his traitor and perform obscenely improbable acts together. What one Cardassian did to another was of no possible concern to her. Let them kill themselves off, it could only benefit the Bajorans. But there was something insufferable about Marak that brought out her most intransigent reflexes.

"We're completing the processing of the suspect now."

"What processing?" Marak demanded. "You caught him, now hand him over!"

"We have procedures on this station, Gul," she said tightly. "We don't just turn over prisoners to anyone. This man's identity has to be established. At the moment, he can't identify himself because he's unconscious and under medical care. And we may have our own charges to place against him: illegal entry into Bajoran territory, assault on a Federation officer, sabotage of station facilities. Those charges will have to be processed before any determination on the prisoner's disposition can be made."

"If I don't get him back *now*—"

Kira interrupted, "If you want the prisoner turned over to your custody, Gul, I suggest that *you* follow procedure and submit an extradition request in the proper form. Beginning with a positive ID. I'll point out that for all the time you've been demanding the return of this man, you have yet to submit his records so we can establish his identity."

"We don't turn over Cardassian personnel records! Especially not to *Bajorans!*"

"Well, in that case, Gul, you can't expect this *Bajoran* station to consider your request! We won't hand someone over just on your word that he's deserted from your ship."

To her relief, he cut the connection, just as her control was starting to slip. But dealing with Marak was enough to strain anyone's self-control. Kira caught herself in the strange position of almost wishing for the days when they had Gul Dukat to deal with. Bajoran popular sentiment claimed that all Cardassians were alike, but Kira knew there were some who were even worse than others, and Marak was certainly one of those.

Well, at least Sisko ought to be satisfied this time. She'd dealt with Marak without making a single provocative remark. Strictly by-the-book. Almost.

It was easy for Sisko. Always so sure of himself. Always with a regulation to cover every situation. Maybe they taught them that at the Starfleet Academy.

Or maybe it's just me, she thought. I see a Cardassian face and something happens to me, inside.

Kira sighed. There was more than one prisoner in detention. More than one prisoner to be turned over to planetary authorities. The provisional Bajoran government had sent official notice that they planned to try Gelia Torly on charges of conspiracy and membership in a terrorist organization. Kira knew she'd be expected to testify. Her words were going to put a fellow freedom fighter into prison. And for what? For loyalty to her cause, to her organization. To her comrades.

Kira closed her eyes and sought her inner balance.

The comm technician interrupted. "Major, there's been a file transmission from the Cardassian ship."

Kira shook her head. It was always something. She called the data up onto her screen: the personnel file on a Cardassian maintenance technician named Berat. She glanced at it without much interest, except for a distinct sense of personal satisfaction that Marak had given in to her demands. "Notify security. Tell Odo we've finally got an ID on the Cardassian deserter."

* * *

Ben Sisko reached over from the conn of the *Rio Grande* runabout to put his hand on Jake's shoulder. He felt sorry for his boy. Jake had been wanting to visit the Bajoran planet, and he'd tried to warn him, but the disappointment was inevitable, he supposed. Much of Bajor's surface was a ruin. Every time Sisko saw it, he had to struggle against a sense of furious outrage, a burning desire to see the Cardassians punished for what they'd done. Wrecking DS-Nine had been one thing. The station, after all, was something the Cardassians themselves had made. But Bajor had been a living world, the home of an advanced civilization. What *right* did they have to come and destroy it?

The sight made him come closer to understanding the Bajorans' motives, a fact that he suspected the Bajorans themselves recognized. It would explain why the secretary-general had insisted on holding this rather routine meeting on-planet.

"Going to be glad to get back to the station, son?"

Jake nodded glumly. Then he asked, "Dad? The Cardassians—are they really *all* bad?"

Sisko was startled to hear his own thoughts so closely echoed by his son. He shook his head. "No, Jake, I don't think so. I know it might seem that way, looking at the destruction on Bajor. But remember, neither of us has ever been to the Cardassian homeworld, either. It's not our place to judge other peoples."

"I suppose not." Jake seemed troubled by something. It worried Sisko, but maybe the boy was just growing up. It was hard to be a parent. You wanted to protect your child from all the universe's cruelty, but bringing him up on a Federation starship—or DS-Nine—made that impossible from the beginning.

Sisko gave a final squeeze to his son's arm and concentrated on his upcoming approach to docking at the station. But when he requested landing clearance, there was a pause as the duty officer exclaimed, "Commander Sisko!"

He could hear some kind of disruption in the background. Was that Kira's voice? What was going wrong *now?* "This is Sisko," he snapped. "What's going on there?"

Another pause. Then a familiar female voice came over the comm. "This is Dax, Commander. We have a slight problem here in Ops. Gul Marak has just transported onto the station. He's rather agitated and insists on speaking to you immediately. It's about the man who deserted from his ship."

Sisko felt a wave of profound relief. Dax: he could always count on her to be in control in any situation. Even on DS-Nine. "Tell Gul Marak," he said with forced calm, "that I'll be on the landing pad in ten minutes. That is, if someone there in Ops will clear my approach to dock."

"The *Rio Grande* is cleared for landing pad two," Dax said with calm efficiency.

Grim-faced, Sisko turned to Jake. "I want you to go straight back to quarters as soon as we dock. I'll have to take care of this."

"But Dad, I—"

"No argument. I'll be stepping into a situation, and it could possibly get violent. I don't want you involved where you could get hurt." He turned his attention back to the runabout's controls, coming in to the landing pad at the maximum velocity allowed by regulations.

A few minutes later he stepped off the transporter pad into Ops. There was indeed an angry-looking Gul

Marak, facing an equally hostile Major Kira, flanked by a pair of security officers. Standing between them was Dax, who greeted his arrival with visible relief.

Marak was livid with rage. Dark blotches stood out on his rough skin. "Commander, this *female* refuses to release my prisoner!"

Sisko hated stepping into these situations where he hadn't been completely briefed and all sides were screaming at him to dispense instant justice—each according to its own notions. From the venom in Marak's tone, Sisko could tell that the female in question must be Kira, but who was the prisoner? The Cardassian deserter? He glanced quickly at Kira, who looked grimly rigid and defiant. A bad sign.

"Major?"

Kira said flatly, "I've placed *this Cardassian* under arrest for attacking station personnel."

Sisko felt a blood vessel starting to throb behind his eyes. He spent just one day away from DS-Nine . . .

Dax, soft-voiced and diplomatic, said, "The Gul transported onto the station to speak with you about the suspected deserter we have in station detention. When he was told that you were returning from Bajor, he attempted to take control of our communications equipment to contact you personally."

From which, Sisko was able to get a fair notion of what had actually gone on. The bruised appearance of the Bajoran comm technician confirmed his suspicions.

But Marak wasn't concerned about such trivial matters as assaulting Bajorans, only his own grievance. "That *female* pretends to have command of this station, over the disposition of *my crew members!* She refuses to let me contact the proper Federation officials—or any other official who isn't *Bajoran!*"

Sisko knew he had to back up Kira's authority—

here, now, in public—regardless of what she'd actually done. Later, in his office, it might well be another matter. He said tightly, "Major Kira is the first officer on DS-Nine. When I'm absent from the station, she *is* in command. And she certainly has the right to arrest anyone attempting to interfere with station operations and assaulting personnel.

"Now, I suggest you go back to your ship, Gul, and I'll discuss the disposition of this case with you later, after I've been briefed on the situation."

Marak's coloring deepened. "I'm not leaving without—"

"Gul Marak, either you beam back to your ship *now,* or I'll have you forcibly escorted to the airlock."

The two commanders faced each other for a moment, but Sisko's security force was clearly waiting for the order. Snarling, Marak contacted his ship and in a moment had transported from the deck of Ops, leaving a universal sigh of relief behind him.

"That man almost makes me appreciate the times when Gul Dukat was here," Dax remarked.

Sisko exhaled forcibly. To Kira he snapped, "My office. Now."

"Dad?"

Sisko turned around in surprise. "Jake? What are you doing here? I told you to go back to quarters. This is an emergency. Now, I'll see you later."

"But Dad—"

Jake's voice was pitched high, and he was clearly upset by something, but he had to know this wasn't the time or the place.

"Jake!"

The tone of Sisko's voice made it an order. Reluctantly, the boy left Ops with a look backward that almost made his father call him back to ask him what was wrong. But Kira was waiting in his office and Gul

Marak was fuming on the *Swift Striker*. There just wasn't *time* for all this!

A moment later Kira was facing her commanding officer. "All right, Major. Tell me about it. And where's Odo? He's supposed to be the one handling this matter. I told you, these confrontations with Gul Marak are exactly what I've been trying to avoid."

Kira took a breath. This was simply a matter of the facts. All her actions were completely justified, and the matter was of no real importance, anyway. Except to Gul Marak. "Marak beamed into Ops, started to make demands. I'd told him already that you were off the station and Odo was unavailable. He's resting now."

"Oh. All right. What happened, then?"

"Marak refuses to deal with a Bajoran. It's as simple as that. When he couldn't find Odo, he tried to contact you on the runabout, but he wouldn't go through a *Bajoran* communications technician."

Sisko shook his head in disgust. "All right, I understand that part. Now, what about this damned deserter? He really is a deserter, I take it?"

Kira nodded. "Odo and Chief O'Brien tracked down the Cardassian deserter, hiding in Quark's place. The Cardassian was armed, he fired at O'Brien—"

"He's all right?" Sisko interrupted urgently.

"O'Brien was only stunned. But the Cardassian turned his phaser on himself. It was on a lethal setting. Occino says that she shot to stun just as the Cardassian fired." Kira hadn't been surprised at the deserter's attempt at suicide. Cardassian punishments were notoriously savage, and Gul Marak was an intemperate commander.

"But I take it he's still alive. Where is he now?"

"Infirmary. Unconscious and under guard. Marak doesn't have to worry, he's not going anywhere."

"So the deserter is under arrest. What's the problem, then?"

Kira felt her jaw start to clench. "Marak has no respect for our procedures. He makes unreasonable demands."

Sisko's expression hardened. "Major, I know you don't exactly get along with Gul Marak. I don't get along with Gul Marak. No one on this station does. But that has nothing to do with the issue at hand. Why does he claim that you refuse to turn over this criminal?"

Kira stood very straight. "Commander, you can view the exchange for yourself. I've recorded it in the log. When Marak called up demanding the prisoner, processing wasn't completed. We had no positive ID, and he was still receiving medical attention."

"You refused to turn him over on medical grounds, is that what you're telling me?"

Sisko would believe that, Kira thought. It was the way they did things in Starfleet, humane even to an enemy. Starfleet could afford such an attitude. Bajor never could.

But it wasn't the truth. "No. I never explicitly refused to turn over the prisoner. I simply insisted that the Gul make his request according to the recognized procedures. That he provide a positive ID. And I warned him that there might be station charges we'd want to file, first. Like assault on one of our officers— Chief O'Brien."

Sisko looked at her. "Major, I don't suppose you're familiar with the term 'stonewalling'?"

Kira blinked uncomprehendingly, said, "No, I don't believe so."

"Never mind, it's mostly gone out of use, even in

Starfleet. Look, Kira, is there any reason to seriously doubt the identity of the man we have in custody?"

Reluctantly, "No. Marak did finally transmit the deserter's personnel file. It's the same man."

"Then you don't have any *real* grounds, now, to deny Marak's request."

"You mean besides the fact that the Cardassian assaulted a Starfleet officer and most likely sabotaged the security grid?"

"Besides that."

Stiffly, "Are you ordering me to have the prisoner remanded to Marak's custody?"

Sisko rubbed his temples. "No. I'll take care of it. That'll be all, Major."

He rubbed his temples again, pressing against the *throb, throb* of the newborn headache. How could he run this station if he couldn't trust his first officer? Not her basic loyalties. He didn't doubt those. But she had spent so many years fighting the Cardassians. Could she be trusted to react objectively, without prejudice? He couldn't order her not to deal with them, not and retain the authority of her position at the same time. And they had to work with Cardassians here on DS-Nine, or the peace was going to fail.

It wasn't that he blamed her for the way she felt. Newly returned from the Bajoran surface, he could sharply appreciate the reasons for it. Only—

A sound at the door opened his eyes.

"Dad?"

Sisko got halfway to his feet. *"Jake?* I thought I *told* you—"

"Dad, this is *urgent!* Is Berat . . . Did they arrest him? Are you going to send him back? You *can't,* Dad!"

"What's this all about? Who's Berat? What are you talking about?"

"Berat! The Cardassian—the one who deserted from that ship. You can't send him back there! You don't know what they're going to *do* to him!"

Sisko was struck almost speechless. "Jake? You . . . *know* this Cardassian?"

Jake had been on the verge of tears, but now a slightly apprehensive expression came into his eyes. "I . . . talked to him. Once. He told me about it. What they did to him. What they did to his family."

Suddenly Sisko made the connection between Jake, the Cardassian, and what Kira had said about the deserter hiding out in Quark's Place. *"Nog!* That's who's behind this!"

But Jake had already incriminated himself too far to back down now. "I promised I wouldn't tell. I swore! I gave my word, Dad!"

His father said nothing. Jake went on, nervously, "Berat was fixing things for Nog. He hid him from the Cardassians. They want to kill him, Dad! If you send him back there, they *will* kill him! They'll *hang* him, and . . ." Jake choked on a sob.

"Son. Sit down. Take it easy." Sisko put his arms around him, led him to a chair. "These things are hard. But the Federation doesn't interfere in the internal affairs of other worlds. It's our Prime Directive. You know that. This man is charged with some very serious crimes. With murder."

Jake shook his head. "Berat told me about it. He said they were trying to kill him. They assigned him to that ship so they could get him out of the way and kill him where no one would see. It was self-defense. They already killed his father, all his family. They *hanged* them . . . they made him watch . . ."

Sisko's brows drew together. "Did he say why?"

Jake nodded. "They said they were all traitors. For withdrawing from Bajor."

Sisko straightened. He remembered the reports on the new Cardassian government, the executions. The confessions he had read. Then it was a political case! That changed everything! "Jake, I'm glad you came to tell me this. I wish I'd known about it sooner." A pause. "I'm just sorry that you didn't feel you could trust me."

Jake looked unhappy. "I promised Berat. He was afraid—"

"I understand that. But now you can see what's happened. Instead of asking for asylum, your Cardassian friend tried to kill himself. He almost succeeded. And he shot Chief O'Brien while he was trying to escape. Did you know he had a weapon?"

Jake nodded again, miserable.

Sisko exhaled. "We're going to have to have a long talk about all this. Later."

"Are you going to do something? Are you going to help Berat?"

"If your Cardassian friend is telling the truth, he has a good case for asylum."

"I should have told you. I'm sorry." Jake looked down at his feet.

"Why don't you go home now? I'll do the best I can, Jake."

"Thanks, Dad. I'm really sorry."

"I know you are, son."

CHAPTER
21

THE FIRST PLACE Sisko went after leaving his office was to Miles O'Brien's quarters.

"Is he all right?" he asked Keiko when the door opened.

"Dr. Bashir said he should rest."

"Commander? Is that you?" O'Brien's voice called from inside.

"Please come in," Keiko invited, but there was a slight reluctance in her voice.

"I won't stay long. I promise not to disturb him."

O'Brien reclined in a chair with his feet propped up on a footstool and a blanket over him. He sat up eagerly as Sisko came into the room, then caught himself with a slight wince. "Ouch! Just a twinge. Hit my head when I fell. It's good to see you, Commander. Will you have some tea?"

Sisko inhaled the aromatic steam coming from the pot on the table next to O'Brien. His own headache was still throbbing slightly. "Thank you, I think I will."

Keiko brought him a cup and poured. Sisko took a sip of the hot liquid. "Ah. That's good!"

O'Brien took a drink from his own cup. "It's herbal. Keiko says it has healing properties." From something in his tone, Sisko suspected his head of operations might have preferred the healing properties of a cold synthale, but he said nothing. The tea was very good. "I'm glad to see you weren't seriously hurt."

"No. Just stunned. Bashir tuned me right back up."

Keiko murmured, "I don't know what he thought he was doing, chasing after a criminal that way, not even armed."

"I'm curious about that, too. What made you think you could find the deserter at *Quark's*, of all places?"

O'Brien gave a small laugh. "Well, you see, it was funny, really. All of a sudden, everything started working right, all over the Promenade. Somebody was fixing things. Then I remembered, when the stowaway first came onto the station, how it had to be somebody who knew how the systems around here worked. So I asked around, and I found out that it was the Ferengi behind the repair racket. Word was out that if it was broken, they could get it fixed—for the right price, of course."

"Of course," Sisko agreed dryly, knowing the Ferengi quite well.

"It was that boy Nog who seemed to be the link. He was the one who picked up the stuff and brought it back, fixed. So, I tracked him down in the casino, saw him go through a back door, followed him . . ." A rueful grin spread across his face. ". . . right into the Cardassian. I didn't have a chance."

Keiko added darkly, "He was lucky he wasn't killed. They say the Cardassian is a murderer."

"We are all glad your husband is safe," Sisko said sincerely. He put down his empty cup. He would have liked more of the tea, but he didn't want to impose on Keiko's hospitality or interfere with O'Brien's needed rest. "But one thing does puzzle me. I've had a chance to see this Cardassian's personnel file. According to it, he'd been demoted for gross incompetence. He'd been on report a dozen times for poor workmanship, among other things."

O'Brien shook his head gravely. "If that's so, Commander, then I'd say it can't be the same man. Whoever did those repairs was a first-rate technician. I tell you, I wouldn't mind having him working for me!"

Sisko raised his brows. "Working with a Cardassian?" He was aware of O'Brien's history, knew that he'd been a witness to the massacre on Setlik III.

But O'Brien looked thoughtful. "The Cardies built this station. We look down on their technology sometimes, I know, but—I've thought about this—maybe we just aren't used to the way they do things. Maybe they might have something to show us about how to run this place." He paused. "Of course, it's too late, now. I guess you'll be turning him over to Gul Marak."

Sisko stood up to leave. "I'm going to see about that right now. You be sure to get that rest." He thanked Keiko for the tea.

On the way to the infirmary, Sisko asked the computer to redisplay the Cardassian deserter's personnel file on his padd. The file was an almost unbroken record of punishments for a wide variety of offenses: incompetence, sloppy work, failure to follow procedures, failure to complete work on time, insubordination—that one appeared over and over again. Either this Berat was the worst crew member in the history of the Cardassian space force, or Jake's story had some basis in fact and the man was being persecuted for some reason deserving of asylum. A political refugee instead of a murderer.

It would have been a lot simpler the other way. The thought made Sisko feel slightly ashamed of himself, but it was true. It would be a lot easier just to turn the deserter over to Gul Marak and forget about him. He had shot O'Brien, after all. Probably committed other crimes while he was hiding on the station, theft the least of them. Sabotage, certainly. Murderer or not, he had certainly proved he was capable of violence. And he was a Cardassian.

A political refugee, he told himself firmly. You *have* to give him asylum.

If that's what he really is.

There was no one else with Dr. Bashir in his clinic office. "I understand Chief O'Brien will be all right?" Sisko asked.

"He should be fine. The stun knocked him out, but scan showed no permanent damage."

"And the Cardassian?"

Bashir looked grave and switched the monitor to show a figure lying motionless on a biobed, held down by a restraining field. "Not so well. His phaser was set to kill. Fortunately, the beam was deflected, but you have to factor in the damage caused by the stun beam. There may be permanent neurological impairment. Of course, this is a Cardassian. Their resistance is higher than ours is. There was less actual burn damage than there would have been in a human, I think."

Sisko raised his eyebrows. "Restraints? Is he conscious?" He didn't look conscious.

Bashir seemed uncomfortable. "It was necessary.

He became violent when he came to. He almost got an edged instrument away from one of the technicians. She was a Bajoran. Things got . . . hard to handle."

Sisko could imagine it.

"So can he be questioned?"

"You can ask. Whether he'll answer you is something else. He hasn't been exactly responsive to me. I've tried to get him to talk to me, but"—he gestured at the patient in his restraints—"you can see the consequences."

Sisko shot him a grave look. "You're a doctor, Lieutenant, not an interrogator. And be glad you're not. I'm going in to see him now."

"There's a guard stationed by the door, in case things get out of hand . . . again."

Sisko looked at Bashir again. "Thank you, Doctor. I'll try to remember that."

The guard straightened up slightly when he saw the commander. He was one of the security reinforcements sent from Starfleet, not a Bajoran, which Sisko thought was probably a good idea. Under the circumstances.

"How's the prisoner?"

The guard glanced inside the cubicle. "Quiet, sir. Right now."

"Hmm." Sisko stepped inside. The Cardassian lay staring straight up at the ceiling. He gave almost no sign of reacting to someone entering the room, not even moving his eyes. But Sisko could see the muscles in his forearms tensing against the energy restraints that held them to the sides of the biobed and the movement of his chest as his rate of breathing increased.

Yes, the prisoner was conscious and very much aware of his surroundings. He knew he was a prisoner.

Taking a breath, he said, "I'm Benjamin Sisko, in command of this station. I believe your name is Berat."

Berat said nothing. His stare stayed fixed on the ceiling panel above his head.

"I understand you've spoken to my son, Jake."

Now Berat did blink. His eyes shifted briefly to look in Sisko's direction. The resemblance between father and son was clear enough. "So. That was how they found me."

Firmly, "No, that was *not* how they found you. Jake only came to me after he'd learned of your arrest. His judgment might have been at fault, but not his honor. He told no one about you. He kept his word."

Now that he had Berat's attention, Sisko drove on to the main issue. "Mr. Berat, Gul Marak claims that you're a deserter from the *Swift Striker*. He wants you returned to face an extensive list of charges, including murder. Now, according to my son, these charges may be politically motivated."

Berat's gaze had returned to the ceiling.

Sisko tried again. "Federation policy does not allow interference in the internal affairs of other worlds. No matter how savage or unjustified their penalties may seem to us. On the other hand, the Federation does recognize claims for asylum. Do you understand me?"

For the first time, Berat turned his head so that he faced his interrogator directly. Sisko suddenly realized how young this Cardassian was and how hopeless his situation must have seemed.

"Asylum?"

"Mr. Berat, I've seen your official personnel file. According to it, you're barely competent to function at the lowest grade of technician. But my chief of operations claims that your technical skills are superior. According to Gul Marak, you're a murderer. My son tells me a different story. Now, which is it?"

Berat exhaled. Now he seemed to be anxious for Sisko to believe him. "My father was a cabinet minister. In the previous government. He favored the peace treaty with the Federation, the pullout from Bajor. But then, when the wormhole was discovered, the Revanche party . . . said they were traitors. My father was hanged. My uncles—most of my family . . . all hanged. I couldn't be charged along with them, I was only an engineer, had never been in Bajoran space. But they wanted to get rid of us all. They stripped my rank. Sent me to Marak's ship, under Marak's orders."

"You don't deny that you killed a man?"

"I didn't know he was dead. But they—Halek— meant to kill me. All along. When he hit me, I knew . . ." He took a breath, started over. "To strike a superior officer is a hanging offense. No matter what the provocation . . . how often . . . It was only a matter of time. I . . ." He stopped, frustrated, unable to express his thoughts coherently.

But Sisko said, "I see. Mr. Berat, do you request Federation asylum?"

Berat blinked rapidly. There was a look of dazed disbelief on his face. Was that all there was to it? "I . . . yes. I do."

"Then I'm inclined to grant it."

"You won't . . . send me back there?"

"No. You'll be safe here." Sisko looked down at the restraints. "Now, if I remove these, are you going to attempt any more acts of violence—against yourself or the personnel of this station?"

Berat mutely shook his head, and Sisko deactivated the restraining field. The Cardassian sat up slowly, with a visible effort.

Sisko went on. "Dr. Bashir tells me that you may still have neurological damage from the phaser effects. So I'm confining you here in the infirmary. Do you understand? There'll still be a guard at your door. I've granted you asylum, but *not* the freedom to roam around this station. This is as much for your protection as anything else. I don't expect that Gul Marak is going to be pleased when he learns what I've just done."

Apprehension clouded Berat's expression. "No, I don't think so, either."

Just then Kira's voice came through Sisko's comm badge. "Commander, the Cardassian deck patrol is here to take custody of the prisoner. Should I send them down to the infirmary?"

Hearing it, Berat tensed visibly and looked around the room as if he were seeking a way to escape.

But Sisko said, "No, Major. Tell them to go back to their ship. I've granted the prisoner asylum."

"Asylum? To a Cardassian murderer?"

A line appeared between Sisko's brows. "Do you have a problem with that, Major Kira?"

"I—"

Sisko's voice took on an ironic tone. "If you meant to turn the deserter over to Gul Marak, Major, you certainly had the opportunity to do so, *before* he requested asylum. I believe you were the one to insist on correct procedures and full identification."

There was a pause. Then Kira's voice, flat and expressionless: "I'll inform the Cardassians."

CHAPTER
22

"NOG! HEY, NOG! Did you hear?"

Jake pushed past the gamblers going into Quark's Place. Nog was at the door, handing out complimentary tokens to new customers. He looked up when he heard Jake calling, and he bared his teeth.

Jake faced him, breathing hard with excitement. "Did you hear? About Berat? My dad gave him asylum! Isn't that great? Now he doesn't have to worry about the Cardassians anymore! They can't hang him!" Jake looked puzzled when Nog failed to react. "Isn't that great?"

"Great! Oh, yes, just great!" Nog snarled.

"Huh? What's the matter with you?"

"My repair business is *ruined,* that's all! They took the Cardassian away!"

"I know, but it's all right now. He's got asylum! He doesn't have to hide anymore!"

"And whose fault is that?" Nog's stare was accusation.

"What do you mean?"

"Who else knew where he was? Who else could lead security right to the room where he was hiding?"

"You mean . . . Hey, *I* didn't say anything about it! I gave my word!"

Nog sneered in contempt, and flipped a gambling token in Jake's direction—one of the lowest denomination. "Your *word!* Now I know how much a human's word is worth!"

Jake felt angry heat rising to his face. "Hey! I never told anyone! Not Odo or even my dad! You want to know how they found out where Berat was? Well, it was *you!* Going around telling everyone you could get their stuff fixed! Chief O'Brien knew he was an engineer! All he had to do was follow you!"

Nog shook his head vehemently. "They never followed me! Not till I showed *you* where he was!"

But Jake took a step back, looking at Nog with a new insight. "You know what I think? You don't care about Berat at all, do you? Just how much money you could make from him. I'm surprised you didn't turn him in to get a reward!"

"At least I wasn't stupid enough to turn him in for nothing! Like a stupid human!"

"I *didn't—*"

Jake's protest was suddenly interrupted by the red flash of emergency lights and the screaming of the alert sirens. Instant, reflexive fear flashed through him, taking him back again to the burning deck of the *Saratoga,* the smoke, the clanging alarms, and his mother lying dead beneath the wreckage on the deck.

What was it now? Another terrorist bombing? A Cardassian attack on the station? Maybe this was Gul Marak's answer to Dad giving Berat asylum.

The public comm shrilled: *"Medical to docking pylon four. All civilians to shelter."*

When would it ever stop?

The dockworker was making wild gestures with his arms as he told Sisko, "I saw the thing blow up! I tell you, it was . . . the flames just blew that whole airlock out! There was this huge *whooooosh,* and the fire just came roaring out! The airlock was all flames! I could feel the heat, all the way across at the cargo platform! I figure a pressurized fuel line must have ruptured or something. Never saw anything like it, not even in the war."

Sisko was about to question him further when a Rigellian woman flung herself at him, screaming, "Why don't you stop this! What's wrong with you? How can you let them do this?"

Appalled at the sight of her burned arms, he tried to hold her off, to keep her from hurting herself as she struck madly at him with her red and blistered hands. Behind him, Kira stood watching helplessly, but then one of the medical technicians was there, gently trying to pull the injured Rigellian away.

The victim saw the Bajoran medic and jerked out of his grasp, screaming, "Don't touch me!" Lunging at Sisko again: "They're all fanatics! They're going to kill everyone! You told us it was safe! You said they weren't terrorists!"

As the Rigelian finally noticed Kira in her Bajoran uniform, her eyes went wide and crazed, but by then the medic had taken out a hypospray, and an instant later, she slumped back into his grasp. Sisko helped ease her onto a stretcher.

The station's officers continued to watch grimly as the last of the bodies was carried out through the airlock. Bashir followed, his hands stained with blood.

Sisko stopped him. "Doctor?"

"I think I can save the ambassador's aide. But three of the crew are dead. Six injured."

The commander let him go. To the rest of them, he said only, "I want the ones who are doing this."

The Rigellians had been one of the first to conclude a trade agreement with Bajor. They had been considered almost certain to vote to accept them as members of the Federation. Until this.

Kira felt an angry, overwhelming shame. Shame at being Bajoran. In resisting the Cardassian occupation, her people had learned their lessons in terrorism too well. They knew how to strike at their enemy for maximum destructive effect, then disappear, leaving no trace behind.

The words from the poster mocked her: *You have been warned.*

How many times had she delivered such warnings herself, to the Cardassian oppressors? But these weren't Cardassians! They weren't oppressors, they had been potential allies—until now. Until the terrorists had struck again.

How could they do this? To the future of their own people? Couldn't they *see* the Federation was their only defense against renewed Cardassian aggression?

"Is that the last of the bodies?" Sisko asked.

A medical technician nodded as she passed by with a covered stretcher.

Then Odo and Kira stepped forward to begin yet another painstaking search for any possible evidence that could lead them to whoever was committing these acts. Before it was too late.

The poster lay on the center of Sisko's desk like another bomb. Everyone assembled for the briefing stared at it, their hands at their sides, as if it might go off. Crudely printed letters read:

> NO MORE WARNINGS!
> FOREIGNERS OUT OF BAJORAN SPACE!
> YOU HAVE SEVENTY-TWO HOURS!

Sisko turned away from it with an expression of deep loathing. He looked haggard and sleepless. "Did you find anything?" he asked Kira and Odo.

Kira shook her head wearily. As usual, the bomber had left no evidence at the site. He was good, whoever he was.

"The trouble is, there are too many suspects. Most of the population of this station qualify. Every Bajoran over the age of ten has some connection with a group the Federation might consider terrorists. I'm a suspect, if it comes to that. If . . ." She looked hard at the others. "If we assume the bomber has to be a Bajoran."

"You have another theory, Major?" Sisko asked.

She nodded. "We've discussed this before. Bajor can't benefit from this violence. But who does? Who do we see openly trying to subvert the delegates to the negotiations? Who keeps insisting that these attacks prove Bajor isn't fit to join the Federation or even associate with other worlds?"

Sisko gestured at the poster on his desk. "What about all these? Signed by the Kohn Ma terrorist group, claiming responsibility."

"I checked that. Except for Gelia, I haven't been able to trace a single one of these signs back to any known member of Kohn Ma. Their leaders emphatically deny any involvement. And Gelia is in a prison cell on Bajor. She *can't* be involved. I think these . . .

things are just a false trail. It's the *Cardassians* who have the most to lose if Bajor enters into trade agreements with these other worlds."

"Not all Bajorans would agree with you, Major," Sisko insisted. "You can't deny that the Kohn Ma still opposes Federation membership, and they haven't renounced violence. How can you rule them out?"

"Because they're the obvious suspects. Too obvious."

"So was Gelia working for the Cardassians?" Odo demanded. "Can you believe that?"

Kira was silent. Gelia Torly might well have planted a bomb, yes. But never for the Cardassians.

Odo went on, "As I see it, the problem still is: Who set off the first bomb? There were no Cardassians on the station when it happened."

"Wrong. There was one."

"Garak? The tailor? How can you say that? His shop was almost destroyed in the second explosion!"

"Right! But Garak was barely injured! He just had a few scratches! Just enough to divert our suspicion by making himself look like a victim. Maybe he thought our investigation was getting too close. And we know that he's worked for Cardassian intelligence before this."

"Major," asked Sisko, "do you have any evidence directly implicating Garak?"

"No. I don't, not yet. But I do consider him a suspect. At least as much as any Bajoran."

"I suppose that's fair." Sisko sighed. "With as much as we've been able to find out so far, he's as likely to be guilty as anyone else."

He shook his head, unable to fully express the extent of his frustration. "I've posted additional security to guard the remaining delegates. But this—" He looked directly at the poster in the middle of the table, then away again. "This suggests that we may be running out of time. Our last warning. In other words, an ultimatum. Seventy-two hours. Three days. Until what?"

"You think they may be planning to blow the station?" O'Brien asked.

"I think we have to assume the possibility. As Major Kira says, these attacks have been political in nature, not military. Warnings. Terrorism, pure and simple. But each time, the level of violence has escalated."

"But to destroy the station! That would amount to suicide!"

"Suicide attacks were hardly unknown during the Bajoran resistance, isn't that true, Major?" Sisko asked.

She agreed reluctantly.

"But I wouldn't put those tactics past the Cardassians, either," Dax added, not simplifying matters in the least. "Their ruthlessness is a matter of record."

"The point is," Sisko said, "can we afford to jeopardize the lives of innocent people on this station? The civilians? The trade delegations?" He took a breath. "I've been talking with the Bajoran ministers about the possibility of relocating the negotiations to the planet. There's been concern that DS-Nine is no longer a secure location for these talks. Unfortunately, the location may become a moot issue. The Rigellians are leaving, abrogating all their agreements. Since this morning, I've been contacted by three more delegations, all of them pulling out of the negotiations. None of them were receptive to the idea of continuing the discussions on-planet."

"What you're saying is: It's already too late. We've lost," Kira said, shaking her head, denying it.

"In light of these developments," Sisko went on,

"I've been considering whether we ought to terminate these talks and advise all the delegations to leave DS-Nine as soon as possible. Perhaps we should even order a general evacuation of civilians."

"Isn't that exactly what they're trying to force us to do?" Kira asked.

"It could be a bluff," O'Brien added.

"It could be," Sisko agreed. "But can we take that risk? With so many lives at stake? At any rate, the Bajoran government agrees. They don't think they can afford the diplomatic risk of having a dozen important delegations blown up during the talks."

He stood up. "Whoever wrote *this* has given us a time limit. Seventy-two hours. That's how long we have to stop them."

CHAPTER
23

SEVENTY-TWO HOURS. Seventy-two hours to find whoever was behind the bombings.

Seventy-two hours with no sleep for any of the DS-Nine crew.

The rumor had swept through the entire station: seventy-two hours to live. All the other bombs had only been warnings. People were lining up in the travel offices, in the freight offices, hoping to find a place on an outgoing ship, never mind the destination. One by one, the heads of the remaining trade delegations had come to Sisko's office, apologizing, but they were sure he'd understand that with the present unsettled conditions, continuing the negotiations was not advisable at this time.

And Sisko would look at his only son, he would see the preoccupied, worried expression on O'Brien's face. The man's wife and daughter were here on DS-Nine: his entire family could be wiped out in an instant. *Get them out of here, send them to safety.* It was the first reaction. But, then, how could you ask others to stay under the same circumstances?

When he felt the jolt to the station, Sisko knew, even before the sirens and alarms started to sound and the news came over the comm, what had happened. Another bomb.

"Emergency! All available security and medical staff to level twenty-two, docking bay five!"

Bay five. Where the Qismilian ship was docked. "Damn them!" he said tightly, heading as quickly as he could to the nearest turbolift shaft. *"Damn* them!"

He cursed the unknown terrorist, the slowness of the lift, the Cardassians who'd built the thing in the first place. He should have transported out to the docking ring instead.

But as soon as he stepped out of the lift, he was stopped by a security officer, who said, "Sorry, Commander, but we've had to seal off this section. There's been a breach at the airlock. Major Kira's orders."

"Are there any pressure suits available?"

The officer shook her head. "Sorry, sir. Medical and operations have priority."

Which was, of course, the correct procedure. But it left the station's commander fuming here in impotent frustration while his officers and staff worked to seal the breach and bring out the injured. He had never felt so useless in his life.

Slapping his comm badge: "This is Sisko. Anyone in docking bay five—can you give me a report?"

A moment later he heard a weary voice, with that echoing tone that meant the speaker was wearing a pressure suit. "This is Kira. It's not good. The Qismilian ship was in the middle of undock procedures when the bomb went off. Their thrusters were already engaged. The pilot lost control momentarily . . ."

"And ran his ship right into the docking ring," Sisko didn't need to hear the rest. He had felt the station shake.

"Casualties?"

"Medical is treating them on board the ship, until the breach is sealed and we can bring them out."

"Are we going to be able to handle it, Major?"

"Yes, I think so. Chief O'Brien got his team working right away. I've ordered security to keep everyone else out except medical and the operations people."

"Good. If there's anything I can do to help, yell. Sisko out."

Addressing his communicator again, he said, "This is Commander Sisko. Until further notice, all docking facilities will be off-limits. No ships will be permitted to leave this station. Security, I want all docking facilities and airlocks checked for explosive devices. That's Priority One."

Only moments after he had given the order, his communicator sounded. "Commander Sisko, I think you'd better speak to the Andorian ambassador. He wants to know who says he can't go on board his ship."

Sisko closed his eyes for a second. It was starting already. "Put him through."

A grim-faced Sisko confronted his senior staff in the commander's office. He'd been forced to come into Ops through a back entrance in order to avoid the throngs of panicky stationers and others waiting to mob him at the lift tube, demanding to know when the evacuation would begin again.

"We were given a deadline," he said, looking from

face to face. "Seventy-two hours before the station is destroyed. Now the question is: Was that last explosion it? Or just another warning?"

"I've finished the computer analysis," said Dax. "According to it, the force of this latest blast was no greater than any of the others previous. It's impossible that it could have done more than minor damage to the station. I doubt if the terrorist could have planned on the Qismilian ship hitting the docking ring. As it is, we only have three sections sealed off."

"So the deadline still holds?"

No one answered. They all knew that their remaining time was measured in hours.

Sisko turned to Kira. "Major?"

"Surveillance on Garak is negative. I still think he might be involved in some way, but he didn't plant that bomb—not during the time we were watching him. If you have no objections, Commander, I plan to bring him in for questioning."

"Anything it takes," said Sisko grimly. "Now, what about the Bajoran government? Have they come up with anything?"

"They've pulled in every known Kohn Ma operative on Bajor," Kira reported. "And they've interrogated Gelia again. She keeps insisting she knows nothing more."

"You think she's telling the truth?" Sisko asked.

Kira nodded. Her face looked worn. "Our interrogators learned their trade in a hard school. Gelia was a dupe. They used her, but they kept her in the dark.

"Right now, I'm concentrating on the dockworkers. Except for the one explosion at Garak's shop, all the attacks have targeted the docking facilities."

"Aimed at the trade delegates," Sisko said.

"It's the best guess we can make." Kira stood up. "I

have at least a score of people waiting in the security office for questioning. If you don't need me here . . ."

Sisko started to say something, then simply nodded. Kira knew what it had been: "There's not much time left." But they all knew that. Everyone on the station knew it. Hour by hour, the time was running out.

On her way to the security office, Kira heard the sound of chanting. A procession came into sight: monks and a long tail of people following them. A part of her wanted to join them, another part wanted to scream at them, "Why are you wasting this time? You should be doing something!"

It was the eternal riddle of the Bajorans, united only by religion. And sometimes not even by that.

Maybe the terrorist was in the procession somewhere. Chanting with the rest of them. Seeking his balance in preparation for what he was about to do. It was a typical Bajoran notion: pray, meditate, then go forth to kill. Kira had done it herself.

Except for the procession, the Promenade seemed all but deserted. People had no time now for the pursuit of ordinary business or pleasure. They were too busy trying to find a way to survive. As the monks passed, across the wide space, in the doorway of his shop, Kira saw the unmistakable Cardassian figure: Garak, watching the worshipers. Their eyes met briefly in a glance of mutual suspicion.

Kira turned hers away first. If Garak was any kind of an effective spy, he'd know they had him under surveillance. But she knew what Sisko thought. That she couldn't be objective when it came to Cardassians. There was no evidence to link Garak to any of this.

And maybe Sisko was right. It was just so hard to imagine how Garak could be working with Gelia, how there could be a link between the Cardassians and the Kohn Ma. It didn't matter. She meant to bring him in anyway. They couldn't afford to overlook even the most remote possibility of a lead.

The sound of chanting was dying away now, and the worshipers started to disperse. Kira saw a robed figure coming toward her. Leiris. He touched her lightly on the ear.

"Nerys, I saw you watching the procession. You looked troubled. Come with me. Let us meditate together."

She pulled her arm back with a certain reluctance. "I can't, now. There's no time. You should know that."

He smiled with that enigmatic look that all monks seemed to acquire—a suggestion of secret knowledge. "If the Prophets wish there to be time, there will be enough time."

At the moment, Kira found the smile slightly irritating, even smug. "If the Prophets wanted to help me, they could find whoever's planning to blow up the station."

Still smiling, he sketched a sign of blessing and started back to the temple, but Kira called out, "Wait!" He paused for her to catch up. "Leiris, I know what you told me, before. But if anyone has come to you, if you know *anything*—"

He shook his head sadly. "You know I couldn't say. No more than I could reveal your inner thoughts to others, Nerys."

"Hundreds of lives could be lost. Innocent lives, Bajorans. If I only *knew!*"

"I'm sorry for your pain. But, for your peace of mind, I can tell you this much. As it happens, no one has come to me to confess any kind of involvement in this matter."

She took his hand, pressed it to her temple. "Thank you, Leiris."

So, she thought as she left the vicinity of the temple, either the terrorist had no qualms of conscience or hadn't brought himself to confess them. Or— She glanced over in the direction of Garak's shop, but the Cardassian tailor was no longer there.

In the security office, the witnesses were waiting to be interviewed, none of them happy to be there. Kira took their statements one by one, questioning them about anything they might have seen or heard near the pylons and bays where the explosions had gone off. It was a tedious process. She had to assure them over and over that there was no evidence against them.

"I wasn't ever even involved in the resistance!" one freight handler kept insisting. "No more than anyone else was! You don't have any cause to come asking me these question, putting me under suspicion!"

"It isn't a matter of suspicion," Kira repeated wearily. "We're just checking to determine how explosives might have been brought onto the station. Knowingly or otherwise. Now, please, Bojja. Is this your cargo manifest? Is there anything you didn't declare? Any package, no matter how innocent-looking? Please try to remember."

As the unhappy Bajoran read through the list of goods, Kira's comm badge interrupted. "O'Brien to security! I found it! I found the bomb!"

Kira jumped to her feet. The freight handler looked up as she started to rush out of the office. "Does this mean I can go?"

"Yes! No! Wait. Finish answering those questions first. Then you can leave."

There was a long moment of awed silence as the station's officers stood in front of the monitor of the power-plant control room. The image of an antimatter-containment pod was on the screen, and planted on it an inconspicuous, drab metal object, smaller than O'Brien's hand. Even at this remote distance, no one wanted to make an unnecessary sound or movement.

Finally Sisko spoke. "You're sure this is a bomb?"

O'Brien was emphatic. "Absolutely. The computer confirms it. All indications are that this is the same kind of device he's been using all along. These components would all disintegrate in an explosion, leave no evidence behind." He laughed hollowly. "If that pod blows, it wouldn't leave any of us behind, either. But at least now we've got it, even if we don't have the bastard who planted it."

Sisko took a large breath, as if he were going to explode with it. "What I want to know is: How in the hell did they get it in there? Don't we have *any* effective security in this place? What are we dealing with? Are these people invisible? Do they have some kind of personal cloaking device?"

At his words, the Bajoran duty technician shrank back against the wall, the better to remain unnoticed. But the commander's attention fixed on Odo. "I want some answers! We've got terrorists running around loose, and with these reactors the way they are—it's a wonder we haven't all been blown up yet!"

"Prophets!" Kira swore suddenly, and slapped her comm badge. "Security, this is Major Kira! Anyone, is a freighter named Bojja, Bojja Riyn, still in the security office? He was in for questioning today."

A voice replied, "He left a few minutes ago, Major."

"Get him back! Now! It's urgent. Bring him back and put him in detention. In solitary."

"Major, what's the charge?"

"It doesn't matter. Smuggling, anything. But do it

now, and *don't* let him talk to anyone! Do you understand, Amran?"

"Yes, Major. Detention. Solitary."

Sisko and the rest were looking at her, clearly in the belief that excessive stress had unhinged her reason. Kira explained, "Bojja overheard when O'Brien called me. Look, whoever planted this device here *doesn't know* we've found it. They still believe it's going to go off in another thirty-two hours!"

"You're right!" Sisko said at once. "We've got to keep this quiet if we still want to get our hands on whoever's behind all this! Constable, you can set up remote surveillance here?"

"I'll take care of it personally," Odo assured him.

Sisko looked back at the bomb. "Chief, what about that thing? Just how dangerous is it, planted in there?"

O'Brien shook his head gravely. "This reactor system is unstable to begin with. That thing in there—if it goes off, there isn't any station left." He stared at the device in the monitor for another long moment. "There's just one more problem. I don't know if I can manage to disarm the thing."

CHAPTER
24

BERAT HAD MADE UP for many sleepless days and nights in the time since his arrest. According to the Starfleet medic, he'd been lucky. Residual nerve damage was only four to six percent, and he might recover perhaps half of that in the next few months, as he healed naturally. "Sleep and rest," Bashir had told him. "That's the best thing you can do now."

And the only thing, here in detention. But Berat had no complaint. As that odd-faced security chief had made clear, he might still be facing serious charges from station officials. But at least the penalties couldn't possibly be as bad as what Gul Marak would have handed out.

Now, at the sound of someone approaching his cell, Berat sat up, still slightly apprehensive. His fugitive instincts weren't quite dead yet.

Seeing the dark-faced Starfleet commander, he stood up nervously. The other, much paler, officer with him looked familiar. Berat's memories of his capture were confused and fragmented, but: *a strange corridor, a brief glimpse of a face, a startled expression, a hand going for . . . a weapon?*

Berat's hand opened and closed, missing the grip of the phaser. This was the man he had shot.

As the two humans came up to the front of his cell, Berat took a step backward.

The Federation officers looked preoccupied, even grim. Berat started to feel a touch of panic. Were they going to charge him with shooting the officer? Or would they revoke his asylum? Hand him back to Gul Marak, after all?

But Sisko said brusquely, "Mr. Berat, I'm here on an urgent matter. This is my chief of operations, Miles O'Brien. I believe you might remember him."

The commander's darkly ironic tone helped Berat regain his mental balance. "I . . ." He forced himself to meet O'Brien's eyes. The human didn't look vengeful, only worried, and very tired.

Berat stammered, "I'm sorry I shot at you. I was . . . I only saw someone in my way. . . ."

But Sisko said impatiently, "Mr. Berat, I understand you were a station engineer. O'Brien tells me you know what you're doing. What I want to know is: Will you help us?"

"Help you?" Berat hesitated.

"I think you're aware of what's been happening on this station. We have a serious bomb threat. We've located the device. It's planted on one of the fusion reactors. I think you know what that means. There are still hundreds of people on this station. I want to know if you can help us disarm it."

"Is it a Bajoran bomb? Who planted it there?"

"Frankly," said Sisko, "we don't know yet who's responsible. It could be Bajoran terrorists. And to be honest, there's a possibility that it could have been a

Cardassian agent. I know we can't force you to help us. But the people who'll die are almost all civilians. Noncombatants, children. Please remember that."

Berat put his hands to his head. "I have to think."

They had called him a traitor, a Bajoran-lover. But he knew it wasn't so. He had never betrayed his homeworld. And the war was officially over now—these people weren't his enemies.

He raised his head. "Where exactly is the bomb planted?"

"On the antimatter-containment pod of reactor B," Sisko answered him grimly.

"Merciless gods!"

O'Brien agreed, "You could say that, all right, and if that thing goes up, we'll all be meeting our gods soon enough."

O'Brien handed Berat his own tool kit. "We managed to retrieve this for you," he said with a slight grin.

"How much did you have to pay the Ferengi?" Berat wondered, only half joking. He had realized by this time that the Ferengi had known all along that he could have had asylum just by asking for it. It did rankle.

"Constable Odo made them an offer they couldn't turn down. Not if they wanted to stay out of detention while everyone else evacuates the station."

Berat stood in silence a moment as they waited for the lift to take them down through the station core. "You told your commander that I was a good engineer? But—you don't know me."

"I've seen your work here and there around the station. It told me enough about you—what I needed to know."

Berat nodded silently. What they had in common

went beyond human and Cardassian. A fuel pump was a fuel pump, regardless of design. And so was antimatter, unfortunately.

When they got off the lift at level thirty-two, he looked around. "I hid out down here for a while. When I first got a look at this station, I thought: The things they say about the Bajorans must be true. Everything was a mess. Then, I saw that the damage was deliberate."

"You should have seen the place when I first got here."

The bitterness in O'Brien's voice made it easy for Berat to imagine what that scene must have been like. He hesitated before saying, "It was hard for us to leave Bajoran space. We put a lot of unrecoverable resources into building a station like this. Then, to just abandon it, hand it over to them . . ."

"You took a lot of resources *out* of Bajoran space, too."

Berat couldn't deny it. He was silent as O'Brien led him through the restricted-access door into the power-plant control room. Then, as he looked around, his face lightened like a man coming home after a long journey. This, at least, was the same as it had always been.

The monitor showed the bomb still in place, inconspicuous and inoffensive-looking among all the banks of equipment, unless you knew what it was.

"How did you find it in here?" Berat asked.

"It took a while," O'Brien admitted. "All the bombs that have gone off so far were too small to do serious damage to the station. So I started to ask myself, if that was all you had to work with, how would you go about blowing the whole place up? When I thought about it that way, the answer was obvious. These reactors have been threatening to blow us up ever since we moved into this place. All it would take was a nudge."

Berat shook his head in disbelief. "I can't quite see how they managed to get a bomb through here. Even one this small. I mean, security—"

"Our security's been stretched a little thin these days," O'Brien said sharply, and Berat had nothing to reply to that, either.

They got into radiation suits, a precaution as natural to Berat as suiting up to go EVA, but he noticed O'Brien grumbling at the necessity. Berat was more concerned with the Bajoran technician watching them watch him. He wanted to turn and say, "I never did anything to you people, I never was even in Bajoran space before." But he was silent, and kept his face turned away.

There were heavy double doors that led into the reactor itself. The two engineers walked through the massive power-storage grid, seething with radioactive sodium, up to the magnetic containment pod that held the far more dangerous antimatter. If the pod was damaged, if the antideuterium slush came into contact with normal matter, the resulting reaction would vaporize the station. In which case, of course, the protection afforded by their radiation suits would be laughable.

O'Brien shook his head. "This system, I've never trusted it."

Berat turned sharply. "What do you mean? This is our most advanced type of generator. Of course, we don't have the limitless resources that Starfleet does."

"Sorry, I mean it just isn't what I'm used to, I suppose." But O'Brien's expression as he stared around at the grid was still mistrustful.

They got down to the serious business of examining

the problem. The bomb was an example of deadly simplicity. Planting it on the containment pod had depressed and activated an arming switch so that any attempt to lift or remove it would detonate the explosive.

"I don't see a timing mechanism," O'Brien said. "It looks like remote control."

"Unless the timer is hidden inside the case," Berat corrected him.

O'Brien looked unhappy at that reminder. "I haven't dared to scan it. No telling what might set it off."

Berat agreed. Without knowing what was inside the case, how the bomb was intended to detonate, there was no way of knowing how to safely scan it. Most devices he was familiar with could be sensitive to X rays, to sonic probes, radio waves, to any fluctuation in the electromagnetic field—you could never be sure what. Even those wires holding down the bomb—what would happen if you cut one of them?

After a long while considering and rejecting all the other alternatives that came to his mind, he said reluctantly, "The best—the safest thing would be to shut down the reactor completely. But that would take—" He glanced at his chronometer. "How much time did you say we had?"

O'Brien shook his head grimly.

"Then the only thing else I can think of is to isolate the problem—remove the pod and the bomb altogether. As a unit."

O'Brien looked worried. "I was afraid you might say that. But removing it, shifting it—won't that set off the bomb?"

Berat frowned. "I don't . . . The mechanism is designed to go off if you lift the bomb from the pod, not if you move the whole thing—not unless it has some kind of gyroscopic detection device. I haven't heard of one of those, but I suppose it could be. But of course we'll have to pump out the antimatter, first."

"What other choice do we have?"

Both of them tried once more to think of something. Finally O'Brien said, "You're fairly familiar with this system, aren't you?"

"I was systems control officer on Farside Station for almost two years—before I was recalled. The basic plans for all our stations are essentially the same."

"Then that's how you knew how to foil our security systems?"

"And which maintenance tunnels to use, where to hide." Regretfully, "Only I didn't count on that reactor section being sealed off."

"Both the A and C reactors are contaminated. It was sabotage. Deliberate. We had no choice. I don't know if we'll ever be able to get them operational again. At least our energy needs aren't that great."

They came out again into the control room. "How do you think we should do this?" O'Brien asked.

"Well," said Berat, stepping up to the control console and pulling off his head protection and gloves. Then he hesitated, looked back.

"Go ahead," O'Brien urged him.

Berat sat down, flexed his fingers slightly. Then he began to call up schematics of the power grid onto the console's screen, moving his lips slightly as he scanned the readings. "The flux level on this containment field is awfully high, did you know that?"

O'Brien did. The erratic magnetic fluctuations of the reactor containment fields had done nothing but lose him sleep ever since he came onto DS-Nine.

Berat glanced back again to O'Brien, with the

Bajoran technician standing mistrustfully next to him. "I'm going to have to pump the antimatter out of this pod and shunt it *somewhere*. I take it sections A and C are out of the question?"

"Completely sealed off," O'Brien said firmly. "The antimatter pods were removed altogether. I tell you, *that* was a job!"

"I see." Checking the readings again, "Then it'll have to be reactor D. It has the most excess capacity."

"We've shut that system down," O'Brien said, worried.

"But the containment-field generators are operational?"

"They ought to be," the technician volunteered.

Berat called up the specifications onto the console. "They are," he confirmed.

"Do it," said O'Brien.

Berat bit down on his lower lip as he examined the figures on both systems. "You can run the station on just one reactor?"

"If we have to."

"Mmm," Berat replied wordlessly, preoccupied by the readings on the magnetic containment-field generator for reactor D. He muttered a number of things about flux and made small adjustments to both the generators. "Give me two percent more. Steady. I don't like that oscillation. There. That's better."

He looked up at O'Brien. "Where do you get your supply of antihydrogen? Starfleet?"

O'Brien nodded.

"Specs?"

In response, the station's operations chief called up a dense display of figures to the console's screen. Berat studied it for a moment, then punched in new adjustments to the containment generators. "All right," he said finally, exhaling. "Activating magnetic pumping system."

On the console, new readings flashed onto the display. A schematic showed the volume of anti-deuterium slush in the reactor-B pod beginning to be reduced, passing through the system of magnetic conduit into the D containment pod. After a few moments the computer's voice issued a warning: "Flux level is up by ten percent. There is a possibility of generator overload. Suggest pumping volume be reduced immediately."

"Bloody hell, we don't have *time*—" O'Brien cursed, but Berat had already started to punch in new adjustments, never looking away from the monitor. Soundlessly, his lips shaped the readings: *Nine point seven, nine point six, nine point five . . .* The flux level on the display declined slowly while the pumping volume continued at a steady rate.

O'Brien exhaled. Berat continued to work at his console, but from time to time he had to clench his fists together tightly to stop the trembling. Finally he looked up at O'Brien, holding out his shaking hands. "I'm going to have to go over to voice command. Nerve damage," he said ruefully, but there was an edge of exhaustion to his voice. "Unless you want to take over here."

"You can override the automatic protocols now with voice command," O'Brien assured him.

Berat looked surprised. "You can? But the computer—"

"I think," O'Brien said wryly, "you may find the computer has had a slight change of attitude. I've had to deal with this kind of problem before."

"Our regulations don't allow modification of the protocols."

"Well, fortunately, Starfleet regs don't cover the

specs on Cardassian equipment. So, we sort of . . . bent a few of them."

Berat's face briefly showed envy before his attention turned back to the console. Indeed, just an instant later: "Warning! Flux level is up by twelve percent. Oscillation increasing. Pumping volume will be reduced—"

"Override! Increase field damping to eight-two. Reduce power to field generator one by point-two percent. All right. Hold that."

"Um," the technician broke in, "that capacitor—"

"Engage backup," said Berat automatically, and the Bajoran stepped up to the auxiliary control, made the necessary adjustment. As soon as the backup unit went on-line, the oscillation started to stabilize.

"All right," Berat said, "that ought to hold it now."

It was impossible to rush the process without risking the very blowup they were trying to avoid, but all three men in the control room were constantly aware of each second that passed. No one knew for certain when the bomb was supposed to go off. There was only the vague reference to seventy-two hours on the terrorist's sign, and more than half of those were irrevocably gone now.

But at last, Berat slumped back in his seat. The monitor showed the containment pod empty, the antimatter transfer complete. He continued the pumping process for several minutes longer, just to be sure the last antihydrogen atom had been flushed from the pod before they shut off the containment field.

The computer warned: "Antimatter levels depleted. Reactor output will be reduced to eighty-eight percent of capacity."

"Acknowledged," O'Brien said. "Now we can go back in there and pull that pod." Berat pulled on his head covering again. O'Brien was starting to do the same, but the Bajoran tech interrupted. "What should I do? Do you need my help?"

"Stay on the monitor. Watch the containment field in reactor D," Berat told him. "It probably isn't used to that level of stress."

"I'll do it."

As the technician took over the seat at the console, O'Brien and Berat went back into the chamber to begin what was essentially, as O'Brien put it, "nothing but plumbing," now that the pod was emptied of antimatter.

It was O'Brien who did most of the physical work of disconnecting the pod, Berat feeling useless and guilty with his gloved hands still shaky. The Starfleet doctor couldn't say just how much nerve regeneration he could expect.

"Last connection," O'Brien whispered. Holding his breath, he took hold of the meter-long pod. Released the last valve. Did the pod move? Yes, and it hadn't exploded in their faces. He and Berat let go of their breath simultaneously. Slowly, so slowly, O'Brien released it the rest of the way. At last it was free, the heavy weight of the pod supported only by the transfer cradle, with the bomb still there on its side, wired into place, still unexploded.

"You did it!" Berat breathed.

"We did," O'Brien corrected him.

"We did!" They were both grinning like fools.

CHAPTER
25

DS-NINE WAS NO LONGER in immediate danger of destruction. The bomb, still attached to the empty pod, was safely in a blast-containment chamber where, if it was detonated, it would do no real harm. There it sat, visible through the monitor, deceptively harmless-looking.

Berat felt slightly nervous surrounded by so many Starfleet officers—and even worse, Bajorans. The female major's expression was almost hostile, and alone among them she hadn't congratulated him on removal of the bomb. He couldn't help remembering he was still a prisoner here, in the hands of those who had been his people's enemies for generations.

"Time is still the consideration," Major Kira was saying. "Whoever set this thing is still expecting it to go off on schedule. We have that long to catch them."

"But in the meantime"—Dax glanced at the bomb through the monitor—"we have this to work on. It's evidence. I'll want to scan it for DNA analysis. And we can compare it to the fragments recovered from the other explosions. If we can find where it came from, that will be a start."

"Then it'll have to be disarmed," said Odo.

"Mr. O'Brien," Commander Sisko ordered, "disarm it if you can. But don't disable it permanently unless you have to." Then he asked, "Mr. Berat? Do you think you can help us again?"

"I have some experience with devices like this," Kira put in.

"Fine. Then you can help Berat and O'Brien."

Kira frowned. That wasn't the reply she'd been expecting.

Berat himself said nothing. He had started to wonder, earlier in his stay on DS-Nine, whether the Bajoran terrorist wasn't largely a myth created by Cardassian propaganda. But here stood Kira, not a meter away from him, admitting to "some experience" with bombs. No question how she had obtained it, who her targets had been.

O'Brien felt the tension. As Sisko and the others left the monitor room, he turned first to Berat, then to Kira, as if trying to force goodwill between them. "Well, let's have the computer scan this bloody thing and tell us what it finds."

"Unless the scan sets it off," Berat added pessimistically.

But it didn't. Instead, the scan image started to appear on the screen. "No timing device," O'Brien noted. "Must be remote control."

"Radio receiver. There." Berat pointed to the screen. Now that he was observing the device more closely, it seemed quite familiar. Almost too familiar.

Kira was staring fiercely at the screen. "So whoever's planning to set this off must be still on the station! They'd have to be, to send the signal. It's not too late!"

Once the scan was complete, Berat explained where it would be safest to drill through the case of the bomb and set a pin that would hold the arming switch in place. Although painstaking, the operation was simple enough, using remote controls under the computer's guidance. Berat stood just behind O'Brien, watching him manipulate the probe. From time to time, he flexed his hands and tried to hold them steady without a tremor.

"There, that's done!" O'Brien said at last, leaning back and exhaling in relief. The pin was in place, the arming switch no longer capable of detonating the bomb. He looked at Berat with appreciation. "You must have done this kind of thing before."

"I have," he said slowly. "In combat engineering school. That . . . that bomb is a Cardassian model."

"You're sure about this?" Sisko asked him.

Berat hesitated. Then, "Yes. The device is Cardassian. It isn't a model that I recognize. And the serial numbers were burned away. But the basic design . . . is Cardassian."

Kira said reluctantly, "During the resistance, we got a lot of our supplies, ordnance, that kind of thing, from raids on Cardassian armories. This doesn't *prove* the terrorist is Cardassian. I wish it did, but—we can't afford to make mistakes in this situation."

"Mr. Berat?"

This was hard. How much should he admit? Was he betraying his homeworld? Had he already done it, deactivating the bomb? Identifying it?

But if there was a plot to destroy DS9, to wreck the peace between Cardassia and the Federation, then he knew who was behind it: Marak. Marak and the whole Revanche party, the ones responsible for his father's execution as a traitor. It was all part of the same plan.

Sisko tried to assure him, "We won't try to force you to disclose any information you think you shouldn't. But the station's safety depends on knowing who's behind these attacks. So we can stop them before they try it again."

Slowly, "I think . . . the reason I didn't recognize it at first is it's a very recent model. There was a new series developed after I was out of engineering school. That was after we withdrew from Bajoran space. I don't see how . . . Bajorans could have gotten hold of them."

The station's officers all looked at each other. Then Sisko said, "Thank you, Mr. Berat. That's all the information I think we need. The security officer will escort you back to detention. For your own safety, you understand. As long as the *Swift Striker* is docked at DS-Nine. Gul Marak has made . . . a number of threatening remarks.

"But I want you to know that we appreciate what you've done today. All of us do."

They waited until he had left the room.

"I don't know," Kira said, "about trusting him."

O'Brien didn't like that. "He risked his life down there in that reactor."

"Either he's lying now, or he's betraying his own people."

"I don't really think so," said Sisko. "There may be more to the situation than we can understand. But that's not our concern right now. Major, it looks like you were right. The Cardassians are behind the attacks. They meant for Bajoran terrorists to take the blame when the station was destroyed."

"And Gul Marak would be on hand to claim the wormhole," Kira added.

"Well," said Odo, "as far as Gul Marak—or anyone else—knows, the explosion is still set to go off in . . ." He checked the time. ". . . twenty-one hours."

"Or whenever they send the signal to detonate," Sisko corrected him. "Remember, all we have to go on is that one poster that said seventy-two hours."

"But they can't set off the bomb while their own ship is still docked here. They don't want to blow themselves up along with the station," O'Brien added. "So we have until the *Swift Striker* undocks, at least."

"If it is the Cardassians," Dax warned. The results of her DNA scan were so far inconclusive.

Kira glanced at her with a troubled expression that none of the others seemed to notice.

"But then what happens when there's no explosion? What will they do next?" Odo asked.

"A good question," Sisko said. "We'll have to do something about that. Unfortunately," he went on, "even without destroying the station, this plot has already done enough harm to Bajor. The trade negotiations are completely disrupted. None of those worlds are going to vote for Bajoran membership in the Federation now, after what they believe has happened. They're all convinced that the Bajorans are fanatics and terrorists."

"But we have the evidence!" O'Brien protested.

"One piece of evidence. And no way for us to prove we didn't plant it to place the blame on the Cardassians."

"Berat saw it."

"And the Cardassians would point out that he's a known traitor who's taken Federation asylum. No, we need to have the Cardassians discredit themselves. Publicly. In front of as many witnesses as we can find."

Sisko looked at all of them, one by one. "And to do that, we have to make them believe their plan is working. We all have to carry on exactly as if we hadn't found the bomb. I see no other way to force their hand."

"What about the evacuation?" Odo asked. "The level of panic on the station . . ."

Sisko frowned. "We can't force people to stay. For one thing, we don't have the security forces to prevent every ship from undocking, if it comes to that. And we *can't* reveal that we've removed the bomb. But we need witnesses. As many impartial observers as possible."

"We can't order the delegates to stay, but we can't guarantee their safety if they try to leave," said Dax.

"Exactly," Sisko agreed. "And with the last two incidents, that's no idle threat. I'll speak personally with all the remaining ambassadors and trade delegations."

He turned to Kira. "Major, there still are some loose ends we have to tie up. Assuming this is a Cardassian plot, they must have had an agent on the station before the *Swift Striker* showed up, to plant that first bomb. I *want* whoever that was. And I want to know how they got that thing past our security to plant it on the containment pod."

Sisko looked back at the monitor, at the bomb. "But I still don't trust our Cardassian friend Gul Marak. I think Odo asked the right question a few minutes ago. What's going to happen when he sees that his bomb hasn't gone off? What does he do then? If the Cardassians were originally prepared to blow up the station one way, they wouldn't hesitate to use a Galor-class warship to get the job done."

Kira clenched her teeth. "And Bajoran terrorists would take the blame."

Odo agreed, "Everyone else who knew the truth would be dead."

"Exactly. That's what we have to prevent." Sisko looked at O'Brien, then at the bomb. "And this thing is what we're going to use to do it."

CHAPTER
26

"I'M AFRAID I don't quite understand you, Major," Odo said.

Kira looked up from her console. "What do you mean?"

"Well, although I try to appear humanoid, I don't have the same feelings you do. I can't really understand the need for revenge. But, you were the one who first thought it might be the Cardassians behind the bombings. You said that Bajorans wouldn't destroy their own station. Now we have the proof that you were right.

"But look at all those names there on your screen: all those people you're holding for questioning. Aren't they all Bajorans? Except for Garak? All the rest of us agree that it was the Cardassians behind the bombs, but you still seem to have doubts."

Kira ran her fingers back through her hair. It was already a mess; she couldn't make it look any worse.

"It just doesn't all fit. I keep running into loose

ends. What about Gelia? She *was* Kohn Ma. She did leave that poster on the wall near Garak's shop. And somebody did give her the order. I have to know who that person was. And I can't just believe it was a Cardassian. A Cardassian knowing Kohn Ma recognition codes?"

"It isn't impossible, you know. People were interrogated. Tortured. I understand the Cardassians are good at that sort of thing. Someone could have let things slip, under pressure, under drugs. You can't be sure."

"I *have* to be sure! And that isn't all. Sisko is right. If it was a Cardassian who planted the bomb, *how* did he get it into the reactor room without being spotted? There's always a technician on duty." Kira shook her head. "There's something here we just haven't got hold of yet. Something we're overlooking—I don't know what."

"Does that mean you aren't going to interrogate Garak?"

"Oh, no!" Kira stood up purposefully. "Interrogating Garak is what I'm going to do right now!"

The Cardassian tailor stood up with a look of wounded indignation. "So, Major, it's you. Finally. I suppose that now I'm going to learn why I'm being detained here like this."

"You're being detained for questioning, Mr. Garak."

"For questioning? Right now? In case you haven't heard, Major, this whole station is scheduled to be blown up in just sixteen hours."

"Oh? You have personal knowledge of the schedule for blowing up the station, do you?"

Garak frowned in annoyance and looked down at the polished nails on one hand. "You know what I mean. You know what the rumors are. People are evacuating DS-Nine! I want to get onto my ship before it's too late."

"And what ship would that be? The *Swift Striker*, maybe? You have an arrangement with Gul Marak?"

Garak replied stiffly, "As a Cardassian, naturally I applied to the Gul when I decided to seek passage off the station. In case you've been too busy interrogating innocent people to notice, Major, let me inform you that space for departing passengers is at a premium right about now."

"Is it, now? But maybe you haven't heard; the evacuation's been called off."

"Ships will still be pulling out. You can't stop them. You can't stop a warship, at least."

"We can try. But, tell me, Garak, just when is the *Swift Striker* going to undock?"

The Cardassian sniffed. "I'm sure Gul Marak is the person you should be asking that question, Major. Not me. I'm just a civilian. I own a tailor shop."

"Simple Garak. Right. You know, Garak, I've always wondered just why you stayed on this station after the Cardassian occupation force pulled out. Did you think we were going to miss the chance to see a Cardassian face every day?"

Still stiffly, "We've gone into this before, Major. I was never a member of the Cardassian occupation force on Bajor. I'm a civilian, a businessman, I had money invested here. Why should I abandon it?"

"But you're prepared to abandon it now."

"You Bajoran fanatics are going to blow up the whole station now! I don't really have a choice, do I?"

"I think you do. You can either talk to me or you can stay right here in this cell until we both know whether this bomb rumor is true."

Garak tensed. "You can't keep me here."

Kira's lips lifted in a slight smile. "Oh? I can't?"

The Cardassian wrung his hands. "All right! Go ahead, do your worst! Ask your questions!"

But Kira stood up and walked a few steps away. With her back to Garak, she said, "I never wanted to believe any Bajoran would go so far as to blow up this station. Not even the Kohn Ma. But *someone* was setting off those explosions. So I asked myself: Just who has more to lose in this situation? Who has more to gain? And do you know the answer I came up with? The Cardassians."

Garak said nothing.

"But if the Cardassians were behind the bombings, they had to have an agent working for them here on the station. Guess whose name is at the top of my list of suspected Cardassian agents?"

She turned around just as Garak exclaimed shrilly, "You think *I'm* the one who set off those bombs? In case you don't remember, I was a *victim* of this terrorism! My shop was blown up, my equipment damaged! I was *maimed!*" His hand went to the nearly healed scar on his face. "I could have been killed!"

"Yes, that was a very good way to divert our suspicion. Make yourself a victim. Plant a misleading message on the walls near your shop. Everyone would believe it was just another Bajoran terrorist, striking out at an innocent Cardassian civilian.

"Or did you make a mistake when you were arming the bomb? Was it an accident? Maybe you just staged the rest of it to cover your tracks."

Now Garak was standing very still, confronting her. "You're wrong, Major," he said quietly.

"Maybe I am. And maybe you'll decide to tell me the truth. You think about it, Garak. I'll be back in—eighteen hours or so."

She turned away from him again, started to leave.

Garak wrung his hands again, bit his lower lip in obvious indecision. "Major!"

Kira paused.

"All right."

She turned slowly to face him again.

"I had nothing to do with those explosions. Nothing. I don't know why my shop was targeted. Maybe it was for the reason you said, but I don't know. I wasn't told. All I know is: There is a bomb set to destroy DS-Nine. I was advised to be off the station by . . ." He checked his chrono. ". . . sixteen hours from now."

"You were advised."

"That's right."

"And the source of this advice?"

Garak said nothing.

"You didn't think of passing your advice along to station authorities? You didn't think other lives besides your own were worth saving?"

"What could I have told them that they didn't already know? There isn't a single person on this station who hasn't heard the rumors. The only thing preventing people from getting away to safety is your security!"

"All right, Mr. Garak. We'll just wait and see just how reliable this anonymous source of yours turns out to be."

"Wait! You're not going to leave me here! Major! I told you the truth! All I know! You can't keep me here! Major Kira!"

But Kira didn't turn back again.

On the monitor in the security office, Odo watched the agitated prisoner pacing in his cell.

"Good job, Major," he told Kira. "It's certainly one

more piece of evidence that it's the Cardassians behind all this."

"But not conclusive proof. For what it's worth, I do think Garak was telling the truth. He wasn't involved in setting any of the bombs. So we *still* don't know who the Cardassian agent is. And that's the one I really want."

Odo was still looking at the monitor. "He thinks he's going to be killed by a Cardassian bomb. It's a form of justice, isn't it?"

"Let him think so," Kira said uncharitably. "Maybe he'll remember something else as the deadline gets closer. As it is, he's safe enough in that cell."

"As safe as the rest of us, at least," Odo corrected her.

Kira didn't argue.

Jake hated it when he fought with his dad. These days, they hardly seemed to see each other at all, and then there wasn't any time to really talk.

But Jake was afraid. Everybody said DS-Nine was going to explode. They were all trying to get away. But some of the ships had blown up when they tried to pull away from the station. People had been killed.

It made him remember when he was just a kid, and the Borg ship had fired on the *Saratoga,* and Mom had died. How it had been, with the smoke and the flames and the sirens, and the ship all broken and twisted. But it was hard to talk to Dad about all that.

Still, he was scared, and he didn't know what was going to happen. Dad said they weren't leaving. None of the Starfleet personnel were leaving—not even Keiko and little Molly.

"Dad," he'd protested, "they're gonna *blow this place up!* In just a few more hours!"

"Jake, you know that's just a rumor spreading around the Promenade."

"Oh, yeah, then why is everybody trying to leave? Why don't you tell them to stop?"

"If ships blowing up in their docking bays doesn't stop them, nothing I say will. Not for long. And it would cause a panic and a riot if we tried to force people to stay. These are civilians. They're free to come and go as they please. But my duty is here."

"Well, what about me? Do I have to stay and get killed just because it's your job to run this stupid station?"

Jake had been sorry the instant he said it, seeing the look of hurt in his father's face. "I'm sorry, Dad. I didn't mean it."

They hugged each other, hard. "Do you really want to go?" Dad had asked, then. "Where? Who would you go with?"

"I don't know. Nog?" But he'd had that big fight with Nog. And he wasn't sure at all he wanted to live with Nog's dad and his uncle Quark. No, he was sure. He wouldn't want that at all.

He wasn't sure just what he wanted, now.

"Look, Jake," Dad said. "Will you trust me if I tell you I have reason to believe the station isn't really in danger?"

"Really?"

"Really. Believe me, Jake, I'd never keep you here if I thought otherwise. The danger is . . . taken care of already. But this is confidential information. You can't tell anyone. Not Nog, not *anyone*. This is important. The safety of everyone on this station depends on it. So do I have your word?"

"I swear, Dad, I won't say anything."

But it was harder than he'd thought, keeping a

secret like that. With Dad gone again, Jake wandered morosely through the corridors. Everywhere he went, people had packed up their things, were frantically trying to abandon the station.

A life spent growing up in Starfleet had made Jake rather an expert on moving out at short notice, and he noticed now that the same generally seemed true of the Bajorans. None of them seemed overly burdened with possessions. He supposed that spending your whole life in refugee camps kept you from getting too attached to places and things.

But now he saw so many people abandoning their businesses, their possessions, their homes. Some of them were crying. He felt terrible, watching them, knowing what he knew.

There was a crowd lined up at an airlock, waiting for a chance to get onto some ship. Somebody was yelling and screaming. Jake went closer.

A man in a purser's uniform was yelling, "No, you can't take all that onto the ship! Ten kilos per person! That's the limit!"

And someone else yelling back hysterically, surrounded by crates and boxes. Jake gathered that they were some kind of exotic imported artworks, and they couldn't just *leave* them here to be blown up, and they weren't even *insured!*

And someone else yelling that they were holding up the line . . .

Jake recognized that voice. He edged closer. There was a small knot of Ferengi, and among them he recognized Nog.

"Nog! Are you leaving?"

The Ferengi boy looked at him in surprise. "Are you still here?"

Jake remembered his promise. "Yeah," he said

sulkily. "My dad won't *let* me leave. He says it's his duty. Just 'cause *he's* the station commander, I have to stay on this stupid place and get killed."

Nog stepped closer, hissed in a whisper, "You could come with us. We could use someone else."

"For what?" Jake asked suspiciously.

In answer, Nog took his hand and pressed it against his own midriff, where Jake felt something hard to the touch. "They have a weight limit on baggage."

Jake understood. The Ferengi were all wearing money belts, probably smuggling gold-pressed latinum off the station. They only wanted to use him. Still, Nog had thought of him, had made the offer. Even if there was profit in it.

"No, thanks," he said. "But aren't you afraid? What if your ship blows up, too?"

Nog whispered secretively, "It's all arranged."

"What's all arranged?"

"The captain made a deal with the terrorists. This ship won't have any trouble undocking."

"The captain knows who the terrorists are?" Jake asked dubiously.

"Shhhh!" Nog hissed. He looked uncomfortable, and not just from the weight of the hidden latinum. "I'll remember you, human. Jake."

And Jake had to leave, right then, before he said something he wasn't supposed to.

CHAPTER
27

SISKO LOOKED through the monitor at the bomb in the containment chamber. "It's live?"

"It surely is, Commander," O'Brien told him. "The switch we disarmed is only what the ordnance people call an antihandling device. It would have set off the bomb if we'd tried to move or tamper with it. But the remote-control detonator is still intact. Whenever the Cardies send the signal . . ." He mimed an explosion.

Sisko nodded decisively. "What I want to do, Chief, is use the Cardassians' own weapon against them. Until they've undocked, they can't send that signal without blowing themselves up along with the station. We have that much time. Now—" He looked from O'Brien to Odo with a strange light in his eyes. "Do you think you can manage to plant that bomb on Gul Marak's ship?"

"Without being detected, you mean?" Odo said slowly.

O'Brien broke into a grin. "Just how much damage do you want it to do, sir?"

"As much as possible. I can't take chances here."

The simple thing would have been to have Odo change himself into the form of a Cardassian and enter the *Swift Striker* through the airlock, as one of the crew. But, aside from the question of passes and ID, the flaw in this plan was clearly demonstrated when Odo showed them how well he could mimic Cardassian features. His face was a raw, unfinished, lumpy thing, no more like a real Cardassian's than his normal appearance was Bajoran.

"Inanimate objects are easy, living things harder. And persons . . ."

"Well," O'Brien had said, "so much for that idea."

But there was always more than one way to attack a starship. The idea came as they scanned the image of the Cardassian ship at dock. "Look at all that debris!"

It was drifting all around the station, a hazard to docking and undocking operations, discarded out of the airlocks in defiance of all station regulations as overloaded ships lightened their loads and jettisoned the personal effects the desperate station refugees had smuggled on board.

"One more inanimate object . . ." O'Brien had whispered, inspired.

Now he floated in the silence of space, with the mass of DS-Nine below him, the wide circular sweep of the docking ring, the pylons arching up from it. He could still remember his first sight of this place, how alien it had seemed, even sinister in its Cardassian design. And now it was home. Things changed, didn't they?

His attention shifted to the *Swift Striker*, the Cardassian ship docked at the nearest pylon, looking very much like it belonged there. More so than the *Enterprise* had ever done, or any other Starfleet ship, he thought reflectively.

They were almost drifting. It had to look that way. O'Brien in his EVA suit clung to Odo, who had taken the shape of an ordinary packing crate, one of many of them out here. Their progress was so slow that O'Brien had time to wonder what was in all these crates, and barrels, and bags. Would any of the people ever be back to retrieve these jettisoned possessions? Would they survive to be able to do so?

A quick jet from his hand thruster corrected their course toward the Cardassian ship and slightly altered the direction of the Odo-crate's spin. O'Brien only hoped the Cardies wouldn't notice. The whole point was to be inconspicuous. Any scan would reveal the fact that the crate was not really a crate. What would happen then was not encouraging to contemplate.

Instead of worrying, he concentrated on the slowly growing shape of the Cardassian ship. The *Swift Striker* was a Galor-class, the most advanced of the Cardassian warships, packed with destructive weaponry. And, like all starships, vulnerable, in part on account of its own mass and capacity for acceleration. It depended on the power of its shields and integrity fields to defend it and keep it intact, but these systems could fail. Having spent a career keeping them functioning, O'Brien knew quite well how they could fail.

Absently, he stroked the case of the bomb he was carrying. Nasty little thing. He shuddered. There was something about an antimatter explosion, the malice of planting the bomb where they had. Above him, the ship's belly started to fill the sky. There were antimatter storage pods on the *Swift Striker,* necessary for the functioning of the warp drive, much larger than the ones that supplied the station's reactors.

But too hard to access. On the other hand, the power linkage to the structural integrity field generators . . .

The crate suddenly extruded an arm, which reached out and snagged a handhold on the hull. Odo pulled them in closer. From this point on, disguise was irrelevant. All that mattered was luck. They ought to be safe, unless the Cardies suddenly decided to run a sweeping scan of their own hull exterior.

Moving cautiously across the ship's surface, O'Brien recalled that argument:

"What if their hull scan picks you up?"

"Commander," Dax had pointed out after a check of her instruments, "the Cardassians aren't scanning their own hull."

Which, in retrospect, was the proof they should have noticed all along. Docked at a station supposedly full of Bajoran terrorists, with bombs going off almost every day, the *Swift Striker,* of all the ships berthed there, was not constantly scanning its hull to guard against sabotage. Because the Cardassians alone knew that the bombings weren't the work of Bajorans at all.

Well, that was hindsight for you—always too late to do any good.

Now O'Brien hoped that Dax had her instruments trained on them at the moment. Their only hope, if discovered, was that Dax could beam them back in time. As to the other consequences, that still didn't bear thinking of.

He followed Odo, more awkwardly because he was burdened with the bomb and his tools, as well as restricted in shape. Odo seemed somehow more natural out here in space, more free. He wondered if it was frustrating to the shape-changer to maintain a single form for so much of the time.

He finally signaled that they had come to the right

spot. Handing the bomb to Odo, he took out his tools and started to remove the hull access plate. The bomb still had the connecting wires that had held it to the containment pod in the station's reactor. O'Brien used them to fasten it to the main power linkage node, then replaced the access plate. That was it. It seemed almost too simple.

Oh, there was still the risk of discovery. The antihandling switch on the bomb had been disarmed, and the Cardassians, if they found it out here, wouldn't have any trouble removing it. But there was only one way it could go off now, and that was if Gul Marak sent the signal to detonate, thinking it was still planted on the station.

Would they do it, he wondered? Or was it only a threat? Hard to believe they'd really do such a thing—even Cardassians.

Odo resumed his crate shape, and they pushed off from the ship, to all appearances just another piece of debris, drifting again, but this time in the direction of pylon five, an empty arch standing out from the station. O'Brien just hoped they got there in time, before the *Swift Striker* took off.

There were only a couple of hours left.

CHAPTER
28

KIRA POPPED a stimulant tab and washed it down with a swallow of bitter brown Kenyan coffee. O'Brien had introduced her to it—a human drink, from their homeworld—and now she wished she'd never started drinking the stuff. It made her hands shake. Or maybe they were just shaking because she hadn't had any real sleep since that last message showed up, now almost seventy-two hours ago.

She was most concerned that the Cardassian agent might have already escaped. Despite warnings, people were still managing to leave the station. But Starfleet personnel were still here, and most of the Bajoran staff, keeping systems working as smoothly as possible, keeping DS-Nine alive.

There were also a number of people still in detention for questioning, and every one of them was protesting as urgently as possible that she had no right to keep them on the station when the whole place was going to go up any minute.

Kira knew that most if not all of them were innocent, and their fears were genuine and well founded—even if false in fact. She had released as many as she could. But she couldn't reassure them about their fates. It would be a disaster if one of them happened to disclose to the Cardassians that the bomb had already been removed. And she was just too exhausted to care any longer. Only one thing mattered now: finding the Cardassian agent, finding whoever had planted the bombs. Making sure they could never set another one.

What kind of Bajoran could work for the Cardassians? Could risk so many Bajoran lives? How could anyone be so misguided?

Kira put down the coffee with a shudder of distaste and went to face her next subject. The woman was one of the technicians assigned to the reactor control room. She was sitting in a position of meditation, but she jumped up nervously when Kira clapped her hands to get her attention.

"Your name is Reis Ilen?"

"Major! This is a mistake! I didn't do anything! You have to let me out of here!"

"You're not being charged with anything. I just have some questions to ask."

"You're asking *questions?* Now? When the station is about to—"

"The sooner I find the answers, the sooner this will all be over."

The technician's nervousness subsided slightly.

"Now, I understand that you're assigned to monitor the reactor control room on the third alternate shift, is this correct? Was there any time in the last ten days that you missed your shift? Were you ever late?"

"No. Never. You can check my time sheets."

"Thank you, I already have. But was there ever a

time during that period when you might have left the control room, even for a minute? Any time the reactor could have been left unmonitored?"

"No! That would be against regulations. There has to be at least one monitor on duty at all times. In case there's a flux surge, or a drop in power levels."

"Part of your duty is to prevent unauthorized access to the reactor chambers, isn't this so?"

"Someone tampered with the reactors, didn't they? That's what happened, isn't it? The reactors are going to blow!"

"We're investigating a lead, that's all I can say."

"No one will survive—"

"Reis! Please. The sooner we can get this over with, the sooner we'll all be safe." Kira hated this, but it was necessary until they found the Cardassian agent.

She shook her head slightly. "Now, on your shifts during this period, was there anyone who could have gotten access to the reactors? Authorized or not? Anyone who came down there at all?"

"Chief O'Brien—"

"O'Brien. Anyone else?"

"No one. Well, of course, the monk."

Kira's eyes opened very wide as a cold shiver ran down her spine. *"What monk?"*

"From the temple. Well, you get nervous, you know, down there with those reactors, thinking you're the first one who'll get it if the system blows up. He's been helping me to deal with it, to meditate—"

"A monk was with you in the reactor control room? When? For how long? What did he do?"

"Major, you can't suspect that a monk—"

"What did he *do?*"

"Well, I'm not sure, exactly. I mean, sometimes when you meditate, you lose track of external things. You know how it is."

But Kira was already hitting her comm badge. "Security! This is Kira. Someone get to the temple and detain a monk named Leiris! Now!"

Reis was still protesting, "But Major, I mean, he's a *monk—*"

By the time Kira reached the temple, the security officer had already reported through her communicator: "Sorry, Major. They say the monk Leiris has left."

"Left the temple or the station?"

"I don't know. They just said he'd left. Earlier today."

So maybe it wasn't too late, after all. "Search the temple."

"What? Major Kira? *The temple?*"

Kira took a deep breath. Why did her people have this blind spot? "You heard me. Search the temple. Respectfully, of course. But if you find Leiris, hold him. And be careful. He may be dangerous."

"Yes, Major." The officer's voice was dubious.

Kira hesitated. Where would he be now? Trying to get off the station, of course, knowing what was supposed to happen. How, though? A monk had no money to bribe a shipping agent or a freighter captain.

But a Cardassian agent . . .

Kira thought of Garak. The *Swift Striker.* Then she was running toward the turbolift that led to pylon six. If only she wasn't too late, if only Leiris wasn't already on the ship!

After all the confusion elsewhere on the station, with people camped out in the hallways, waiting in line for passage on any ship they could find, the corridors in this section seemed deserted. These parts of the station had never really been brought back into normal use. And even though people were desperate to leave DS-Nine, they weren't quite desperate enough to seek passage on a Cardassian ship. No Bajorans, at any rate. Only Garak, still locked in his cell, wanted to board this ship. And it looked as if Garak was actually innocent, after all.

The agent wasn't a Cardassian. He was a Bajoran traitor.

Kira supposed she'd been as blind as any other Bajoran, incapable of suspecting Leiris just because he was in a religious order. She *knew* his views, his past associations with terrorist groups, even Kohn Ma. He was the one, the only one, who could have known those recognition codes. But she'd dismissed him automatically as a suspect. He was a *monk.*

And if she was too late, if he was already on board, then there was nothing she could do. Frustration made her grind her teeth against each other. In a flash of ironic insight, she suddenly thought that she could even understand Gul Marak, in one way, because right now she wanted to march onto the *Swift Striker* with drawn weapons and drag Leiris bodily off that ship.

She backed away, around a corner, out of sight of the lift doors. "Security. This is Kira. Has there been any sign of Leiris?"

"No, Major. It's like he's disappeared."

Disappeared onto that ship. Tapping her communicator again, "Ops, this is Kira. Has the Cardassian ship requested clearance for undock yet?"

A moment later she heard Sisko's voice. "This is Major Kira?"

"Yes, Commander."

"The *Swift Striker* requested undocking clearance only twenty minutes ago. Is there a problem?"

Kira was aware that Ops was full of foreign ambassadors, importuning Sisko with their demands and interfering with operations. They couldn't take a chance of sensitive information reaching the Cardassians. She answered carefully, "I'm just not sure if all the passengers have boarded the ship yet."

"The passenger you were speaking of?"

"Correct. Um, has Chief O'Brien completed the . . . airlock maintenance?"

"All maintenance is complete. We can clear the *Swift Striker* for undocking—unless you see a reason for further delay."

"No. If the passenger misses his ship, he'll just have to make other arrangements."

"Understood, Major. Good luck."

Kira stared at the turbolift door. Either Leiris was already on board, or he wasn't. If he was—it was too late. But if the Prophets had listened to her, he'd be hurrying to board now, or else he'd be left behind. She thought again of Garak in his cell. How frantic he'd be if he knew the *Swift Striker* was about to take off.

And Leiris knew where the bomb was planted, knew there was no hope for anyone still on the station when it was detonated. Odo's staff was monitoring the reactor, just in case he came back to try to disarm it at the last moment, to save himself.

Is that what he would do? Kira shut her eyes for an instant. Leiris. She thought she had known him, once. Of all the people she would have never suspected. *Why?* What possible reason could he have had to serve the Cardassians? What conceivable motive to betray his own people?

And when she opened her eyes again, she saw a figure hurrying toward the lift, almost at a run. He was wearing drab coveralls, not a robe, but Kira recognized the traitor monk. She checked her phaser and, in a low voice, ordered the computer to record what was about to happen. Then she stepped out into his path.

"Afraid you're going to miss your ship, Leiris?"

He stopped, as stunned as if the Orb of the Prophets had just materialized in front of him, instead of Major Kira Nerys. His face looked very pale. Then he forced a shaken smile. "Well. Major. I see you've managed to overcome your inner conflicts and ambiguities. You've chosen your side."

His eyes were on her phaser. Kira noticed that her hands weren't trembling any longer. "What about you, Leiris? Did you suffer any inner conflicts about becoming a Cardassian agent? Or were you working for them all along? Even during the resistance?"

He laughed ruefully. "Oh, no! I was as loyal to the cause of freedom as you were. Dedicated to Bajor's independence, enduring hardship, deprivation—all of it. Just like any good little Bajoran."

"Then—*why?*"

"For this." As he reached a hand into the carryall over his shoulder, Kira tensed with her finger on the phaser's trigger. But what Leiris pulled out was a heavy pouch. With a sharp, bitter laugh, he tossed the contents—gleaming gold—high into the air.

Kira's attention was distracted just for a single instant, but it was time enough for Leiris to grab for the phaser hidden in his bag. Just as he fired, she dropped down and rolled to the side, back into the shelter of the cross-corridor wall.

He was running for the lift, but Kira fired her own weapon—too soon. The blast missed, and Leiris managed to duck behind a deserted kiosk before she could shoot again.

Between them was the empty corridor and beyond it the turbolift. Kira stood between the traitor and his only hope of escape. She hesitated. One mistake already, and she'd almost lost him! Maybe she should call security for backup.

But just then Leiris broke from cover in a desperate

attempt to reach the turbolift. Phaser fire beamed from Kira's weapon and impacted on the deck just ahead of him. No. Leiris was *hers*.

She called out, "Leiris! You mean you betrayed Bajor for Cardassian latinum?"

"That's right. Why—are you shocked?" He looked at her hopefully. "I don't suppose we could come to an understanding, Major? You can have the latinum, all of it, as soon as I'm gone. Just let me get onto that lift. No? Ah, well, I didn't suppose so. You're a patriot, aren't you, Nerys? You're above such petty material temptations.

"What about this offer, then? Let me go, and I'll tell you where the bomb is hidden, exactly when it's supposed to go off. What's more important— arresting me or saving this station for the Federation?"

Kira laughed. "You're too late, Leiris. Your bomb is already disarmed. I don't suppose your Cardassian employers will be very pleased when they find out about that, will they?"

A pause. Then he said, in a resigned voice, "So. I see."

She couldn't see him behind the kiosk, wasn't sure what he was doing. "Leiris. Tell me, why did you do it? For the money? That *can't* be the only reason."

"Why did I do it? No, it wasn't just for the money. What is money? Just a few pounds of gold-pressed latinum. No, it was what it could buy me. A way out of here. Into a different future."

"I don't understand."

"Don't you? Maybe you wouldn't. During the resistance, Nerys—what were you fighting for all that time? What was all that suffering about? Bajor? Let me tell you: We may have defeated the Cardassians, but we lost Bajor. Our world will never be the same.

Our religion will never be the same. Do you think all those temples they demolished will ever be rebuilt? In the name of the Prophets, the Orbs are nothing but alien artifacts now! Heaven is the Gamma Quadrant. Bajorans don't worship the gods anymore, they worship the Holy Wormhole! They worship foreigners and their foreign silver and gold and latinum!

"People like you, in love with the Federation, you keep telling yourselves that we won the struggle. But we didn't. We lost our world, we lost ourselves. When we had the Cardassians to fight, at least we knew who we were. Do you want to see the future of Bajor? Look around, look at this *station*. We won't have temples on the new Bajor, we'll have gambling halls and sex holosuites and foreign imports and space academies.

"I already lost once, Nerys. I lost the Bajor that I struggled to preserve. Why should I lose again? Why should I suffer for something that's already gone? So I took money from the Cardassians. Why not? Is that worse than taking it from the Federation, or the Ferengi, or any other aliens?"

Kira retorted, "But you did lose again, didn't you, Leiris? You betrayed your own people, and what do you have to show for it? There's your latinum on the floor. There's your Cardassian ship, taking off without you. Where's your new future now?"

There was no reply. "Leiris?"

A weak voice answered, "Enjoy your victory, Major Kira. I have to say . . . I'm glad . . . I won't be around. . . ."

"Leiris?" Kira suspected a trap. As she hesitated, her comm badge sounded. "Major Kira? This is Sisko. I want to advise you, the *Swift Striker* has just undocked."

"Thank you, Commander. And I have our traitor here. He knows he's not going anywhere now."

"Good work, Major! Do you require assistance?"

"No. No, thank you, Commander. The situation is under control.

She tapped the badge to shut it off. "Leiris? The *Swift Striker* just pulled away from the station. It's all over now."

Again there was no answer, and Kira realized that it was all over for Leiris in another way than she had meant. She stepped out into the lift corridor and approached the kiosk. When she came around it, she saw Leiris's body sprawled on the floor, eyes fixed and staring at death. His phaser lay discarded next to him.

She knelt, picked it up. The weapon was not set to lethal. There was no obvious wound or cause of death on Leiris's body. But his heart—she touched her fingers to his pulse—had stopped.

Some monks, she knew, had developed their powers of meditation to the point where they could stop their bodily functions at will. She wondered if that was what Leiris had done. Not to have to face another defeat.

Still kneeling, she closed his eyes.

CHAPTER
29

SISKO'S EYEBROWS ROSE as he saw Kira coming into Ops. There were deep shadows of exhaustion surrounding her eyes, and her shoulders seemed to sag with weariness. "Major, you should get some rest. Is your suspect in custody?"

"The suspect is dead. But I have his confession on record."

Solemnly, Sisko called up the recording from the computer and viewed Leiris's last moments on the main screen. When it was over, he glanced at Kira, seated at the first officer's console. Despite the fatigue that showed on her face, her expression as she stared at the viewscreen was as hard and implacable as stone. He was aware that she had known the dead monk as a spiritual advisor, even an old friend. His betrayal must have affected her, no matter that she wasn't showing it openly.

Later, maybe, he might be able to talk to her about it. Offer what comfort he could. But there was no time for that now. Already, even before the recording was finished, a number of ambassadors had started to express their reactions, not all of them in temperate language.

It had been the course of least resistance to allow them into Ops, a decision that Sisko was already regretting. They questioned his decisions at every turn, interfered with normal operations, and frequently turned on each other to squabble over some trivial point of politics or protocol.

On seeing the final image of Leiris, the Klingon made a low growl deep in his throat, fingering the handle of his ceremonial sword. "It is well for the traitor that he is already dead."

"So, the bombs were set by a Bajoran terrorist," the Rigellian declared in a tone of vindication.

"Working for the Cardassians. Paid off with gold," the Tellarite sneered.

"You believe that transparent lie?" the Rigellian demanded.

Sisko hesitated to interrupt their quarrel. These were the people he had to convince. These were his witnesses.

But the Qismilian was lashing her tail, a dangerous sign. She looked from the viewscreen to Kira, then to Sisko. "Commander, is this true, what she says? The bomb is found? The danger to the station is over? If this is so, then *why are we kept here?* Why are we not told this?"

Kira went pale and started to speak, but Sisko was quicker. "It is true," he said, weaving together a fabric of lies and truth he hoped would convince them, "that we did locate and disarm one explosive device. But there may well be others. As you should well know after your tragic experience, Madame Ambassador."

"But you insisted that we remain on the station,"

the Tellarite said, frowning suspiciously. "You, personally, guaranteed our safety."

Sisko shook his head. "I'm afraid, if you recall, that what I said was I could not guarantee your safety if your ship attempted to leave."

"Klingon warships do not run in fear of terrorists," that ambassador stated firmly, glaring around the room as if he were challenging anyone to dispute him.

"Are you calling us cowards?" the Aresian bristled.

Kira wanted to close her eyes, she wanted to sleep. The quarreling of the foreign trade delegates was reaching a high pitch that was bringing back her headache. Her job was finished, with Leiris dead, but it would have been unthinkable not to be in Ops when they finally confronted the Cardassian.

Trying to ignore the disruption, she glanced around the room. There, quiet and inconspicuous in one corner, was the commander's son. He seemed anxious, as if he understood what was happening here. But—suddenly Kira stood up. What was that he had?

The boy started at the sight of her. "Major Kira?"

"Jake? Just what is that thing? It looks like Cardassian equipment?"

The boy's expression was slightly defensive. "Berat fixed it for me."

"Could I see it?"

He handed it to her. "It works. Only I don't understand much Cardassian—"

"But I do." She turned the unit over, flipped through its frequencies. Cardassian voices came through, faint but clear. It was routine comm traffic: navigation data, orders from security to maintenance, from bridge to engineering . . .

Kira's eyes went wide as she recognized Gul Marak's voice.

Just then, Commander Sisko shouted out loud, "Quiet!" and the deck of Ops went suddenly silent.

Poised on the point of drawing swords, the ambassadors turned to stare at him.

"Security will evict the next person to cause a disruption of any kind. The lives of everyone on this station may depend on your silence." He paused to emphasize the order with a dark scowl.

Then, "On screen. Let's see the *Swift Striker* again."

At the sight of the Cardassian warship, menacing on the huge overhead display, the belligerent mood of the ambassadors faded. They all were well aware that the ship's weapons banks could easily obliterate an undefended space station like DS-Nine. Suddenly, it seemed all too probable, especially if Leiris's confession had been true.

Staring up at the image, Sisko felt the full, oppressive weight of responsibility. It all came down to him now: the man in the commander's seat. If he failed, if he had been wrong, then it would mean more than just the loss of DS-Nine and all the lives it held. The onus of the crime would fall on the Bajorans, and no world in the Federation or its allies would object when Gul Marak seized the Gamma Quadrant wormhole for the Cardassians.

It was frightening to think that the only thing which might prevent this was a single bomb, an object so small that a man could hold it on the palm of his hand. If O'Brien had done his work well, it was now planted somewhere on the *Swift Striker*. And there was only one man who could set it off, only one man now alive who knew the correct code and frequency to detonate it.

"Commander!"

Sisko turned to see Major Kira, holding out a small

object. He recognized a Cardassian communicator. "What the . . ."

Kira hit a switch, and there, plainly, came Gul Marak's voice confirming a course setting for his navigator. Sisko's eyebrows raised, and then a grin broke out on his face.

He looked up to the main viewscreen. "Get me Gul Marak."

The voice from the communicator: *"Sisko on the comm? Flakk it, why now? What does he want?"*

"Yes, yes, I'll talk to him. Put him through."

Now all of Ops was silent, almost holding their breath, straining to hear the voice coming through the small comm unit.

In an instant, the face of the Cardassian commander appeared. He didn't look as if he had expected to hear from Sisko, but neither did he seem displeased at another opportunity to gloat over the enemy commander. "Well, Sisko. So, have you changed your mind? Are you asking me to come back and evacuate your crew from the station? But don't you think you're a little too close to the deadline? I'm not sure if I ought to risk my ship."

Sisko's speech was formal and rather stiff. "We're searching for a fugitive, Gul Marak. A suspect in the bombings, a man pretending to be a Bajoran monk, using the name Leiris. We have reason to believe he might have boarded your ship."

Kira adjusted the Cardassian comm unit, and a voice came through: *"The Bajoran traitor? No, he never came on board. Good riddance, I say!"*

On the main screen, Marak laughed. "You amaze me, Sisko! You really do. Asking me to return a Bajoran fugitive! Well! What do you say to a trade, then? My traitor for yours? Or have you forgotten about that inconsequential matter? The Cardassian murderer that *you* gave asylum? Well," and suddenly Marak scowled menacingly, "I can assure you that I *have not.*"

"Then you have this Leiris in custody?" Sisko asked, ignoring the threat and hoping that his voice conveyed a sense of urgency. He hated this business of deception, but it was necessary.

"Unfortunately, no. It's too bad, isn't it? We might have been able to make some kind of deal."

"Maybe he stowed away somewhere on your ship. Our information was very clear."

Now Marak was sounding impatient. "Sisko, believe me: if there were a *Bajoran* on my ship, I'd know about it!"

Sisko took hold of his seat and leaned forward. Behind him, the watching ambassadors held their breaths. "Gul Marak, our situation here is desperate. We think this man may have planted another device somewhere on the station. It could go off at any time now. It's already been almost seventy-two hours since we found the warning. We need to be able to locate this bomb before it's too late!"

From the comm unit came faint but clearly scornful laughter.

"Well, then that's your problem, Commander," Marak sneered. "You should have evacuated your personnel earlier. I tell you again, for the last time: We don't have the man. Anyway, what makes you believe a *Bajoran* would ever think of escaping on a Cardassian ship?"

"We have evidence. Cardassian-minted coins were discovered with his possessions. They were gold-pressed latinum."

Marak's eyes narrowed. He snorted, "Cardassian latinum? That's your evidence? That's all you know?"

"We've checked our records. It seems that this

monk, or whatever he was, had prior connections with the Kohn Ma. When our security officers searched his quarters, they found the latinum. Unfortunately, they weren't able to apprehend the suspect himself."

From the comm unit: *"Program the detonation sequence. Here's the code."*

Now a grin appeared on Marak's face, growing slowly. He reminded Sisko of a shark about to snap its jaws shut on its prey. "I see the efficiency of your security officers hasn't improved, Sisko. Maybe you should hang one or two of them up for a few days, as an example to the rest. It works wonders for morale. Anyway, this terrorist is probably somewhere at large on your station. Or maybe he escaped already on some other ship. I don't really care.

"But I tell you what, Sisko. Here's one final offer. Surrender Deep Space Nine to me. Officially cede the Gamma Quadrant wormhole to the Cardassian government. Then we can talk. Otherwise, I'll enjoy watching you all die."

"You seem very sure of yourself, Gul."

"Oh, yes, I am. This is your last warning, Sisko. The deadline is up. Surrender the station now or start counting down your last seconds."

Slowly, "That sounds like a threat, Marak."

"Take it any way you want. You don't have any other choice. Frankly, Sisko, I'm only making this offer because I'd rather have the station's facilities intact. It *is* Cardassian, after all. And it makes a convenient base of operations for whoever controls the wormhole. As you well know. Otherwise I wouldn't bother." He laughed. "Whatever you do, the wormhole is Cardassian now. As it would have been, all along, if it weren't for the acts of traitors."

"So you did give Leiris the latinum. And the

explosives. He was your agent on DS-Nine. It was all a Cardassian plot to get control of the wormhole."

"Detonation sequence is set. Frequency eight eight four three two."

"Eight eight four three two. Ready."

In the background, the Klingon ambassador took hold of his sword hilt, but he caught himself and kept silent.

Marak had stopped laughing. "Suit yourself, Sisko. But I like our story better. Bajoran terrorists blowing up their own station. Killing Starfleet officers and their own civilians. Who'll ever doubt it? Everyone in the galaxy knows what the Bajorans are by now." He held up his hand, one finger poised over a control on the ship's command console. "This is it, Sisko. Make up your mind. Do I get the station, or blow it up?"

That was it, Gul Marak had confessed. It wasn't too late. Sisko half-rose from his seat. "Marak! I'm warning you. Don't do it!"

"You're warning me?"

"The bomb—it's not planted on my reactor now. It's on yours!"

Marak laughed again. "A good try, Sisko. But not good enough!" His finger stabbed down onto the control, and at that moment the image from the *Swift Striker*'s bridge broke up into a random pattern of static on DS-Nine's main viewscreen.

For an instant, there was an awed silence in the Operations Center. Only O'Brien breathed, "The bastard really did it!"

Then the image re-formed into the external view of the *Swift Striker* against the dark backdrop of space. The real damage to the ship wasn't visible—there was only a small area on the hull where the bomb had gone off and the plates were twisted and blown.

But over Jake's comm unit came the sound of Cardassian voices, swearing in panic, frantically issuing orders.

"What's wrong? What's wrong?"

"There's no power!"

"Engineering, curse you—report!"

"It's the main power linkage node in sector forty! It's blown!"

"Bypass!"

"The structural integrity field isn't holding! I read total power loss!"

"Cut engines! Full stop!"

"I'm trying to bypass!"

"Damn computer! Override! Override!"

"Pressure loss in sector eighty!"

From her scan console, Dax's cool voice reported, "I'm reading massive energy loss. The structural integrity field isn't holding—no, it's completely down now. The ship is decelerating, but I'm starting to pick up hull integrity failure on the right wing."

Everyone stared at the visual screen. The Galor-class warship slightly resembled a ray from Earth's oceans, with two wide-swept wings forward. Now, at the edge of the right wing, there were hull plates pulling loose, parting under the unshielded stress of acceleration. With the structural integrity field down, the *Swift Striker*'s own mass was pulling it apart.

"Very good work, Chief," Sisko said to O'Brien with a coolness he didn't quite feel. Inside him was elation tempered with horrified awe. No one who had ever served on starships could view this kind of destruction unmoved. Even if Gul Marak had unequivocally called down his ruin on himself. A ship was dying out there. Men inside it were dying.

He still held the comm unit.

"We're losing atmosphere!"

"The right wing is breaking up!"

"Abandon ship! Abandon ship! All nonessential crew to the lifeboats!"

"Can you contact the ship?" Sisko asked communications.

"Their communications are dead, Commander."

Tearing his eyes away from the disintegrating ship, he looked again at the small communicator, found the switch to transmit. "Gul Marak, this is DS-Nine. Do you need assistance?"

In a moment he heard Marak's voice, harsh with rage. "Curse you, Sisko! Cardassians would rather die than accept aid from you and your Bajoran scum!"

"One lifeboat away," Dax reported from her station.

Sisko nodded. He could see it on the main viewscreen. As the *Swift Striker* broke up, more of the small craft pulled away from the stricken ship, heading back under their own power toward Cardassian territory, going home in failure and disgrace.

"Lieutenant Dax," Sisko ordered finally, "I want you, Chief O'Brien, and Dr. Bashir to take the runabouts out there and see if you can find any survivors."

Sisko didn't mention the fact, but everyone knew it would be nonsurvivors they were most likely going to find among the wreckage of the Cardassian ship. The victims of its commander's treachery.

CHAPTER
30

"FLUX LEVELS: NORMAL."

"Field oscillation level: optimal."

"Antimatter injection rate: normal."

"Power output: ninety-eight point eight percent of capacity."

Miles O'Brien looked up from the console, grinning. "Well, I never thought I'd hear *that* as long as I was on DS-Nine."

Together, he and Berat had replaced the antimatter-containment pod on reactor B and refilled it with slush antideuterium, and the entire system was now back on-line.

Berat had a pensive expression. "I wonder . . ."

"What?"

"If I'll ever be able to work on one of these again."

"Look, I meant it when I offered you that job here. The commander agreed. We need someone like you on this station, someone familiar with these systems, trained to operate them. Hell, you've done this all before, you'd be better for the job than I am."

"I couldn't have handled that computer override."

"Sure you could. You just have to get out of the habit of letting them think they know best."

Berat allowed a grin to appear briefly on his face. But then: "No. I'm Cardassian."

"Does that matter? You're a damn good engineer, Berat, that's all I care about."

"Here, on this station, it would always matter."

O'Brien had nothing he could say to that. In silence, they packed away their tools, went to the turbolift. "How are the hands?" he asked finally, on their way up to the habitat ring.

"Still getting better. Your doctor says I can expect ninety-eight percent recovery now." He paused to flex his fingers. "You have good equipment, a good doctor."

"Bashir? I suppose so. When he remembers that he's a doctor and not the latest gift from God to humanity."

The lift doors opened onto level eleven. "Want to go have a drink, or something?" O'Brien asked.

"I—" Then Berat noticed someone coming across the floor of the Promenade. He stepped back into the lift. "No, thank you. I want to check the news reports back at my quarters."

Major Kira came up to O'Brien, glanced at the now-closed door of the lift. "So how's your Cardassian?"

"He does good work." O'Brien shook his head. "He wants to go home."

"Can he? Go home? After what he did here?"

This issue had come up between them before. "We should all be bloody glad he did what he did."

"I am glad. But I just can't help thinking—Cardassians died in that ship."

269

O'Brien looked away. He knew he was at least as responsible for those deaths as anyone. But then he turned back to Kira. "You think Berat's a traitor for helping us? Like that monk?"

"No. Not like Leiris. There just wasn't any excuse for what he did. There couldn't be."

O'Brien said slowly, "This happened to me. Not too long ago, in fact. My first commander was Captain Ben Maxwell, on the *Rutledge*. I would have followed that man into hell, no questions asked. But something happened to him, later. His family was killed in the war by the Cardassians, and it started to eat at him.

"We were at peace with Cardassia by then, and he was commanding the *Phoenix*. I was transporter chief on the *Enterprise*. Captain Maxwell started attacking Cardassian ships—unarmed ships, some of them—without orders, without provocation. There were hundreds of deaths. Cardassians were charging the Federation with breaking the peace.

"Captain Picard had to go after him. To save the peace, to save Cardassian lives, he had to be prepared to fire on another Federation ship, with all the crew on board.

"Now, tell me—where's loyalty in a situation like that?"

Kira was silent a moment. "Did he? Your captain? Did he open fire?"

O'Brien looked distant. "Someone managed to talk Maxwell into surrendering." Then he seemed to shake off his mood. "A synthale or something, Major?"

"No. No, thanks, Chief."

Kira crossed the floor of the Promenade. In the doorway of his closed, darkened shop, Garak watched her with a resentful expression. But Kira was too preoccupied to think of Garak at the moment.

She stood in front of the doorway to the Bajoran temple. It was round, rayed like the sun, like life, like eternity. It had a center.

From within came the voices of monks chanting. The familiar sound filled her with an irrational anger and grief. How could they? How could they just go on as if everything were normal, as if nothing had happened?

She held her head. She could almost feel the touch of his hands on her, the sense of calm that touch had brought, the inner peace. Had it all been a lie? A delusion?

Angry tears stung her eyes. You weren't just a traitor to Bajor, Leiris. You betrayed me. You betrayed my faith.

"Major? Can I help you?" It was a monk in his saffron robe.

"No, thank you. I just came in to meditate for a moment."

"Of course." The monk bowed and withdrew.

Kira took a breath, let it slowly out. She closed her eyes and sought her center.

Crossing the Promenade on his way up to Ops, Ben Sisko noticed bright colored lights flashing from the open doorway of Quark's casino. From inside, Quark's sharp little eyes caught sight of him pausing there. The Ferengi scurried to the door.

"Well! Commander! Care to come in for a quick flutter? A short drink?"

"Don't tell me you're back in business already?"

"Have to set a good example for the local business community," Quark said smugly. "Get the flow of commerce started again around this place. In case you didn't know it, Commander, trade is the lifeblood of any civilized community. When people have their lives back in order, we'll be ready for them."

"Ready to take their money. Very commendable, I'm sure," said Sisko dryly. "And I suppose that if the Cardassians had taken over the station again, you'd still be setting up shop for business as usual?"

Quark grinned, totally unabashed. Profit was profit, and gold-pressed latinum didn't know whether it was Cardassian or Bajoran. "Why, of course, Commander! An experienced entrepreneur knows how to survive these minor setbacks."

"Hmm," Sisko muttered, leaving Quark to set up his tables and his games of chance. It was annoying, but he had to acknowledge that Quark, actually, was right.

Most of DS-Nine, in fact, was pulling itself back into working order. The station was used to a state of constantly recurring crisis. And the core of the staff, both Starfleet and Bajoran, had never abandoned their posts. Sisko was proud to have commanded them.

He was deep into work in his office when a sense of commotion down on the main floor of Ops made him lift his head. Then he uttered an intemperate word. There was his chief of security coming off the lift with two criminals in custody: his son, Jake, and the boy's companion in wrongdoing, Nog.

He slapped his comm badge. "Odo, bring them up to my office!"

Jake, as usual when he felt guilty, had his eyes aimed down at the floor, while Nog, well-known for his quick escapes, was squirming in Odo's grip on his ear ridge.

"Well, what it is this time?" Sisko demanded, looking like a storm cloud.

"I caught them out on the docking ring, in the parking bay for the crawlabouts."

"What!?" The crawlabouts were small craft used in the maintenance of the station's exterior. While they did not, in fact, crawl on the surface, the power of their tiny thrusters was negligible. Still, those boys had no business taking them out.

The storm cloud grew darker and more threatening. "Jake!"

The boy looked up with an expression of misery on his face. "Honest, Dad, we weren't going to do anything *wrong!*"

"Not wrong? Unauthorized entry into the equipment area, taking it out with no permission, not even telling anyone what you were doing? Like station traffic control? Don't you think there's a reason we have regulations around this place? A million things could have gone wrong, and no one would even know you were out there!"

"I'm sorry. I guess I didn't think—"

"Didn't think! Just what on Earth did you think you were going to *do* out there with those things, anyway?"

"Well, see . . ." Jake paused, swallowed. "There's all this *stuff* floating around out there. People tossed it out of airlocks when they were leaving the station and couldn't take it with them, and everything. And it's just, out there, you know. Just floating around. And getting in the way. And, well, so Nog and I figured we could go out in the crawlabout and scoop some of it up. You know, they've got grapplers and nets, and all that. I mean, kind of like cleaning up the place! Getting rid of the junk."

Sisko was still scowling. "And what were you planning to do with all this junk after you'd picked it up?"

"Well . . ."

273

It was Nog who spoke up eagerly, as Jake hesitated, "Salvage! It's a salvage operation! One of the oldest principles of interplanetary law states that if cargo is jettisoned or abandoned, the first person to find it can claim salvage rights."

Sisko held up a hand. "I'm acquainted with the principles of salvage law, thank you. Just what were you two planning to do with these salvaged items, then? I do hope you're aware that in common law, the act of salvage, contrary to what many persons erroneously believe, does *not* confer title on the persons who acquire the goods."

"Well, I—"

"The original owners have the right to claim their belongings, after payment of an appropriate salvage fee."

Nog, who had started to look unhappy, brightened at the mention of a fee. Sisko sighed inwardly. It was clear whose idea this scheme had been. The Ferengi boy was a true disciple of his uncle Quark, constantly thinking of material gain. Less than a day after they were back on the station, he'd already conceived of some scheme to profit from the misfortunes of others. Nog represented the antithesis of everything Starfleet stood for—and this was his son's constant companion on DS-Nine.

But it was his duty to pronounce impartial judgment on both of them. "You're right, in a way, Jake and Nog. We do need to clear away the flotsam and jetsam cluttering up the traffic lanes around the station. But those goods belong to the people who live here on DS-Nine. They *will* be returned to their proper owners. Freely returned.

"As for you two, you'll both be assigned to assist an authorized operator to do the job. Consider this your assignment until the job is finished."

Both boys looked dismayed. "But . . . what about school?" Jake asked in a disbelieving voice.

"School has been suspended until normal station operations resume."

Nog glanced quickly in the direction of the door, but Odo had placed himself in front of it. "I, uh, think my uncle needs me to help him in the business," he said nervously.

"I'll speak to your uncle myself," Sisko said mercilessly. "Once I've explained about the fines and penalties for attempting unauthorized appropriation of station equipment, I'm sure he'll agree that this is the best alternative."

"But—"

"That will be all. Jake, we'll discuss this matter later, in private, when I get back to our quarters. Where you will be waiting for me. Clear?"

"Yes, sir," his son said unhappily.

"Constable, you'll make sure these two report to Chief O'Brien at the start of the next work shift?"

"I'll make a point of it," Odo said firmly, approving the punishment. He escorted the miscreants from the office.

Sisko leaned back in his chair and shut his eyes. From the hallway he could still faintly hear the retreating voices:

"It's *your* fault! If you hadn't . . ."

EPILOGUE

SEVERAL DAYS LATER, Sisko's comm unit warned him, "Commander, it's Gul Dukat!"

Sisko got to his feet just as the Cardassian commander came through the door of his office—as usual without any kind of knock. "Gul Dukat! It's good to see you here again. Why don't you sit down."

Dukat had a thinner, sharper look to him now, and a slightly confused expression as he accepted Sisko's offer of a seat. "Things seem a little different around here this time. Everyone seems almost glad to see me. Out there in Ops. Even that Bajoran Major Kira of yours actually spoke to me without snarling."

"Mmm, well, things do change, I suppose. And speaking of change, I understand you were under arrest for a while under the Revanche government."

Dukat grinned fiercely, which gave his face a distinctly predatory look. "And they lived to regret that!"

Sisko didn't really want to hear about it, but Dukat went on, in the apparent assumption that the Starfleet commander shared his zest for revenge. "Your friend Marak was executed just before I left home! It was quite a spectacle; you should have been there to take credit. You're a tricky enemy, Sisko. I'll have to remember that. In case we find ourselves on opposite sides one day. Unlike now, of course."

"Your people aren't very forgiving, are they?"

"We can't afford to be. Marak lost his ship, he failed in his mission, he blackened our reputation before the entire Federation. He deserved to die. Which reminds me. The Revanche party may be discredited and out of office, but the Cardassian Empire still maintains the claim on the Gamma Quadrant wormhole. And this station."

"And of course you realize that as the representative of the Federation, I'm forced to deny that claim."

"Of course."

They understood each other.

"Now," said Dukat briskly, "I understand you gave asylum to a young acquaintance of mine. That—I do appreciate that. I would have given anything to see Marak's reaction when he heard."

"Asylum appeared to be justified under the circumstances." Sisko tapped his communicator. "Have Berat sent up to the commander's office, please."

To Dukat, he said, "My chief of operations speaks quite well of him as an engineer. He's even asked him to stay on here, as an officer on DS-Nine."

Dukat raised his eyebrows skeptically. "A Cardassian officer, serving under Bajorans?"

"Oh, well, it was a thought, anyway."

Berat entered the room uncertainly, but his face lit up when he saw Dukat. "Gul!"

Dukat stood, and the two Cardassians clasped each other hard around the upper arms in an emotional greeting. Sisko wondered if they were somehow related.

"Boy, your family will be glad to see you come home!"

"They're alive? Who—"

"I saw your cousins Karel and Tal in that hellhole they stuck us in. Just eight days ago, we stood together and watched Marak hang. We all thought of you then, and your father, and the rest of them. But we never expected to find you alive, and certainly not *here!*"

Berat sobered a moment, glanced in Sisko's direction. "I was lucky."

"Now," said Dukat, "I've got you a berth on my ship. You don't have to spend any more time in this place."

"Then . . ."

"What?"

"The charges. I mean, Sub Halek did die."

"Don't worry about it. We've had your rank restored, retroactively. As far as the service is concerned, Halek forfeited his life the first time he laid a hand on Glin Berat." Dukat slapped the younger Cardassian hard on the shoulder. "I'm glad to see that you made one of them pay, at least."

He glanced at Sisko. "We won't take up any more of your time here." He headed for the door.

But at the last moment, Berat turned back. "Commander? You'll say good-bye to Chief O'Brien for me?"

"I'll do that," said Sisko, somewhat surprised.

"And, um, tell him thanks for the offer? But—I'm going home. But I hope I'll see him again, someday, when I can come back."

"Oh," said Gul Dukat, grinning, "I think Commander Sisko knows that we'll be back. And soon."

Which, like it or not, Commander Sisko supposed he did.